PRAISE FOR HELEN MARSHALL

"Stories subtle and unsettling: Helen Marshall clothes the uncanny in new flesh and then makes it bleed."

Kelly Link, author of *Pretty Monsters*
and *Stranger Things Happen*

"Masterful horror. In Marshall's dark landscapes, the metaphors are feral and they'll turn on you in a heartbeat."

Mike Carey, author of *The Unwritten*
and co-author of *The Steel Seraglio*

"The stories in Helen Marshall's *Hair Side, Flesh Side* occur in the interstices of our most fundamental relations. Brothers and sisters, parents and children, lovers find the space between them grown strange, shifting, as the familiar becomes the site and the source of startling transformation. Elegant, unsettling, these stories leave the reader no less changed than their characters. Highly recommended work."

John Langan, author of *House of Windows*
and *Technicolor and Other Revelations*

"Helen Marshall's *Hair Side, Flesh Side* is a revelation. Her collection of expertly drawn characters with their historical longings are depicted with a compelling intelligence and achingly soft touch, and their stories are as compassionate as they are disquieting. *Hair Side, Flesh Side* announces a major new talent in dark fiction. Indeed, these are stories that will be imprinted on the inside of your skin."

Paul Tremblay, author of *The Little Sleep*
and *Swallowing a Donkey's Eye*

"Darkness can be as beautiful as light, and rarely is that perfect diorama of light and shadow more lyrically and elegantly rendered than it is here, in Helen Marshall's debut short fiction collection, *Hair Side, Flesh Side*. These stories are a literary storm sweeping in across the water, with lightning flickering at its heart and a promise of fury yet unleashed."

Michael Rowe, author of *Enter, Night*

"Helen Marshall writes assured, accomplished prose that is as chilling as it is beautiful, and the stories she tells are as daring as they are unexpected. This superb first collection is set to make waves."

Tim Lebbon, author of *Echo City*
and *The Thief of Broken Toys*

"*Hair Side, Flesh Side* is a quirky, kinky treat. We haven't had a writer like this for a while—secure and erudite and sexy. I hope this book influences because we need more."

Tony Burgess, author of *Pontypool Changes Everything*
and *People Live Still in Cashtown Corners*

HAIR SIDE, FLESH SIDE

BY HELEN MARSHALL

INTRODUCTION BY ROBERT SHEARMAN

ILLUSTRATIONS BY CHRIS ROBERTS

ChiZine Publications

FIRST EDITION

Distributed in Canada by
HarperCollins Canada Ltd.
1995 Markham Road
Scarborough, ON M1B 5M8
Toll Free: 1-800-387-0117
e-mail: hcorder@harpercollins.com

Distributed in the U.S. by
Diamond Book Distributors
1966 Greenspring Drive
Timonium, MD 21093
Phone: 1-410-560-7100 x826
e-mail: books@diamondbookdistributors.com

Library and Archives Canada Cataloguing in Publication

Marshall, Helen, 1983-
    Hair side, flesh side / Helen Marshall ; introduction: Robert Shearman.

Issued also in electronic format.
ISBN 978-1-927469-24-8

    I. Title.

PS8626.A7668H35 2012   C813'.6   C2012-904987-5

CHIZINE PUBLICATIONS
Toronto, Canada
www.chizinepub.com
info@chizinepub.com

Edited by Sandra Kasturi
Copyedited and proofread by Clare Marshall

Produced with the support of the City of Toronto through the Toronto Arts Council.

We acknowledge the support of the Canada Council for the Arts which last year invested $20.1 million in writing and publishing throughout Canada.

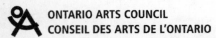

ONTARIO ARTS COUNCIL
CONSEIL DES ARTS DE L'ONTARIO

Published with the generous assistance of the Ontario Arts Council.

Printed in Canada

For my dad.
Love is memory enough.

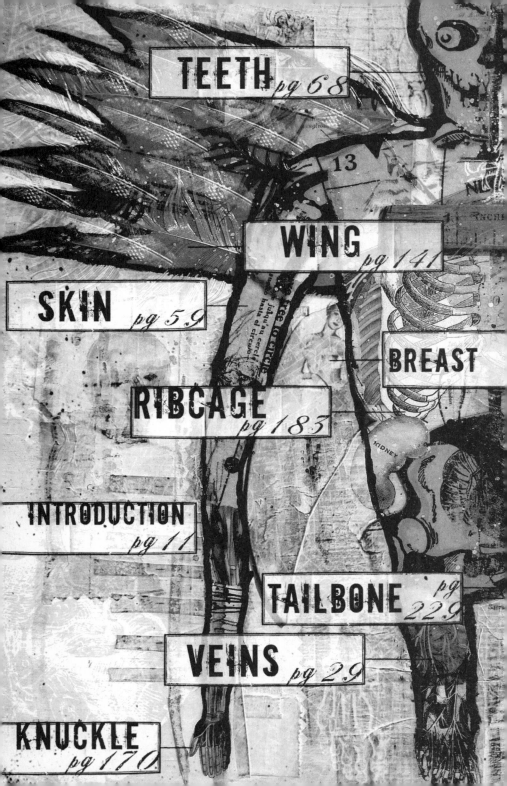

TEETH pg 68

WING pg 141

SKIN pg 59

BREAST

RIBCAGE pg 183

INTRODUCTION pg 11

TAILBONE pg 229

VEINS pg 29

KNUCKLE pg 170

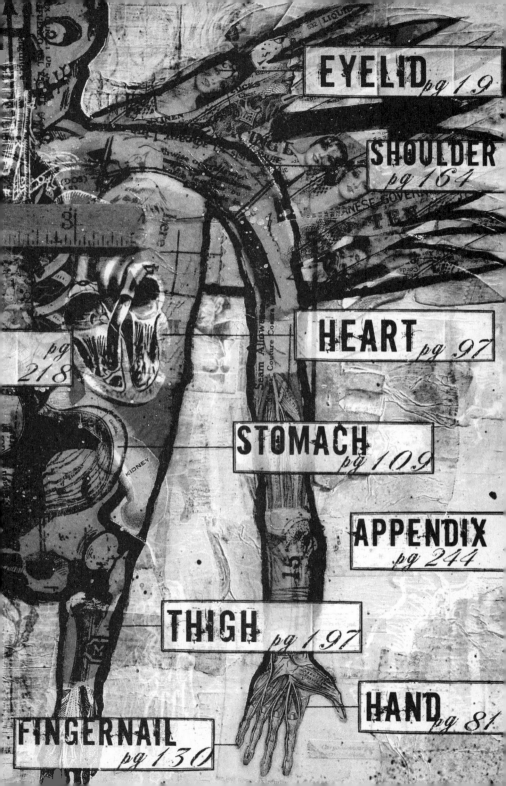

EYELID pg 19

SHOULDER pg 164

HEART pg 97

pg 218

STOMACH pg 109

APPENDIX pg 244

THIGH pg 197

HAND pg 81

FINGERNAIL pg 130

To our bodies turn we then, that so
weak men on love reveal'd may look;
Love's mysteries in souls do grow,
but yet the body is his book.

—John Donne, "The Ecstasy"

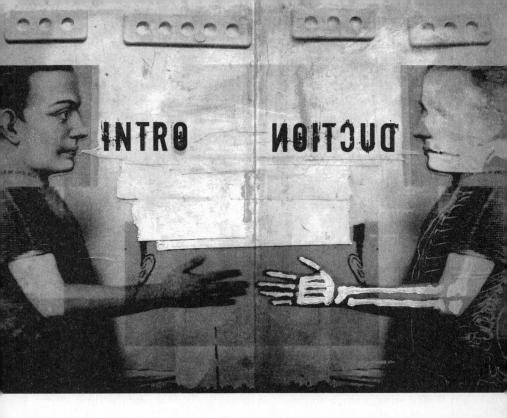

INTRODUCTION

Don't go to a museum with Helen Marshall. And whilst you're at it, don't take her to an art gallery either, or anywhere there might be statues or quirky bits of architecture, nowhere you might come across pieces of old pottery. Because such things fire Helen's imagination. They inspire her. And you might be showing genuine interest in a particular painting, or some pile of old rubble, and then she'll open her mouth, and out will pour all these new story ideas. Crazy flights of unreality that are both macabre and deeply human, stories in which history and art collide with real people, people with ordinary problems and ordinary lives, and how the entire world is changed in the process. It leaves you exhilarated. It leaves you exhausted. And frankly, once in a while, all you wanted was to just look at the nice painting.

And you realize that the painting has been wrecked forever, because the whirlings of Helen's mind have overwhelmed it rather, and you're never going to be able to look at it in the same way again. This can sometimes be rather annoying. This afternoon we've been out to the Natural History Museum in London. I thought I'd show her all the spiders. I thought that would keep her brain quiet. Helen doesn't like spiders. And, for a while, I thought I'd got her. She just sort of stood there in front of the blow-up photographs and flinched. But then she turned around. She began to look at the school group that had trailed in after us. And she told me this story about what it would be like if she suddenly fell pregnant and gave birth to a whole flotilla of children on a day trip, all wearing uniforms and Day-Glo caps so they'd be recognized by their teachers. She grinned at me then, blinked so innocently behind those glasses that make her eyes look big and studious, and I admitted defeat, and off we went to another exhibit.

Helen is prim, and pretty, and puckishly sweet. She does not look like the vessel for fictions that push against the boundaries of sanity. In my mind's eye she seems to sum up every nice teacher I had at junior school, all the ones I wanted to impress, all the ones I had a crush on. She looks so wholesome butter wouldn't melt in her mouth; no, worse, I'd think her entire face has been specially constructed for the refrigeration of dairy products. I have known Helen a couple of years now, and we speak often, and I've read all her stuff, the wayward and the seriously wayward—and I still find it hard to contain my surprise at the dissonance between the Helen I see and the Helen I read, the Helen who's a dear and cheeky friend and the Helen whose stories can frighten me so.

But I want to return to that image of Helen as a teacher. That there's something professorial about Miss Marshall should be clear enough; when she's not writing her weird fiction and poetry, she's looking over fourteenth-century manuscripts as she completes her doctorate in medieval studies. Most people who write within this genre draw upon the usual sources of old creaky horror tales—Helen does it from an academic celebration of art. This is a book about books—and books as they used to be, as treasures, as handwritten labours of love and duty, as something otherworldly that came with their own rules and mysteries and must never be taken for granted. The ghosts of Jane Austen and Geoffrey Chaucer stalk these pages, both thematically and literally. Helen writes about art from a time when it truly mattered, when—as you shall see—it was genuinely stuff of life and death.

And I know that the academic influence might suggest stories that are dry and dusty. Not a bit of it. There is something fleshy about Helen's writing—deliciously, disgustingly, of the skin and bone and messy organs. She writes of books made from the bodies of dead children. Peeking under flaps of skin on a modern-day editor there is found a missing nineteenth-century manuscript. A plague spreads around the world turning people into the pieces of art they cannot but help imitate. And with the same professorial instincts that allow Helen to analyze her medieval texts, so she turns upon her own wild fantasies and examines them from every angle, and makes them real and urgent and moving. Many is the time that Helen has told me one of her story ideas, and I've thought it was ridiculous, too clever, too bizarre to work. And a few weeks later she'll show me how she's found all the blood and beating heart of it, and there on the page will be something so very true, and touching, and funny, and wise.

I feel especially proud to be writing this introduction. I was in at the birth of most of these tales—in some instances I can honestly remember the statue or museum exhibit we were standing by when the idea first came to her. She has been the very closest of friends—the writer with whom I'll share my first drafts, just as she shares hers with me, whose instincts are so much sharper than my own, who'll tease at plotlines with me for all sorts of strange oddnesses over Skype at three in the morning. I think writing's a bit of a sod, actually; Helen approaches it with a reckless enthusiasm I find inspiring. And over the time I've known her I've seen Helen change from someone who rather liked to dabble at her fictions when she could make the time, to a thrilling full-blooded writer bursting with an ambition to be the best bloody writer she can be. I know no other writer quite as sharp, odd, or as clever as Helen—I know of no one either who writes about everyday emotions of love and loss with such honesty. I've been rereading this, her first collection of short stories, over and over as she's been writing it. It feels good that it's being let out into the world so that everybody else can join in.

But, for all that. Don't go with her to the museum. Seriously.

—Robert Shearman
London, June 2012

HAIR SIDE, FLESH SIDE

BLESSED

It was three weeks to her birthday when the big box came—each of the moving men taking an end, grunting and sweating as they heaved drunkenly to the spot where Chloe used to park her new two-wheeler. She had been told to move it to the backyard where it now leaned up against the fence, exposed to the elements, shining ribbons soggy from last night's rain. But that was okay, because she knew what this was, what it *had* to be, and she was so tingly with excitement that it didn't matter if the gears of her bike rusted out.

Chloe's parents took her by the hand, one on either side, her mum on her right, her dad on her left, and they walked her into the garage to see. "It's for you, honey," her mum—her other mum—said with her biggest smile, "it's just for you."

"It's from Italy," said her dad. "We brought it all this way to celebrate. We know your birthday's not for another couple of weeks, but, well, sweetheart, we wanted you to have something early—"

"—something from *us*—" her mum cut in.

"—before you have to go back home."

And they looked at each other encouragingly and they looked at her encouragingly, but Chloe was hardly listening because she was looking at the box. It was very big—as long as her bed, made of thick wooden slats with HIC JACET SEPVLTVS written in bold red letters.

"Go ahead, sweetheart," said her mum. "Go on and open it. Henry, tell her to open it."

"It's okay," said her dad. "Here, sweetie, fetch me the crowbar."

And Chloe brought him the large hooked crowbar, and he fit it into the lid of the crate and, after some more grunting and heaving, off it came with a pop. A kind of horsey smell filled the air, a smell like dirt and old things that made Chloe feel all warm and tingly. "Is it—?" she asked, but her dad was lifting her up onto his shoulders.

"Shh, honey, see for yourself."

At first, all she could make out was the layer of straw and the cloud of dust that leapt into the air as her dad began to root around. It glittered in the sunlight streaming through the garage door, but she still couldn't see what was *inside* the thing, not through the settling dust and her dad's rooting arms, and she had to hold tight around his neck so she didn't fall off. But then, then there was something peeking through, brown and leathery, something that might have been a football, except it wasn't a football because her dad was still clearing and Chloe saw it, a *face* and more than that, a face with pale, stringy hair tangled up in the straw and a brown, leathery neck and thin, twiggy arms and thinner, twiggier fingers.

Her dad bounced her on his shoulders and then heaved

her off again so she landed gently on the ground, and she stood tip-toed until she could see over the top of the crate. Chloe fingered the straw shyly, not daring to touch it yet, not daring to stroke the soft leathery skin.

"For your birthday, kiddo," he said in a warm, excited voice. "You're almost seven, and we wanted you to have this—"

"Lucia of Syracuse," her mum interrupted. He gave her a look, but it was an affectionate look, one that showed he didn't mind much. "Died 304. A real, genuine *martyr*."

Chloe's mouth opened in a little "oh" of delight and then she reached out and let her index finger brush against the brown leather cheek. It was rough like a cat's tongue in some places and smooth as fine-grained wood in others where the bone peeked through. "She was about your age, sweetheart, when they came for her. Wanted her to marry some rich governor who thought she had the most beautiful eyes in the world. But, oh no, she wasn't having any of that. Do you know what she did?"

"She plucked out her eyes," Chloe said, barely a whisper, as her finger traced the smooth curves of the eye sockets.

"That's right," her mum beamed. "That's exactly right, sweetheart. Now there's a real saint for you, a saint to be proud of. Not just any martyr had that kind of panache."

Her dad nodded sagely, and Chloe nodded too because it was *true*, this was something, this wasn't one of those knock-off relics that some of the other kids got: there were about five girls in her grade alone who claimed to have Catherine of Siena, and that was nonsense, there was only one Catherine of Siena and they couldn't all have her. Melissa Johnstone admitted she only had a finger bone, and it was a hand-me-down from her older sister's Theresa of Avila anyway—*her* parents couldn't afford a whole new saint, not for their third kid.

But Chloe could tell just by looking that this was the *real* Lucia, that this little girl, a little girl her own age, had been good and kind and best beloved of all. And then, *there*, it happened. Chloe felt a warm rush of heat and all the hairs on her arm stood up. This was it, this was the moment! Out of the crate stepped a little girl the same age as Chloe, with long dark hair and olive skin and a beatific smile.

"You won't be lonely now when you visit, sweetheart," her dad said. "Lucia will be here waiting for you."

And afterward they took Chloe inside and Lucia followed serenely, smiling at her with only the faintest stains of blood on her neck where the Roman had stabbed her, but she didn't seem sad and so Chloe wasn't either. There was birthday cake and it was her favourite—double-chocolate with thick brown icing that seemed to fizz on her tongue—and she was even allowed a second piece. At the end of the night, when she had had as much cake as she could fit inside her, and her eyes were starting to drift shut, they tucked her into bed. They stood, one on either side, her mum on the right, her dad on the left, and the third, Lucia, a faint ghostly little-girl shape by the window.

"Can she come home with me? Please, dad?" Chloe asked dreamily, but her parents shared a look, a special look, and her dad crouched down beside her.

"I need you to listen, sweetheart." He looked up at her mum for support in the way he did sometimes. "You can't tell Clare—well, your mother, your mum back home— about this. Okay, sweetie? It's important. This is a *special* present. And because it's a special present you need to keep it a secret."

Chloe looked at her dad, and his eyes were so sad, so she promised. And when she fell asleep, she dreamed of Lucia, bathed in golden light with her beautiful blank eye sockets, and she forgot the sadness in her father's eyes and she didn't think about what it would be like to go home.

In the end, they let her take a finger—only a pinkie—from Lucia's right hand where the sinews were weakest with age; it snapped off like a broken twig. She just had to promise, cross her heart and hope to die, that she would keep it secret.

"Your mother—Clare—at home, she wouldn't like it if she knew," her other mum said as they packed her overnight things back into the little pink suitcase she had brought with her. Her other mum was tall and beautiful with soft, soft hair that she sometimes let Chloe brush; her mother back home didn't like it when Chloe talked about her. "Your father said you were good, you'd be careful. And you'll come back, won't you, sweetheart? To see Lucia?"

"She can't see me, Mum," Chloe replied as she folded her pyjamas, "she gave away her eyes."

"Even so," her other mum said, and she kissed Chloe on the forehead.

Lucia went with her, of course, but with only the little boney finger she appeared as the faintest of faint outlines, barely more than a whisper of a shadow. Chloe didn't care though; Lucia filled her with a sense of light and warmth, and no matter how dark it was she never felt the night terrors with Lucia there. She kept the finger in her pocket when she went to school, and she only showed it to Melissa because Melissa had a finger too. "But you're not supposed to have one yet!" Melissa squealed with wide eyes. "It's not your birthday."

"It is too. My parents only see me once a month. It's my *special* present."

But Melissa only muttered darkly, "You're not supposed to. Now you'll get two because you have two mums, and I'll only have a lousy finger." She wouldn't look at Chloe for the rest of the day, and as Chloe sat in her desk, trying to figure out her multiplication homework, she could see the outline of red standing out darker on Lucia's neck and she knew there would be trouble.

Later that evening, her mother—her mum at home— received a call from Melissa's mum and that was it, she demanded to see the finger. "This was a gift from *them*, wasn't it? Well. That's just like them. They know you aren't properly seven yet and they're trying to get a present in early." She paced about the kitchen wielding a wooden spoon like Goliath's club. "I won't have any of that. I won't have any second-class finger-bones in *my* house." Chloe tried to tell her that they didn't mean anything by it and that it was all right, she didn't need a second saint, but her mother rounded on her fiercely. "That's what you think, is it? You don't want mine. Fine. You can make do without any." Then her mum snatched the finger out of her hand and threw it into the garbage disposal; it disappeared in a terribly grinding of gears so loud that Chloe had to cover her ears. The little ghost-girl—just like that!—vanished like a burst soap bubble.

"Oh, I bet you think you're *so* clever," Chloe overheard through her locked bedroom door that night as she hugged her covers to her chin. The dark seemed so much darker now, like it had all crowded into the room when her mother closed the door. "Saint Lucia—ha! What, because she's got your eyes? She hasn't, you know. They don't look a thing like yours and if they did, well, I'd pluck them out myself and send them to you. You think she likes saints, do you? I'll get her a saint. I'll get her Joan of bloody Arc—there's a saint for you, there's someone who really counted, not one of those timid little virgin saints."

And she did: it might have cost a fortune but her mother—her mum at home—had the Seine dredged for ashes and three weeks later on her birthday, she presented Chloe with a heavy glass pickle jar filled with Parisian mud.

"That'll teach him," she said, grinning sharply at Chloe. "You want to try martyrdom, try *burnt* at a stake." And they sat side by side, a half-eaten slice of carrot cake between them, the candle licked clean of icing, and her mother glaring at the jar, waiting for something to happen.

By ten thirty it was getting quite late, and Chloe was getting sleepy; it was past her bed time, but her mother gripped her wrist fiercely. "She's there, it just takes longer, she was roasted alive for Chrissake. But she'll come. She'll come, and you and I are going to wait here until she does."

And they did. And ten-thirty became eleven. And eleven became eleven-thirty. And when the last chime sounded for midnight, with a harrumph, her mother pretended not to look when Chloe slipped her arm away and climbed the stairs to her bedroom, closing her door herself, even with all the darkness crammed into the little room.

But in the morning when she wandered downstairs in her pyjamas for breakfast, there was a watery shape sitting at the table with close-cropped boy-hair and a chainmail shirt.

"Good morning," Chloe said shyly as she took her seat, but the French girl stuck up her nose and refused to make conversation.

"*Où sont mes ennemis?*" she asked. Her mother made her carry a thermos full of mud to school that day, and all her friends wanted to know was it really Joan of Arc—all of her friends except Melissa, who made it quite clear that they weren't friends at all anymore, not if Chloe had two saints. And Joan didn't speak to Chloe, not even once, and she never smiled.

Chloe didn't like Joan very much. Oh, she tried to because here was another girl and she too was best beloved, but, well, Joan was *fierce.* She smacked Chloe's fingers with the flat of her sword when she reached for a cookie, and whenever Chloe tried to put on a dress, Joan would shake her head and scowl at the hemline; worst yet, on days when she was particularly cross she would set herself afire. Then she would writhe about as her skin went black and crispy. She would look at Chloe accusingly, her eyes burning with righteousness, as the flames consumed her hair like a halo.

Chloe tried to tell her mother—her mum at home—but she would only look on with approval. "That's the way it's supposed to be, isn't it? *Real* martyrs have standards; *real* martyrs won't put up with nonsense, no. It's good for you to have a little discipline in your life, really, Chloe. I won't be there *all* the time." And Chloe supposed she was right. Even so. At night, when the room was dark with shadows and Chloe could feel the night terrors coming on, she still found herself wishing that the fire in Joan's eyes helped just a little bit.

On Friday morning, Chloe packed up her pink suitcase and waited by the door for her dad to pick her up. She had been looking forward to the visit all week: she had been extra good and extra kind, and Joan hadn't had to immolate herself even once since Tuesday. Her mother, though, had taken to pacing in the kitchen: she was always like that the day of a visit, always tense and strange, prone to fits of tears followed by scolding followed by remorseful hugs that were always a bit too tight.

"Come here, Chloe," her mother said, and that thing—whatever it was that only came on visit days—was there in her eyes. She placed a glass of something black and sludgy in front of Chloe. "I want you to drink this, darling, I made it for you special."

"I'm not thirsty, Mum," said Chloe, but even though she didn't want to, she could see the tips of Joan's hair starting to light up like little fuses and so she closed her eyes. She gagged and she coughed and she sputtered, but she managed to drink it all.

"Good," said Chloe's mother, "there's a dear." And she hugged Chloe very tightly.

Then her dad rang the doorbell and Chloe ran to him and flung her arms around his neck. Her mother said nothing, she never did, but Chloe didn't mind because he was picking up her suitcase, and then they were out the door. But in the car Chloe began to feel quite ill. "Would you like something to drink, sweetheart?" her dad asked, but Chloe said no, she didn't. "Are you hungry? Do you need to pee?" And Chloe still said no, but something strange was happening to her skin, first it started to itch and then it started to prickle with sweat and then it started to *burn*.

"Dad," she said.

"What's wrong, sweetie? Should I pull over?"

"Dad," she said again, but this time her voice sounded small and frightened and Chloe couldn't recognize it because all she could hear was, "*Mon père, mon père.*"

Chloe spent the weekend in bed with a fever of 105 degrees. Her mum—her other mum—laid washcloths on her forehead but nothing helped, nothing stopped that feeling of fire licking at her skin, of her hair shrivelling up. Sometimes, she would catch sight of Lucia by her window, shaking her head sadly, serene, the blank spaces of her eyes as dark and as cool as a well. And then she could only whisper, "*Mon Dieu, aidez-moi, aidez-moi.*" Then her parents would exchange glances between them and they looked so scared and small beside the bed. Chloe wanted to reach out to touch her mum's hair, but she was afraid the flames that licked her fingers like birthday candles might devour her all up.

Chloe could hear bits of the phone conversation floating up to her through the floorboards, not even words anymore, but just bits of anger and sadness and fear and fury all tied into one. They couldn't take her home. They were afraid to move her. They didn't know what was wrong. And so on Sunday her mother came, and when Chloe saw her she didn't seem small like her parents. She seemed huge, hulking, massive; her legs were like two Ionic pillars, and her face seemed carved from marble, it was so firmly set. She glared until her other mum fled the room. "What have you done, Henry?" her mother said. And her dad hung his head miserably and he slunk out too. Chloe could feel the fire burning on her skin, searing flesh, blackening bone.

Her mother sat down by the bed where her other mum had kept the washcloths. She touched her daughter's hair the way she did when Chloe had been very young. "I love you," she said. "My little girl, my darling, and I'm sorry this is so hard. But it's not supposed to be easy, is it? Real love isn't ever easy. Sometimes it's hard and sometimes it hurts but if it's real love then you don't ever leave, you don't, no matter how much it hurts. I want you to know that. I'm here with you now, my darling, and I won't ever leave." And her mother stroked her face lightly with fingers that were hard and sharp as broken bones. "This is their house and they want you to pretend that it is yours, they want you to pretend that you are their child, that you belong to them. But you don't, love, you are my daughter. Your hands are my hands and your fingers are my fingers and your eyes, oh my darling girl, your eyes are my eyes."

And she cradled her daughter's head gently in the crook of her arms, and the pain was bad, it was very bad. But Chloe loved her mother very much and she was willing to bear this pain for her mother, she was willing to let the fire devour her if that was what her mother wanted, because that was what love was: it was fire and it was torture and it was being hacked to pieces, and broken fingers and knives and hammers and pitchforks and spears, and it was being drowned and it was being suffocated and it was being locked up in dark, dark places. Chloe knew that, she knew that in the deepest bit of her. And she loved her mother enough to bear the pain, really she did, enough not to ask why or for how long she would suffer, for how long she must bear the weight of her love.

But even so. Even so. Chloe looked up through the halo of fire into her mother's eyes, wet with tears—real tears, because she hated seeing her daughter in pain. She reached up gently, shyly, and she felt the skin cool beneath her fingertips, and then—it was hard because she hated the darkness, and she was afraid, she was truly afraid, but she could see Lucia standing by the window, and Lucia looked so beautiful, calm, patient and kind, everything she had ever thought love was—and so Chloe plucked out the eyes from her skull, just like that, like a soap bubble popping, and it was done.

SANDITON

They were in the elevator, Gavin's voice surprisingly deep and gruff, but his smile was so charming, it lit up his entire face. He touched her lightly on the arm, and she was happy for the warmth of him, but wryly wary. He was married. She knew that. He pressed the button for his floor, and Hanna felt the ground dropping away beneath her, again when he slipped his arm around her waist, not too firmly, gently really, and it was the warmth of it she loved.

"I've had too much scotch," she whispered.

"Surely there's no such thing when you're among writers."

"We're not among anybody now. They're still downstairs."

"I know."

The door pinged open: the hallway decorated with bright

yellow wallpaper with paler fleurs-de-lys in velvet; the carpet red, shaggy; sconces well-lit, almost as well-lit as Hanna felt. Her steps muddled a little bit, the carpet soft under her shoes, and Gavin's arm steady around her. She leaned into him, closed her eyes, breathed out and moved away, unhooked her arm.

"Coming in?" he said, his voice catching in the smallest way.

"Of course not."

"Right," he replied. And then: "Why not?"

"Because you're married." Hanna paused. "And I'm not, at least not to you."

"Right." But his hand was still hovering near her, and she didn't move away from him or the door. "The thing is, you're the most interesting person down there, and the rest of them are a bit of a mess right now. If you go back down, you'll only end up playing mother to a bunch of old farts trying to figure out how to write for the BBC. Or get their novels published. Or get their published novels adapted for the BBC. Better to stay here and play the wife."

"You're very charming, but no."

"Fine," he said again, but he still hadn't moved away from her, and in fact the distance between them was getting smaller, micro-inch by micro-inch. "It doesn't have to be about sex."

"It doesn't?" Hanna replied, and she enjoyed the startling vibration of the electrons between them, wondered about all that kinetic energy piling up; it had to go somewhere.

"Sex is overrated."

"Not with me."

"Tea then?" he asked, quirking an eyebrow.

"What, in your room, at four in the morning?"

"I'll put on the kettle. I saw tea bags in here earlier." He used the space to take out a plastic key card and slide it into the surprisingly modern lock. At her last hotel, they gave her a three-pound key that she had to return whenever she left. It could only be retrieved when she handed over her passport for inspection.

The lock whirred and clicked, and Gavin opened the door.

The room was largish and decked out in the same colours as the hallway, but the lights were off, discarded luggage making muted shapes in the darkness. Gavin moved closer for a moment, and Hanna didn't quite move away, letting him bump up against her as he slipped the key into a second slide. The lights flickered on, low for the first five seconds and then burning up to full illumination.

His hand touched the small of her back, and Hanna took a step in, but didn't quite move past the entrance hallway and into the body of the hotel room.

There was a small round table with a tall plastic boiler— the kind Hanna had in undergrad for mac and cheese— a basket with assorted teas, sticks of dehydrated coffee, a biscuit wrapped in plastic. Gavin fitted the plug into the three-pronged socket.

Hanna looked around at the now-illuminated luggage: a big brown suitcase, half-filled with books, clothes spilling out, socks; the smell of aftershave was slightly chemical.

Gavin turned back to the kettle. "Shit," he muttered, "the light's not on." He tapped on it half-heartedly. And then back to Hanna: "Did you really want tea?"

"Coffee would have done."

"Right." He collapsed into the chair and Hanna eyed him warily. The scotch was starting to kick in a little, and she realized she actually did want the coffee; the world was a bit unsteady. "What's it going to be then? Mother or wife?" he asked, that charming smile of his.

"Or editor?"

"Editors are boring. Do you really want to correct my punctuation right now? You can go and join the lot down there, they love editors. Until they have them."

The jet lag was wearing Hanna's good sense rather thin, and she liked the feeling of being in the room, watching him fumble with the kettle, and knowing that neither one of them needed that kettle to work. And the deep growl of his voice was . . .

She finished the biscuit and sat down on the edge of the bed, next to the suitcase. She took out one of his books, admiring the cover, the beautiful French flaps. "Gavin Hale. A writer at the height of his craft. A book not to be missed. From Simon Hatch no less." Flipped through the first chapter before laying it, carefully, beside her. Looked at him.

"The punctuation really is quite bad. Even I couldn't fix it."

"So don't fix it." He didn't get up. He dragged the chair he'd been sitting on over with his legs until he faced her, and they were really quite close together. And then he reached out and touched her hand, very gently, opening up the fingers and sliding his hand in.

"I can't," she protested.

"You might."

"I won't."

"Perhaps."

"I—" And then he leaned forward, stopping her breath, kissing her lightly on the lips. "—might." Her eyes were mostly closed, and when she opened them, his head had moved away scant inches. He was watching her, waiting. There was a smile—that goddamn smile, Hanna thought—like the Cheshire cat's, slipping onto his face and then off again.

"It wouldn't be professional," she said, but this time she let herself smile back, just a little.

"That's mostly the point."

She let go of his hand. He waited. Then she reached out with both hands, took the front of his shirt, and slowly tugged it closer to her. "Good," she said.

Hanna lay back in bed, limbs tangled in damp covers, and Gavin was beside her, sheathed in polished sweat. The suitcase sat overturned on the floor, the books scattered out onto the carpet, but other clothes had joined the mix. A lacy pale blue bra, her conference jacket, the shirt Gavin had been wearing very recently. Hanna's breathing was still a bit scattershot, and Gavin had that smile on his face again as he leaned over to kiss gently her collarbone, and then he moved a touch lower to the beginning of the swell of her breast, and then lower, and then to the nipple, which made Hanna lean back further into the pillows. She made a small noise.

"So the wife then," she said after a moment. He looked up from what he was doing, and Hanna ran a finger along his fashionably stubbled chin.

"Or the editor if you'd like."

"That was very nice."

"My professional evaluation?" He asked playfully, kissing her finger.

"The punctuation was very good."

"I think I read that review once. 'The punctuation was very good.'"

"Reviewers are terrible people. They don't hold a candle to editors."

Hanna watched him pause over this, thought he would make another rejoined. Instead, he said, "You can stay the night."

"I can't."

"You might."

She opened her mouth to speak again, to say something else, but then she closed it. "I'll be back in a moment." He kissed her again and then rolled onto his back with a sigh, as she untangled herself from the covers. She slipped around the corner, and then into the bathroom. She closed the door, locked it.

Hanna let out a breath, and ran the tap. The slightest tremors of a hangover were starting to tighten the circumference of her skull, pushing on her brain. She pooled the water in her hand, and then rinsed out her mouth. She was bleary-eyed. Tempted by the idea of not needing to go home. Hanna spat out the water, and then looked up into the mirror. Something caught her eye, a smallish discoloured lump on the side of her neck, no bigger than a dime. She squinted, touched it with a finger. The skin was dried out, rough, but the space itself was numb, as if all the nerve endings had been disconnected.

She shook her head, tried scratching it with a nail. A queer sensation ran through her body, as if the area was simultaneously hypersensitive and blanked out with Novocain.

"Gavin?" she called uncertainly.

"Yes, my darling?"

There were sounds from outside the bathroom, but Hanna had to squeeze her eyes shut to remain steady on her feet. The handle jiggled but the door was still locked. He knocked softly. "Hanna?"

She shook her head again to clear it, and then opened the door for him. Gavin was casually leaning against the frame, but there was something subtly wrong with the pose, a slight strain in the shoulders.

"What's wrong?"

"It's . . ."

He moved behind her, and slipped his arms around her waist, kissing the nape of her neck. "No regrets, I hope?"

"No, it's not that. There's something here—" Her finger brushed the spot. Numbness. Tingling. "—can you see anything?"

Hanna was a bit scared. She had read numerous accounts of women discovering small lumps on their breasts, had a friend at college who got cancer, and had to take a year off for chemo and recovery. There had been a list of people who had signed up to go with him, visit the hospital and keep him company. Hanna hadn't been one of those people. She had liked him well enough, but the whole thing was a bit grotesque, and then he had lost his hair and his face had swelled until his head looked like an egg balanced on his neck.

Gavin reached up and took her hand in his, moving it away from the spot, then leaned in close to look. "Do you have a tattoo?" he asked after a moment.

"A tattoo?" she asked, couldn't understand the word. *It's cancer*, she thought, *not a tattoo*. Something that wasn't part of her yesterday.

"It says something here: *Sanditon*. Is that Greek?"

"Why the hell would I have Greek tattooed on my neck? Do I look like I grew up in fucking Oxbridge?" she asked, and her hand trembled in his. She could see his face again in the mirror, and he was looking at her, face a bit tense as if he could feel their relationship going strange, growing real. The eyes were colder, and the smile had slipped away.

"Look, I'll get your things. You don't have to stay the night."

"I—" she said helplessly, wanting something from him, seeing he wasn't going to give it to her. She tried for a smile. "I don't think I should. I'm not the wife." A pause, and then the barest hint of a question. "Only the wife stays the night."

He looked her over, nodded carefully and kissed the back of her neck, ran a finger down her spine, and Hanna felt it like a chill.

"You're more fun than the wife. And the editor, for that matter." He went from the bathroom. She stared at herself in the mirror, the dark spot, but she didn't want to touch it again. Gavin brought her clothes to the bathroom entranceway, and she put them on as fast as she could, trying not to let her shirt touch her neck as she buttoned it up. She couldn't figure out the jacket so she just slung it over one arm, and then she was out of the door, and standing in the hallway with the pale gold fleurs-de-lys, chest tight, feeling the fear for real now that she was by herself.

Carcinos. Carcinoma. The Greek words for cancer, she thought, and then, *Screw Gavin and his books and his beautiful voice and his cat's smile and his wife, damn them all to hell and chemo and let* him *be the one. He* has *a family, and that's why you have families, so you don't need anyone to sign up to sit with you while you die.*

And then she caught her breath, and she got in the elevator, and she went home.

Home was not really home. Home was a tiny room she was renting at the edge of Cowley, just outside Oxford, while she conducted research and met with potential authors for Belletristic, Inc. It was approximately five feet across, eight feet wide, with a recessed nook holding a desk, carelessly painted, makeshift shelves, and a window incapable of closing. The bed had no sheets, but tight, stabbing springs that she had to learn to weave her body around when she first arrived.

Hanna's own suitcase was large, black, filled with tightly rolled t-shirts and a few nicer things for professional use, Gavin's neatly typed manuscript handed over for her editorial inspection and a somewhat smaller sheaf of paper, her own unfinished notes on a novel. As she unpacked, she stowed the t-shirts in a rickety chest of drawers and spent five minutes wedging the suitcase between the uppermost bookshelf and the ceiling. It was too big to fit anywhere else, and if it wasn't stowed she would have had less than a hand's span of room to stand in.

When she lay on the bed, springs pressed sharply against her legs, the suitcase stuck out a full foot and a half over edge of the shelf. Hanna worried that it might fall on her while she slept, so she checked it again, but it held firm, and did not budge. It just loomed over her, disproportionately large against the cramped, cracked ceiling.

At first, she didn't think about Gavin, about the darkened mass on her neck. But then she did, and she rooted around in the top drawer, amidst the power adaptors, her passport, and other paraphernalia, until she found a hand mirror. She tried positioning it at different angles, and with her shirt off she could just about find a clean line of sight, her hand shaky, awkward.

But it was there, and it was slightly larger than she remembered it being. Hanna breathed deeply, her shoulders rising and sinking, the bed creaking beneath her. She put the mirror away. Then she reached up, fingers snaking along her collarbone, exploring the side of her neck. She could feel the roughness, a slight sponginess as she put pressure against it, that same feeling of simultaneous tingling and numbness. A hard scarab shell, scab-like. She forced her nail into it. The tingling intensified, but it didn't feel bad—just very, very strange. Slowly, she dug the nail in until she could feel the edge of the thing against her finger. She dug a little bit more, scratching, getting the other fingernails involved. Then something peeled away, flaking off between her forefinger and thumb. She brought it around for inspection, leaning down on the pillow, the dark shadow of the suitcase in the background of her vision, in the foreground a paper-thin scraping of something—she didn't know what—with the word "Sanditon" in a kind of languished, cursive scrawl.

Hanna picked up the mirror, repositioned it, but as she gazed at the spot she could see—something, the spot was dark but not as if it were bruised or discoloured or some kind of dysplastic nevus, but more like a shadow, like there was no surface at all, a hole in her neck—yes, when she moved the mirror she could make out the edges, not tears or scratches but a thin bank of skin around—nothing. Nothing.

––––––––––––––––––––

Hanna didn't know what to do, she had never seen anything like that. She sat on her bed, the phone receiver heavy in her hand. She thought about calling her doctor back home, but she didn't know what to say, and she couldn't go to a doctor here, she couldn't remember what her health plan was and if it covered overseas medical. Probably not. Her publishers were cheap, and cut corners where they could. Like this room. Like the standby plane tickets from Toronto.

In the end, she called Gavin, his number written on a business card he had given her when they met yesterday before the conference. He hadn't looked like his author photo; somehow the photographer hadn't captured the energy, the expressiveness of his face, the charisma that came only in movement and animation. But she was alone in a city where she didn't know a single soul.

The phone rang several times. A woman answered.

"Hello?"

"Hi," Hanna started, suddenly unsure of herself. "It's Hanna Greeson. I work for Belletristic, Inc." She paused. Considered hanging up the phone.

"I'll just get Gavin on the phone, love."

A voice distantly called. Hanna could make out the sound of a dog barking. Maybe children in the background. Or a television. Some sort of extra noise that her room didn't have.

And then Gavin's voice came over the line: "Hanna."

"Gavin," she replied. "So that's the wife."

"And you're the editor."

"Right," she said. "That's right." She could feel that the phone call was unwelcome, but she didn't want to hang up. She couldn't remember exactly where he lived, somewhere near Holland Park, maybe. "Look, Gavin, I'm going to be in London tomorrow and I wanted to talk to you."

She heard a door closing at the other end, and then the noises were muffled away. Then Gavin's voice, reserved, querying: "Talk."

"Yes, talk. There's something—something I need help with."

"I'm not much good in the helping department. Ask around. Ask anyone. I'm bloody useless."

"Gavin, I—"

"Really, Hanna, it was very lovely to meet you at the conference, but—you know how these things go, when the cat's away . . . There's really nothing I can help you with." His voice sounded final. Hanna could hear the click coming.

"Listen to me, Gavin," she said softly, intensely. The kind of whisper you don't ignore. "I said I'm going to be in London tomorrow and you can meet me at the Euston Flyer at three, or you can put the wife back on the line, and I can stop being fucking *professional*."

Hanna took a morning bus into London. She had wanted to shower but she was afraid of what might happen with the water dripping off the edges of the opening in her neck. She had stolen some saran wrap from the communal kitchen and tried taping it like a band-aid in place. But the tape kept peeling and wouldn't hold properly, so eventually she gave up on the whole thing and did her hair in the sink. She put on makeup, dressed nicely, wanted to look good for him, for Gavin Fucking Hale. She didn't know why, but she did it anyway.

She couldn't sleep on the bus. She kept wedging her neck between the window and the seat to hold it steady, but then she was worried that she was pulling too much at the skin. At last she just settled her head back, and read the book that Gavin had given her. It was clean writing, serviceable prose with just the right amount of pathos, the perfect, quirky dialogue—all up to snuff; her publisher would be proud. An old woman with pinkish-dyed hair caught her eye, smiled, nodded at the book. Hanna pretended not to see.

When she arrived in London, she picked out a seat near the back where she had a good vantage point. She didn't know if Gavin would come. She didn't know if she'd make good on the threat, and was half-curious to find out.

Hanna spotted him, eighteen minutes late, a few minutes before she had decided to take out her cell phone to see if she could goad herself into calling. He made his way over, face looking dull, more like the author photo.

"Well," he said, "I'm here so you can call off the charge and put down your weapon. I'll come in peaceably if you only ask politely."

"Gavin." She put away the phone, waiting as he took his seat. "I'm glad you came."

"Ah, my dear editor. What shall it be, business or pleasure?" And then to the waiter who had wandered within distance: "We'll have two scotches. On me. Neat, no ice." The waiter nodded, and disappeared the way that good waiters do when they can sense an awkward situation. "Neat and tidy," Gavin continued, meaningfully, but this time to Hanna.

"I didn't know who else to call." Now that Gavin had come, Hanna realized she didn't have any idea what to say next, how to begin the conversation.

"Let me start. An autograph, maybe?" A little mean, snarky. "No, something else then. A second draft on the new manuscript? Notes and first impressions?"

"What about a second fuck?" Just to break his stride. He was making her angry.

"And then a third and a fourth and when would it end? We might as well *be* married at that point and then who the hell would edit my books? The wife can't do it." His stride unbroken, and even charming in spite of himself. "It'll be dogs and cats in the street. The lion and the lamb all cuddled up. The end of freedom, democracy, and Her Majesty out of work, pumping gas for a Paki kebab seller." He leaned back in his chair, took a sip from the scotch that had appeared magically on the table.

"Fine," she said.

———

They were in the bathroom, Hanna with her skirt up around her waist and Gavin holding her up, pinned against the side of the stall as he machine-gun thrust into her. A door opened, and then Hanna heard it closing again quickly, barely, over the sound of her panting and Gavin's deep-throated grunts.

Then they were finished, and Gavin was slumped down on the toilet, a happy, sweaty smile on his face, running a hand over her bare buttocks, pulling Hanna close until she was resting on his knee.

"Aren't you quite the surprise?" he said hoarsely, a little smugly too. "Fancy a second turn?"

This time Gavin spun Hanna around, her breasts pressed flat against the door. Hanna was afraid that the lock might give, the problem with ladies' bathrooms in old pubs where the doors didn't seem to fit the frame. Gavin pounded away behind, and his hands were at her waist, and then one cupping a breast, and then the other at her neck. Then she could feel something tearing along her shoulder, and warm numbness filled her so fast she thought she had already released.

But Gavin had stopped, she realized. His hand touched lightly upon her shoulder. He was saying something, softly, almost scared.

"A gentleman and a lady travelling from Tunbridge towards that part of the Sussex coast which lies between Hastings and Eastbourne, being induced by business to quit the high road and attempt a very rough lane, were overturned in toiling up its long ascent, half rock, half sand." Hanna didn't know what it meant, was almost lured by the unknitting of her thoughts, the pulse of pleasure still having built to a nice warmness, mingling with the numbness starting at her shoulder. She felt happy for a moment, but Gavin was still speaking. "There is something wrong here, said he, but never mind, my dear, looking up at her with a smile, it could not have happened, you know, in a better place, good out of evil. The very thing perhaps to be wished for. We shall soon get relief—"

"What's that?" Hanna murmured drowsily, forgetting she was leaning half-cocked against a mildly graffitied bathroom door.

"What do you mean, what's that?" Gavin asked.

"That—a gentleman and a lady travelling . . ."

"How the hell should I know?" He tugged on her arm, simultaneously pushing and pulling away from her. Then he was tugging up his pants, buckling his belt, as Hanna leaned against the side of the stall, trying to get her breath, not really enough room for the more elaborate elements of Gavin's attempts to put his clothes back on.

"Gavin, what's wrong?" The numbness fading away. Panic returning, fear. The sense of inevitable breakup, people drifting apart. "Did I—?"

"No," he answered. "Look." He unlatched the door, and there was that push-pull as he took her wrist, guided her to the bathroom mirror. She tried to hitch her skirt back down, and almost tripped.

Then she was in front of the mirror, and Gavin was running a finger along her shoulder, but there was no warmth to the gesture. Hanna looked, and at first she couldn't see it, but then she noticed the fault line running several inches to her clavicle. The edges of her skin had puckered up like old paper and there seemed to be nothing on the other side. Gavin reached up to where the fissure began, where a strip of something onion-thin, almost translucent, had curled up. He bent his head closer, tugging very gently on it. "*There*, I fancy, lies my cure, pointing to the neat-looking end of a cottage, which was seen romantically situated among wood on a high eminence at some little distance, does not *that* promise to be the very place?" He was reading, she realized, and then she could see that on the underside of the flap was a very tiny scrawl.

She pulled away from him without even thinking, her heart a misfiring jackhammer, and there was an awful tearing sound as the strip came away in his hand. She knelt down, grabbed the jacket she had left behind in the stall and wrapped in protectively around her shoulders.

"Whatever it is you're doing, I want you to make it stop."

"Whatever *I'm* doing?" he asked, but distractedly; he was staring at the piece that had torn away.

"I won't call your wife, I promise."

"Bugger my wife, Hanna," he said. "The old lady has nothing on you. She's made of nothing but laundry lists and children's paintings and cheap romance novels. If I cut her open I'd expect to find nothing more than a list of things she had forgotten to pick up at Sainsbury's, and maybe a notice about an overdue fine. But this is—"

"What?"

"—this is bloody Jane Austen."

Hanna did not go home to the tiny room in Cowley. Gavin set her up in a hotel room close to Victoria station, on a street filled with similar Georgian-style, whitewashed façades that hosted numerous other anonymous hotels. The manager knew Gavin, that was clear, and provided a room large enough to fit several of her Cowley apartment rooms inside. The space was comfortable, the bed soft and plush, the manager suitably unctuous, if a touch overly familiar.

Gavin guided her in, his demeanour having taken on the excited, manic glow of a kid at Christmas.

"You'll be fine here, darling," he said, drawing open the blinds, and then shutting them again quickly. "The least I can do, considering your . . . I'll have your things brought up from Oxford tonight."

Hanna nodded and sat down on the bed. Her shoulder wasn't sore, exactly, but she found herself wishing he would just go so that she could have a proper lie-down, clean herself up.

"But, Hanna, just in case—" She looked up at that. "—I don't think you should really go outside, not in your condition. Stay here. Rest up, fortify your reserves, and I'll have my doctor set up the appointment. Shouldn't take more than a day or two."

"I don't want to go outside," she replied.

"Of course not. Good." He wandered away from the window and came to stand nearby, still looking around the room distractedly. "As I said, shouldn't be more than a day or two. And I'll be in touch." She nodded, was surprised when he leaned down and kissed her on the mouth. Sought after some witty thing to say to him in response, because he was now looking at her eagerly, intently, for a touch longer than he should have been. He seemed to catch himself doing it, and he cleared his throat. "Take care, my darling, and don't worry, not about a thing. I'll take care of it all."

Then he was gone, and Hanna could feel the weariness taking its toll. She rolled onto her side, couldn't be bothered to get underneath the covers, and then for the first time it what seemed like a month, she slept—

—was woken up to the sound of her phone ringing.

"Hanna, Hanna, is that you?" Her publisher. "Hanna, something extraordinary is happening." The voice was cheery, chirpier than Hanna remembered it being.

"What is it, Miri?" she mumbled into the cell phone.

"I've just received a call from James in Brighton. And he received a call from someone by Vauxhall. Something's going on with Gavin Hale—something big. Everyone's buzzing about it, but no one knows what it is. All very hush-hush. But you saw him in Oxford, didn't you? Did he say anything?"

A stab of panic. Hanna propped herself up onto the pillows, trying to clear the mugginess from her brain. "No," she said quickly. "He didn't say anything. We just talked work. Regular work. The manuscript he was shopping around."

"Was he—I don't know—surely he must have said *something*?"

"No, just what you'd expect."

A pause on the other end. Some of the chirpiness was disappearing from Miriam's voice. "Can you find out what it is? You're—where are you staying?—close to London, that's right. See him. Set up a meeting. See if he'll cut us in."

"I don't think that's a very good idea."

"Hanna, you're twenty-eight years old and I know like every other twenty-eight-year-old working for crap pay, you've probably got an unfinished manuscript of your own stuffed away in a drawer, mounting student debt and the ache to *do* something real, to put some beautiful piece of fiction out into the world without it getting shat on, and maybe earn enough to feed yourself." Miriam's voice was picking up speed like a freight train. "And like every other out-of-grad-school hire, I can tell you that you know *nothing*. Not yet.

"Listen to me, your job status is about as close to probationary as it can be, and none of those pretty dreams are going to come true unless you can do this *simple*, fucking job. You're in London. This is what we need from you. That's *why* you're in London."

Hanna swallowed. "Right." Silence on the other end. "I'll see what I can do."

She hung up the phone. Her shoulder began to ache.

"I've cleared it with my agent, and I've got a deal all prepped and run through the legal mill," Gavin told her excitedly.

"I don't want a deal," Hanna replied. "I don't even know what the deal is *for*. I don't know what's *happening* to me!"

The hotel room had felt increasingly small over the last twelve hours, and Hanna had been pacing it back and forth like some kind of large predatory cat locked in a cage. This was the first bit of raw meat that had been dangled in front of her since Gavin had left her there, and she couldn't help but take a swipe at it. She just wanted to see something bleeding.

"Something extraordinary, my darling. One of the world's greatest authors, the peak of her career, just a pinch past forty and she's writing up a storm, really gaining momentum with these quirky little romantic comedy things she's been putting out there—and you know what?—the people love it, they're just falling all over themselves to find out what happens with all those stuffed-up, bloody aristocrats and then—BANG!—bile and rheumatism until her mind could no longer pursue its accustomed course, and it's all gone forever except that last, unfinished manuscript. *Sanditon*."

"*Sanditon?*"

"She was going to call it *The Brothers* for George Crabbe but—" He finally caught the long look that Hanna had been shooting at him, and perhaps he sensed something of the tiger in her. "Yes," he continued, a little abashed. "*Sanditon*. The unfinished manuscript, only twelve chapters that she wrote, but you, my dear, you—"

He stopped, his face caught in an expression of absolute rapture. Hanna didn't like the way he was looking at her.

"I think it's all there."

45

"What, the manuscript?"

"Yes, *the* manuscript, the whole bloody finished novel, there—"

"Gavin, that's impossible, crazy, *where is the doctor*?"

"The doctor?" Pulled up short.

"Yes, you imbecile, the doctor, the doctor, the fucking doctor you promised me!" Hanna practically shouted the words at him. She felt close to tears. She had been terrified to look at her shoulder, afraid that perhaps there would be nothing there after all, that it would just be some malignant melanoma and that the rest of it was all something dream-whipped up by the tumours pushing on her brain, spreading everywhere. She had dreamed that someone was feeding her through a paper shredder, and she had woken up screaming. Some of this finally seemed to get across to Gavin, and he stopped the triumphant parade, the gleeful little biography lesson and finally looked at her properly. She could see him doing it, re-evaluating her, shifting the categories in his mind.

He crouched down in front of her, and took her hand in his. "Hanna, darling." He stroked the sensitive flesh between her thumb and forefinger, brought her hand up and kissed it gently. "Something extraordinary is happening, miraculous. It's about more than doctors. It's about art and beauty, something coming back to us from beyond—I don't know, from beyond where—something we were supposed to have, that the world was supposed to have."

He kissed her hand again, and then reached up to gently touch her face. His eyes were wide, the feverish excitement gone for a moment, and Hanna couldn't tell if it was calculated or not, but she found herself slumping into him, into the warm embrace of his arms.

"It will be all right, my girl. There's a kind of magic to it all, miracles don't happen every day, and I'll be right here, I'll take care of you." He stroked her hair lightly, gently. "It's an extraordinary thing and we can't stand in the way of it. You understand, don't you?" He pulled away just the barest amount, and their eyes locked, his were liquid and brown and Hanna thought she could see the slight reflective sheen of what might have been tears in his eyes.

Hanna wanted to say that she didn't understand, why the hell should Jane Austen choose to write her last words on the inside of a twenty-eight-year-old editor, almost two hundred years after her death? That wasn't a miracle, that was fucking poor planning.

But Gavin was kissing her now, very gently, just a little nibble at her lower lip, and she found she didn't care quite as much as she thought she might, and maybe he was right anyway, maybe it was a miracle and all this was happening for some reason beyond her. And he kissed her again, and then that spot right behind her ear, his breathing a tickle in her hair, and then lower, and then—

"I just need to see it, Hanna," he whispered, "just to be sure, to know for sure, that I'm right. You understand, don't you?"

It had been a week. Her suitcase still hadn't arrived. She imagined it back in the tiny room in Cowley, shoved against the ceiling, the makeshift bookshelf beginning to sag now, hers and Gavin's papers beginning to muddle all together. Gavin had brought her a fresh set of clothes at least, but they didn't fit quite properly, a little tight across the chest, a little baggy around the waist, and Hanna was almost dangerously sure that they might have been things stolen from his wife's half of the closet.

She'd received three irate phone calls from her publisher, but she'd let them all go to voicemail. She consoled herself with the knowledge that she did, in fact, have the insider knowledge Miriam was looking for, even if she couldn't share it just yet. Gavin had warned her not to. Said he would talk to his lawyer first, make sure everything was kosher, and that she was protected. It turned out that she *wasn't*—a boilerplate bit of her contract gave Belletristic, Inc. the first right of refusal to anything she produced or obtained while 47 working for them. It was unclear which clause *Sanditon* would fall under, but it was clear that some part of the contract had it covered. So the lawyer had recommended a temporary gag order, and she'd listened, putting everyone through to voicemail except her parents, and stopped answering e-mails.

Her initial fear had begun to transmute into a waiting tension, and then boredom, and then curiosity. She had started trying to capture pictures of the novel with her cell phone. The outside bits were easy enough, where the skin had peeled back from the fissure, but she didn't want to cause any more damage. She fingered the papery tissue carefully, with her right hand, used her left hand to zoom and snap. The first twenty pictures were awful, but after several hours she found that she was starting to get the hang of it.

With the load of clothes, Gavin had also dropped off a copy of the 1925 Chapman transcription of the original manuscript, now housed in King's College, Cambridge. She had read through it eagerly, but in the end she found herself increasingly bored. There wasn't much of it, not enough to truly get the shape of the novel beyond the description of the town for which the novel was named, and its various, colourful inhabitants. It wasn't *Pride and Prejudice*, she thought, but it was something. And perhaps the missing bits would flesh it out, get to the real crux of the narrative.

She began to transcribe the images she could get out of the camera. It wasn't very much, though the writing was surprisingly dense. She finished what she could in about a day's worth of meticulous photographing and transcription. And then the boredom returned, hours of it, just sitting, reading and rereading the copy Gavin had left and then trying to match it up with what she had on her computer.

Hanna didn't know how it happened, exactly, but she found herself tugging on the skin just a little bit, to read several lines that had been obscured in shadow. And then just a little bit more. Soon she found there was a wide enough space that she could just fit in the edge of the slim phone if she was very careful. It felt strange, but not painful, rather a tickling sensation at the edge of the remaining skin and then nothing on the inside. Without a light, though, her cell phone didn't have a good enough camera to make out very much else, just dim shapes, the curvature of the inside of her skin.

But, still, she had plenty of new material. Hanna could intermittently pick out scraps of dialogue and narrative that hadn't been in the original. It wasn't all in proper order, after all, and trying to read it was something like putting together a jigsaw puzzle.

When Gavin arrived on the fifth day, Hanna was debating whether or not she might be able to get a little bit more brightness on the camera phone if she could manoeuvre herself closer to the bathroom light. She was standing up on the sink, shirtless, her shoulder pressed toward the ceiling and the cell phone held awkwardly in her right hand, snapping away like mad.

She almost fell onto the sink when she heard the door open. The ceramic cup holding her toothpaste crashed to the floor, and smashed apart.

"Hanna?" he called from the doorway. "Are you all right, darling?"

Hanna crouched down gingerly, careful to mind the bits of pottery, and popped her head out around the corner. "I'm fine. Where the fuck have you been, Gavin?"

His mouth crinkled with a smile, and his brow crinkled with a smug look. He tugged her in for a very passionate, if quick, kiss before releasing her. "I've been showing off the pages, that's where the fuck I've been. And—you know what?—they love them, everyone bloody loves them, want to know where we've been getting them. I've gotten half a dozen calls from Rosemary Culley of the Hampshire Jane Austen society, demanding to know where I found it and if I want to publish with them; and all the big boys, of course, James & Sweitzer, Great Auk, Door Holt, and that's just in Britain. The Americans can sense there's something going on, and even if they don't give two figs for Jane Austen, they can smell the money. Not that we'll go with the Americans, of course, not really theirs, is it? I mean, it's ours, of course, well, it ought to be—"

"And the Canadians?" she asked.

"Foreign rights, that's obvious. But there are no major players there, wouldn't make any sense to shop it around for the first print run, let them wait for it, they don't need it first—"

"I'm Canadian, Gavin," Hanna said pointedly.

He had the good grace to look abashed. "Of course, we'll consider every offer." He paused, checking to see if she was mollified, and then dismissing it. "But that's not really the point, is it? It's not about the money, it's about the culture, rediscovered, the unexhausted talent of the nation's greatest writer—"

"Shakespeare?"

"—Shakespeare, who is Shakespeare? A balding man with a passion for soliloquies, perhaps he had a couple of real zingers, *Macbeth*—*Hamlet* was a bit too slow if you ask me—but nothing like the human drama of Austen, the subtle play of wit, understatement, the clever critiques of a society straightjacketing itself out of all the good bits of life."

Hanna could see that he had worked himself up into a frenzy of speechifying, but the patter sounded clean, a little too clean—rehearsed maybe. The kind of thing you might deliver in an interview or on a talk show.

"I'll need the next lot of papers," he added. "The work you're doing is extraordinary, just extraordinary, my girl. My editor. My perfect editor." He paused for a moment, noticing at last that she had her shirt off. "What's happened here?" He reached toward her, fingering very gently the flaps of skin, more than there had been the last time he had been there.

"An experiment," Hanna replied, smoothing it out of his grasp and back over the gap in her shoulder. She moved out of range, feeling his speculating gaze on her back, to where she had kept some safety pins. Deftly, she slid the pins through the double flaps of skin, pinching closed the hole so that it would not tear further. "I don't know how else I'm supposed to get anything else out of it. There's only so much I can read on the outside."

"Right." He nodded, still speculating. "Of course. Can't just cut you open, can we?" He laughed. She did not.

The next day he returned with a new camera, one mounted on the end of a snake tube. He had duct-taped a very small LED light to the tip of it. He sat her down on the bed, and carefully unhooked the safety pins, slid the camera in. Hanna held her laptop on her knees. She sat very still, afraid to move. And then the pictures began to flood in, a little grainy at first, but there was so much more than she had been able to capture herself. She felt herself getting caught up in the excitement of it all, catching little snippets that she knew she could slot into the jigsaw puzzle of the narrative.

Gavin was breathing heavily, his mouth very close to her ear as he tried to manoeuvre the camera around. He kept shifting his weight, making the bed creak, and throwing off her balance. But she didn't move. Kept very still for what seemed like hours. She had to pull herself up straight so that her stomach, sagging a little from the English food and the lack of exercise, wouldn't wrinkle and distort the images on the inside. Finally, he pulled out the little camera.

"Well done, my darling." He beamed at her, and this time she did smile back, good and proper, but her eyes were already drifting back to the manuscript, the long scrawls of words written around the slight concave dimple of where her spine stretched out the skin of her back, the flat of her shoulder blade, the hollowed insides of her breasts.

———

The weeks had crawled by, and now Hanna was watching Gavin on television, with some late night talk show host with a polished look to him: steel-grey hair, charming and a little self-deprecating, in a neat grey suit. Gavin was well-turned-out, and his bearing showed off his confidence to best effect. He was talking animatedly. "*Sanditon*," he said, "she called it, and I quote, 'the very spot which thousands seemed in need of.' And now we have it."

She muted the volume. The real Gavin was lying next to her in the bed, had stayed over for the last few nights. Hanna was glad of it, had found that the standard assortment of complaints she typically brought to bear against her partners didn't quite bother her so much. Perhaps it was the general loneliness. Perhaps it was because he was married, and didn't seem as demanding as she would have imagined. Sometimes he seemed to forget about the sex altogether, caught up in a blur of telephone calls, the occasional phone interview or, as she was watching just then, major media appearances. What had been an energetic bit of fucking, punctuated by happy moments of productivity had soon blurred into less frequent heavy petting and a little more kindness. He read to her from the manuscript, practised his interviews with her, got her to ask him questions, and waited, patiently, for her evaluation of his performance.

But not right then. Then he was nuzzling her shoulder, careful around the pins, didn't want to hurt her, he said. By this point, Hanna didn't know if it actually was hurting or dangerous. The doctor had never come, despite assurances from Gavin that he would pop round tomorrow or the next day. Not malice. It wasn't even deception—not real deception—but she could see the question drifting out of his mind two seconds after she'd asked it, not sticking in there as a real concern at all. And so it had become less real to her as well. The manuscript was almost finished, and there would be time for doctors after that, and money too. Gavin had negotiated an advance of half a million pounds, almost unheard of, and his phone had rung off the hook for about a week—enquiries from Jane Austen's estate, more pressing queries from the librarian at Cambridge demanding that he stop the press releases until the veracity of the document could be determined, requests from researchers, book dealers, rival agents, rival lawyers—until he got a second phone, giving the number only to his agent, his lawyer, Hanna, and his wife.

"You're beautiful, my darling, well and truly beautiful."

Hanna smiled, touched the silk-wire hairs on his chest. "And you are a man who gets paid to make things up for a living."

"Am I?" he asked plaintively. "I had forgotten. It seems as if I'm only parroting other people's words, a publicist for the dead." His eyes flicked to the screen.

"I believe I'm the one who is supposed to be feeling sorry for myself. You should be cheering me." She quirked an eyebrow, curious at the change of tone.

"Right," he said. "That's why I began with the bit about you being beautiful. Which is true, by the way. Every word of it."

"I'm the editor," she answered. "Not the wife. Don't make me the wife."

"Ah, the crux of it all."

"Cruxes are for editors, I was taught."

"Crosses are for wives." He paused. "To bear, that is. I am my wife's cross, she says sometimes."

Hanna said nothing.

"I think I might not go home tonight."

Nothing.

"I think I might not go home ever again." He whispered.

Television-Gavin was saying something witty to the camera, and, muted, Hanna just caught the close-up on his face, smiling. She thought about that smile—the cat's smile—slipping on and off again, the warmth of him beside her. Felt a little sad.

"I think you should go home."

The next day, Hanna left the hotel room. The unctuous hotel manager, attentive to the last, stopped her at the door.

"Mr. Hale said that you weren't to leave." His voice apologetic.

"Mr. Hale is not my fucking *keeper*," Hanna hissed. The manager took a step back, and she took the opportunity to walk out the front door.

She took the bus from Victoria station to Oxford, this time without a book, without anything to do. After a while, Hanna took out her phone, began to check the missed messages—an overflow of worry, excitement, sometimes anger until the voices themselves became increasingly indistinct, just a mass of things wanted from her, things offered to her. She was fired, apparently. Her mother wanted her to come home. Something from Gavin at the end that she pointedly ignored.

There was a weight lifting from her, as she stared out the window, watching the hills roll by, a patchwork quilt of dark green shrubs and lighter tones of grass, fields, the strange light of the shifting mass of clouds a clear sign that rain was coming. But it was England, and there was always rain coming, so she just watched the clouds, mottling from silver to black to white, shades and textures she never saw in the sky back in Toronto.

Hanna made her way up Divinity Road, and turned off at Minster, the smell of roses and heavy humidity in the air. She barely recognized the house now, but when she unlocked the door to her room everything was where it had been before. She was worried that someone might have put her things out by the side of the road, even though she had paid up for four months in advance.

Carefully, she climbed up onto the bed and unwedged her suitcase from its cramped space between the shelf and the ceiling. She had forgotten how small the room was, and it smelled musty now from the windows being closed in the summer. The bed was unmade, the towel she had used to wash her hair before she went to London hanging from the inside door knob. Dry now.

She put the suitcase on the floor, and lay down on the bed.

Someone was knocking on the door to the room. Hanna opened it cautiously, mostly expecting to see Gavin standing in the entranceway, but it was an oldish woman, formerly pretty, with smallish breasts and a rounding waistline.

"The wife," Hanna guessed aloud.

"The editor." The woman quirked her head, smiled, and she was prettier than Hanna had imagined at first. "May I come in, love?"

Hanna gestured her in, but there was really nowhere for the two of them to sit, not with the suitcase taking up most of the available floor space. The woman did not try to sit, standing a little awkwardly. Hanna caught her looking around the room, her eye taking in the peeling ceiling, the narrow walls. "Sorry," Hanna apologized. "I've apparently lost my job. But it didn't pay very well to begin with—thus, the room."

"Gavin tells me that you stand to make a good deal of money soon, you and he. Are you going somewhere?" She nodded to the suitcase, and Hanna took the handle, tipping it up vertically so that there was a little extra space.

"Home, I think."

"Not on my account, I hope?" The woman's gaze was sharp, but then she smiled again and sat down heavily on the bed. Hanna sat down beside her, not quite as heavily, still unsure of the bearings of the conversation, unable to navigate it.

"No—" she began. "It's just been a long time. I miss it."

The woman nodded. "Well, you're a pretty girl. I imagined you would be, common as any young lady in the kingdom with a tolerable complexion and a showy figure—" Quoting now from the book. "—very accomplished and very ignorant."

Hanna didn't let herself show any sign of emotion at the jibe. "He showed it to you then? The pages?"

"That's not new, love. The original, the bit we already had." Mrs. Hale turned away then, and began to dig through a large, overstuffed purse she had brought with her. Eventually she took out a manila envelope tied shut with string. She unwound the string carefully, not drawing out the suspense on purpose, but Hanna began to feel it anyway, something like dread. The envelope had an address on it, and a name, JAMES MARTEN, M. D.

Finally, Mrs. Hale slipped out a series of photographs—x-rays, the shapes white and grey against a background of black, oddly reminding Hanna of the clouds earlier. But then as she looked further, she began to make out letters, little scrawls. Her eyes had gotten surprisingly good at reading this kind of text, fitting the superimposed images together, separating them into sensible bits and re-arranging them in order.

It was a love letter. To Hanna Greeson, the most darling editor in all the world. She couldn't make out all of it, but what she could read was most definitely Gavin's—clean writing, serviceable prose with just the right amount of pathos, the perfect, quirky endearments. But tiny, distorted, imprinted on the insides of his tissue.

"He came home complaining of a pain, oh, months back now. Around the time he went to Oxford. And met you, I expect. Dr. Marten investigated. We were worried about colon cancer. His father went that way, younger than he should have. He was about Gav's age. We were both very scared.

"But then the results came back and it wasn't cancer, and Gavin said he had found something, he had a major project due, something big. Yes, he showed me some of the pages. They were good. Very good. And it was all very exciting, a huge relief, something to take our minds off the things that had almost, but not quite happened. But he didn't come home one night. I wasn't surprised really. Sometimes he does that when he's working. God knows, we have enough money and with the kids around it can be hard for him to get writing done, so when he's in one of those moods and there's a deadline coming, sometimes he'll just rent a hotel in town and stay on until the work is done. Or so he's always told me.

"But then the doctor's office called. I was half-sure that they had been wrong the first time, and it was cancer after all, but no, something else. They showed me the photographs. I didn't know what it was."

She was silent for a long moment. Hanna looked again at the images, Gavin from the inside, made strangely unfamiliar when she saw all the curves and the angles backward. And the writing, of course.

"He told me. He told me about the pages. About everything." Mrs. Hale looked up and Hanna found herself returning the look, unwilling to speak. And then, unexpectedly, she rested her hand on Hanna's.

"It's okay, love. Really it is. You weren't the first, and I have no doubt there will be others. It's just his way, and I've made my own peace with it. It's what we do—wives, that is. It's what marriage always meant to me, and it's why I married him. Because he needs someone to care for him, for all that bundled enthusiasm and pride and ego and sometimes kindness. He's not a bad man.

"And the truth is—the real truth, between us women— is that I'd rather have *Sanditon*. Even if Gavin never wrote another word, the world would keep turning, there are plenty of Gavin Hales in the world and no one would really mourn." Her smiled quirked up, reminding Hanna of Gavin's smile, the way two people can come to look alike when they have shared a life together. "But then there's you, my dear, and then there's Jane. And maybe the world can't live without her. Maybe that's what it all means."

Carefully, Mrs. Hale reached for the photos, took them from Hanna's numb fingers, slipped them back into the envelope and placed it on the bed beside them.

"He might come for you."

"I'm going home. Tonight," Hanna said.

"He might come anyway. But I hope not. He's a good husband, despite everything."

Mrs. Hale stood, took her oversized purse and left.

Hanna was alone in the room. The envelope was beside her, but she found that she didn't want to look at it again. She could hear the footsteps going down the stairs, listened as the front door quietly clicked shut.

Then she unzipped the suitcase, and searched around inside for her own manuscript, the pages not entangled with Gavin's after all. She counted out each one, finding herself reading bits and pieces as she went, automatically reassembling the words in her head, the shape of the unfinished story. Hanna found she liked it still.

And then she slipped off her jacket, unbuttoned the blouse beneath and slipped that off too. The pins had kept the skin from tearing much further, but she could feel the perforation running down farther, almost to the swell of her breast now. She undid the pins one by one. She pulled back the flaps of skin. The ink smudged a bit, but she didn't need to be so careful now that it was all fully photographed, the words recorded. She found that she could peel away most of her shoulder, that queer feeling of numbness and excitement all wrapped up together.

And then she rolled up her manuscript, and she slid it through the gap, could feel the slight pressure of it against her ribs, on her pelvis. It felt right there. She reinserted the pins again, closing up the gap, thought better of it, and took out the tiny traveller's sewing kit she kept in the top drawer. Bit by bit, she stitched together the edges until they just about fit, only a few times when she had to tug the skin close to match up ends that didn't quite join up any longer. She could feel the weight of it, the way the pages settled against her inside, the words face-to-face with Jane's, pressed together, ink rubbing on ink in the darkness inside her skin.

[skin]

A TEXTURE LIKE VELVET

To Jeffrey M. Beeler, Professor, St. Hugh's College, Oxford
Delivered—after some delay—October 4, 1945

To Jeffrey:—
It is my most fervent hope that this letter reaches you, although it is impossible for me to know in what state I shall be upon your receipt of it, if any action on your part might prove beneficial, or indeed, wise. I do not know if the University is aware of all that has transpired. I do not know if this letter shall be burnt, or simply scoured for some sign of guilt, if it is read at all. Please read it, Jeffrey. I am afraid.

They have given me this paper, this scrap upon which to write and although I do not know to what purpose it

shall be put afterward, it is the only recourse left to me—
me, whom you chided so pitilessly, whom you swore would
never sit an exam while you lived and breathed, whom
you so staunchly opposed, for whom every road was made
steep, every word harsh, every test stringent and inflexible,
the one you goaded, forced, exhorted so severely that no
choice was left to me but to know the works of Aeschylus
and Hesiod, Archilochus and Alcaeus and Sappho—all
those great masters whose words have survived through
the painstaking efforts of scribes and scholars such as
yourself—as completely, as minutely, as you yourself did.

This is a feeble Prologue, I fear, and if you have not scoffed
at the notice of the sender, then I hope the carelessness of
the prose has not turned you further against me. (*Avoid
cacophony and* hiatus, you might have written, *let your
sentences be short and uncontaminated by such emotional
discourse. We are rational animals, are we not? To the point,
Miss Bahr, to the point!*)

And so—to the point!—I have been engaged for some
time in a study of a certain manuscript come to light
recently in the Bibliotheca Estense in Modena, a small
volume written on a fine vellum, much damaged by fire
but still clearly one of the earliest copies of a work thought
to be attributed to Aristotle. My research indicated—
and those colleagues of mine I call friends at the Royal
Society have verified the results, checked transcription
after transcription—that the book can be reliably placed
near Heliopolis in origin, housed, I had hoped, in the lost
Library of Alexandria.

I can imagine your scepticism at such a claim:
Overreaching, Miss Bahr—your constant criticism!—*align
the evidence first and let such conclusions as come naturally
follow upon it*. And perhaps such chastisement is deserved.
Perhaps. Nevertheless, it was not the contents themselves
nor, indeed, even the provenance of the book that was the
thing. No, the parchment—the stretched and tattered skin,
barely readable, discoloured by fire yet still beautifully
resilient after all these years.

In May, I departed for Cairo at the request of the Society. My passport was stamped, my visa checked in triplicate and the manuscript eyed hairily by authorities who neither understood its value nor my own purpose. "Where is the *ustatha*? The professor?" they would ask, your perfect echoes, deaf to any protestations that I was as skilled a researcher as any.

Finally, a small, svelte man with immaculate English arrived to take me to the Museum of Egyptian Antiquities. Khaled Nassar, he said his name was, and he was a godsend, though he and I had much cause to dispute the term. *Thou shalt not consent unto him, nor hearken unto him; neither shall thine eye pity him, neither shalt thou spare, neither shalt thou conceal him*, says the Torah, but what do such words mean in a strange land, far from home? It has always been this way for my people. But I digress. . . .

At the Museum my true work began. That intoxicating blend of excitement and curiosity you praised alone of my virtues, driving me forward even as exhaustion dragged my mind from those soaring pinnacles of knowledge, which we have glimpsed in the gelid mists of our studies. I was alone, utterly alone, but for my rescuer, my liaison with the Museum. He helped me negotiate the streets of that wretched city, sweat crawling down my spine, and taught me the few words of Arabic that helped me survive. In the evening, he would bring a strong, sweet coffee which we drank to the dregs together, discussing the struggles of research, the petty bureaucracies that exist in all Universities. Between us, there was that flash of friendship that comes when two minds strike against each other, flint on steel; and I remember the way his eyes might crinkle like foolscap when he laughed, the softness of his voice made thick by the strange accent I had only recently learned to negotiate. With the others I felt a stranger but with him, with Mister Nassar, that strangeness was not something to be feared but something to be celebrated— *Therefore love the stranger, for you were strangers in the land of Egypt.*

Mister Nassar brought to my research an exhaustive knowledge of the writings of antiquity, but more than that, he had a brother in Giza who working with a team of French scientists. He had agreed to sample the manuscript and perform the necessary tests to verify its authenticity.

It took five days for the results to arrive from Giza, five days of the breath of Hades on my neck as I tried to fill my time reviewing my students' Michaelmas papers in a hotel infected as by much by fleas as by the refugees pouring into the city daily, five days of cryptic responses from my liaison: "Soon, *ustatha*, it will be soon." The paper, when it came, was heavily worn and bore many official stamps. I opened it carefully, reverently—indeed, it was that very document that has brought me to my current, wretched state. For I learned that my little codex *had* been housed in the Alexandrina Bybliothece, but that was it not all. . . .

The fateful words of dear Mister Nassar are burned into my mind forever: "The skin, *ustatha*," he said. "It is not sheep." And then he touched my hand. "Human."

It may seem a little thing to you, Jeffrey, that touch. A kind of well-practised ritual among friends, like breaking bread, a social nothing whose language is so banal, so often read, that the words mean nothing. Perhaps I should say nothing of it, perhaps it would be safer to admit nothing. But he had never touched me before that, and so the shock of it, to you a simple thing but to him *taboo*, forbidden, to me— it was electric! That touch. Those words. "The skin, *ustatha*."

A book written on human skins.

A chill still runs up my spine when I think on it, even in this place, whose blank, dull walls leave me insensate, whose twilight is perpetual. I have been a scholar for some years, and I have given all of my energies and most of my eyesight to the study of books. When I sleep, I smell the musty scent of their pages; when I wake, my fingers explore them, probe their bindings, the threads that stitch them together. I know the soft velvet of the flesh side and the smooth, oiled surface of the hair side. I have studied the pattern of follicles, traced the network of veins that undergirds our most precious documents, the records of civilization, the rise and fall of human knowledge, and the Torah, most sacred of all precious texts. I have devoted my life to recovering the irrecoverable and rebuilding what was lost, searching out its ghosts and giving them flesh within monographs and articles.

There is an old passage I remember having found, marked out in one of my undergraduate books, a simple image, you may recall, but a striking one, drawn from some apocryphal commentary, some pseudo-Dionysius or other such Church Father:

In this way Christ, when his hands and feet were nailed to the cross, offered his body like a charter to be written on. The nails in his hands were used as a quill, and his precious blood as ink. And thus, with this charter he restored to us our heritage that we had lost.

It seemed very beautiful to me, always, that image of Christ's body stretched on the cross like an animal skin, like parchment; the blood, the wounds, the pierced heart, that holy alphabet, the covenant, mankind's heritage, lost, restored to us through the purest form of sacrifice. . . . It *should* have been a thing of beauty, an act of the greatest love, but I cannot think upon it now without shuddering. . . .

I looked to Mister Nassar, and he to me, and in his eyes I saw the traces of something crumbling, the vast architecture of a world dissolved into dust. It hurt me to see it. It hurt me to know that my eyes mirrored the same transformation. And with that pain, something else. His hand touching mine.

That was twelve months ago, and it could have been twelve years. He and I, joined by the strange bonds of discovery, left Cairo that day, clutching the codex but borne down by the weight of its presence, for we knew, deep in our hearts, that it was not just one book.

Indeed, Mister Nassar's connections were invaluable, and discreetly, we were able to obtain samples of manuscripts from across the country—from Plato,

Pythagoras, Aristophanes of Byzantium, Apollonius of Rhodes—all those great men you so adore, towards whose study you have given most of your life and, certainly, all of your kindness. For one and all, the answer was the same. "The pages, the skin of them," he had said. "Human."

In the intervening months, we visited many archaeological sites, studied the ancient midden heaps of Heliopolis, Sharm El-Sheikh and Aswan. The travel was difficult, dangerous even then despite the British victories. There were soldiers everywhere, the British, the Egyptians . . . but somehow it meant nothing, we read the news sparingly, fearing it might divide us, I, a woman of Britain and him, a native of the country, but in truth we were absorbed entirely in the work at hand. It was necessary—you see that, don't you, Jeffrey? You, at least, would understand!— we had to know.

Beneath the layers of thousand-year-old refuse were bones, bones, bones, so many of them that it sickened me. Whole villages had been wiped out, their inhabitants sacrificed to the altar of the great gods of our civilization. A single codex could have required as many as three hundred hides, the young valued most highly for the smoothness, the freedom from blemishes. A seven-year-old child could provide enough for twelve folios; an adult, perhaps sixteen, though the quality would suffer for it.

History's secret, the silent conflagration, we called it, as we huddled in tents that clung to the edges of the desert. It became *our* secret, and we whispered it to each other again and again. "Skin," Mister Nassar would repeat, until the words meant nothing and the charred midnight air snatched them away.

What would you do, Jeffrey, with the weight of that knowledge hanging upon you? What would you do if you were offered a chance to set it right? The press of a button and that slaughter of innocents prevented? Would you have the strength of will to silence Aristotle, to let the words which shaped civilization go unremembered, unpreserved, reduced to whispers and empty air?

It was men who did it. Men who desired books, who knew these things must last, that it meant more than those hundred thousand lives.

The pyramids were built on such sacrifices.

We could not bear that knowledge, Mister Nassar and I. As we walked through the densely cloying mass of the city, we saw nothing but books: the face of the old man who sold us pomegranates, the rind torn open to expose the sweet seeds beneath, nothing but a length of skin to be taken from the body, scraped, hung on a wooden frame, and whitened with chalk. That woman wailing for her brother killed by the Germans, would her grief be better written in ink? More legible? More permanent?

It was not so different when we touched, in the evenings when the desert grew softer, the air hazy and us both drugged senseless with the horror of it, his hand on mine, the skin of him nothing but another book, his body an archive laid out before me, before my blindly groping hands. . . .

I heard in one of the provinces a woman was stoned for adultery. There was a madness falling upon the land then, we could feel it. Mister Nassar would whisper, "We must be careful. We must be careful, *ustatha*." And other things, softer things, there in the desert, when we were alone. It is the softness of him that I will remember, the way the light played upon the curve of his bones, the network of almost blue veins on the underside of his wrist, the smoothness of that skin, its beautiful, dark colour.

They came for me in a small village where we were excavating: the men with their heavy boots and their guns. They said my visa had expired, that I was not to have left the Museum, I was not to have travelled, alone, with a man who was not my kin. Mister Nassar laid a hand upon one of them in protest, a touch, a simple thing, and they were on him like animals, beating him, kicking him, and I yelled for them to stop, I told them I would come, if they would please, just stop hurting him. . . .

Oh, Jeffrey.

They have held me for many days here. I do not know how long. Too long. I have not seen Mister Nassar for some time. Khaled, my love, yes, I believe he is dead. A man came in a clean white coat and I gripped a piece of wood in my mouth and pushed and pushed and pushed, and I held the child in my arms for only a moment, saw the fingers flex, each one tiny and perfect, the dark thatch of hair, the brown eyes, the skin the colour of milk stirred into sweet, black coffee. They took the child, Jeffrey, they took my daughter from me, *his* daughter.

Come to the point now, Miss Bahr, you will be saying now, *in the wake of chaos, Reason, even then!* Perhaps you are impatient at the narrative, perhaps you are doubtful or perhaps, simply, you do not care. What should it matter, you might ask, this precious research, this great secret of History, this silent conflagration of the innocents? For dead is dead, you might say, and sheep or child, History would have swallowed them regardless, in plague or famine or war. Dead is dead. At least something of them lives on. In their skins. In the books.

But it is more than that, is it not? Must it not mean more than that?

After weeks of pleading, begging, they have given me these scraps that I may write to you, Jeffrey, that I might bestow the terrible gift of knowledge upon you—my reluctant, recalcitrant teacher, the guardian of History's most precious treasures, you, Jeffrey. This is my gift to you.

I am afraid.

The light is dim. My eyes are weak and strained, and the shapes of the letters blur in front of me. I write more by touch than by sight now, these hands of mine groping across the page, smooth, so smooth, with a texture like velvet, free, I hope, of blemishes, the colour white except where the chalk has rubbed away, where it is coffee-dark. I am afraid, Jeffrey, that as my hands move, they will discover in those scraps the shape of a child, or a lover, or a bullet hole.

This is, I fear, the last thing I will write. But I don't care. It is coming now. The charnel house. Oh, Khaled, my love.

But I want to be heard, I want it to be remembered.

And thus, with this charter he restored to us our heritage that we had lost.

I do not want to vanish into this darkness so completely. It is selfish, I know, all these words, at the end, knowing what I do. But I am afraid, Jeffrey. I am afraid to stop writing. I thought you stripped all fear from me in those hallowed halls, in the great libraries, but I am afraid. I am nothing. I am nothing, but I want to be heard. It doesn't matter. Please, Jeffrey.

I must write.

I must write.

The parchment . . .

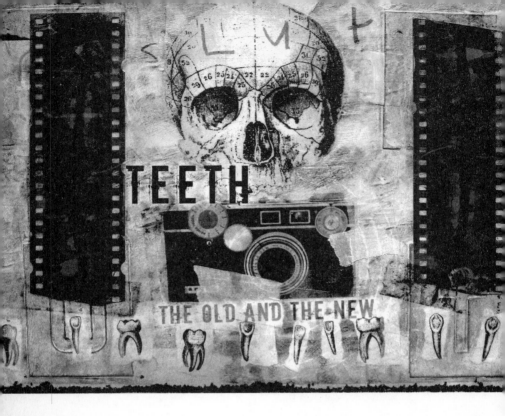

[teeth]
THE OLD AND THE NEW

The catacombs were dark, and Becca felt a chill settling over her entire body the moment she emerged from the narrow, spiralling staircase. She could hear a rheumatic gurgling in the distance. Or perhaps it was close by. It was very hard to get a sense of the space, and Becca wanted to reach out and take John's hand but the staircase had been too narrow, so she had had to go it alone, John in front, enthusing about the quality of the light, the patterns of the shadows on the stones.

John loved the play of the light on the stones here.

"Look at this," he said. "We don't have anything this old back home." He patted the walls affectionately. "Nah, everything's brand new—so shiny it could be made of plastic. But this—" *pat pat* "—this is the real thing, this is *old*. This reeks of history."

Becca looked around a little bit sceptically—not too sceptically, she *wanted* to be here, really she did, or rather, she wanted to be with John and John wanted to be here, and so, by association, she wanted to be here as well. She made an encouraging noise, kind of like an *ooh-aah* all run together. The stones really were old . . . very old. They had that sort of rough-hewn look to them, as if they were carved by peasants. They probably were, she thought. Not a sandblaster or an electric drill or anything like that, just hammers and chisels, or maybe even fingernails—who knew what the peasants might have been given to work with?

"But that's the problem with North America, isn't it?" John asked. "Nothing old, nothing that sticks around that long. Nothing but teepees before the Europeans showed up, and they don't last for more than a couple of years at best. Maybe you get a lighthouse here, a church there, but that's nothing. This is it. Right here." John had a happy look in his eyes, and so Becca smiled with him, and she *oohed* and *aahed* at the walls and the creeping dampness, and the smell of rot and dead things that had lived and died years and years before her country had even become a proper country.

But then they hit the bones, and the rocks were nothing—the rocks were meaningless, because here were over six million dead Frenchmen (and women, probably, but Becca couldn't remember if women were buried properly back then—maybe it was just the men, but the women *had* to be buried, didn't they?).

And the bones were . . . something. They were lined up, row upon row upon row of them, all these smiling bone faces with black eyeholes like another set of little caves for her and John to explore. But that's what the brochure had said, some unreadable stuff in French and then in big letters: STOP! THIS IS THE EMPIRE OF DEATH!

There were so *many* of them—that's what amazed Becca the most, how many there were. Six million. Six million people had been buried here in the catacombs. Becca couldn't even fathom that number. If she squinted she could almost pretend that they were rocks, that they hadn't been people at all, they were just rocks that might look a little bit person-shaped.

Becca didn't like the way they smiled at her. It was creepy, all that smiling in a place where over a six million dead people had been put on display.

When John slipped his hand into hers, Becca almost yelped, and she was thankful that the hand gripping hers had flesh and was warm and even a little sweaty. She was glad for it, that warm hand. So glad she gave it a little squeeze. Then Becca looked at John, she smiled but a shiver ran over her spine when John smiled back because right behind him were row on row of eyeless, skinless heads smiling right along with him.

Paris was beautiful in a way Becca hadn't expected it to be. Montmartre. The Eiffel Tower. All those lights winking at her from across the dark cityscape. She hadn't thought much of Paris, really, until John had said he wanted to go, had always wanted to go, and that he wanted *her* to go with him. Then Paris seemed magical, everything about it seemed magical—the city of light, *la Ville-Lumière*, he had called it.

Becca thought quite a lot of John, had always thought of him. She used to watch him while she was at the photocopier back when she first started working for the firm, fetching coffee and the like. Becca suspected that John hadn't thought very much of her initially. John was one of those easygoing handsome sorts who tended to work at firms, effortlessly charming in conversation, with little streaks of silver running at his temples. John never spoke to her, but that was all right because John was married, and so Becca watched him while she did the photocopying. She didn't talk to him. Others did. There were always people stopping by his office for a chat or a coffee. His wife, sometimes, with bags of take-out food from Pusateri's or some other expensive place. They'd eat together in the office. She'd sit on the desk, and she'd kick her legs, long legs, perfectly slim beneath some sort of frippy little summer dress, and John would look at her and smile. She was a pretty woman. Prettier than Becca, with small slim hands and blonde hair Becca would have killed for.

Not Becca though, she never talked to John. She was just an intern, so she didn't exist, his eyes just skipped over her. When they rode together in the elevator there was nothing but silence between them, he wouldn't even look up, not once. He only had eyes for *her*, his beautiful, blonde wife.

One day, it was news around the office that John wasn't married anymore. No one quite knew what happened—if she'd left him or what or why or for whom. But the ring was gone, and so was the charming smile, and the little streaks of silver became a bit more than that, like someone had smudged them, like he had aged ten years overnight. Becca felt sad as she watched him after that, people didn't stop by his office anymore, they didn't bring him coffee. Well, they did at first, all curious to know what had happened, but John would simply get a look on his face—a sad look— and then he would smile a sad smile, and they would feel bad that they had asked, bad that they were disturbing him. Pretty soon, they stopped visiting altogether.

Becca felt sad for him too, sad for the way he shuffled around the papers on his desk as if he didn't quite know what to do with his hands, as if he had forgotten why they were there, ringless. Once, when he was out on his morning smoke break, she snuck into his office and she left a coffee for him—two sugars, the way he liked it. She waited by the photocopier. She copied things. She decided that she had copied those wrong, that there was a smudge on the page, and her boss wouldn't like a smudge on the page. So she copied those things again. But then that load didn't look quite right either, so she decided there must have been something on the copying panel. Becca made quite a show of cleaning the copier, and she copied the pages a *third* time because that was what her boss would have wanted. John didn't come back to the office though. And the third set of copies didn't have a smudge. Not even a hint of a smudge, nothing smudgy or blotted or wrong with them at all. So Becca fiddled for a moment, hoping for something, for *anything* to be wrong with them, but there wasn't so she retrieved her papers, and left.

"How about a photo?" John said, smiling, but he wasn't really looking at her, his eyes were rapt with the camera.

"I don't think so." She said it with a smile so he wouldn't think she didn't want a picture taken with him, just that she didn't want a picture with . . . *them*. All of them.

"Just one. It'll be nice. Just one? I don't want to forget this. I don't want to forget our first trip to Paris. We want to remember this, don't we? We'll never see anything like this again, and just think, we can be a part of it for a little while. We can show the folks back home that we were really, *really* here."

Becca didn't want a picture, but John wanted it, and she wanted John to be happy.

"All right," she said. She squeezed his hand and let him manoeuvre her to the nearest shelf of bones.

"Not that group," John said after he had held up the camera. "The light's no good there. Try this one—well, maybe this one. Much better ones here. Whoever did that lot wasn't good," and he laughed. "Probably didn't get a promotion for that lot of bones. Must have been the dull one out of the bunch."

Finally, it was right and John was happy and he held the camera up and said, "Smile!" So she smiled and he smiled— and when he turned the camera around to show the tiny digital display, a thousand dead Frenchman smiled and winked alongside her.

John didn't come back from his break. Becca watched his office from her tiny desk—it wasn't a proper desk, just a table set up for her. From where she was seated, she could see the steam rising from the coffee, and then, after a little while, there was no steam.

He didn't come back after lunch either, and when Becca went to do the afternoon copying, the coffee was still sitting there, untouched. It had to be quite cold. It had been several hours. But she didn't want to give John cold coffee, did she? What if he thought she did it on purpose? What if he got back in the afternoon from an important meeting with his divorce lawyer and he found a cup of cold coffee? *She* used to drop off coffee, he would think to himself, my wife, Laura, whatever her name was, *she* used to drop off coffee and now I won't ever have a hot coffee in my life, only cold coffees for me from now on. As if a broken heart wasn't enough.

That would be a little bit cruel, a little bit sad. And Becca wanted him to be happy. John deserved to be happy. He was a good man, a kind man, the kind of man you ought never to leave. And so she left the copying to go, and she went back into the office.

She just meant to grab the coffee. Just the coffee and that was it. But then she couldn't help it, she saw on his desk a photo—a photo of a woman smiling. Laura. Or whatever her name was. His wife. The picture didn't look old. It looked quite recent, and she was smiling at the photographer, really smiling, not the kind of fake smiles that most people did for cameras. It was a real smile, and there was so much love in it, more love than Becca had ever put into a smile before. Most of her smiles were littler things than that, she didn't show her teeth ever, she thought they were big and horsey. But Laura had nice teeth. Nice little even rows of super-clean, white teeth.

Becca found herself hating that picture. Why would he even have the picture up still, when Laura, or whatever her name was, had left him—had just up and vanished? She picked up the picture, and she slipped it out of the frame. There it was, on the back: *Laura*. That was her name after all. Laura. No date, no other words, just Laura. Laura was a bitch, Becca thought, how could she have left him? She was a slut. Becca didn't like the word, would never say it out loud, but somehow it seemed right. Becca picked up a magic marker, and she wrote across the back of the photo *SLUT* in wobbly writing. Then she put it back into the frame, but you could see the word, *SLUT,* all across that smiling, perfect face. And then in the corner, Laura. Just a name, nothing more.

Becca picked up the coffee cup. It was cold. She sipped it, and the coffee was sweet, too sweet for her, but it was just how John liked it. She drank the entire cup.

She couldn't leave the picture there. How would John like it if he were to come back to his office and find the word *SLUT* across his picture? The ink was starting to bleed through, black smudges growing darker and darker across Laura's face. Becca slipped the picture frame into her purse, and she went out to the copy machine.

It was quite close to closing now, and Becca was looking forward to getting out—light and sunshine, bottles of wine, a quaint European hotel room. . . .

The tourists had trickled off but John's enthusiasm hadn't. Not even a little. Row on row of the faceless heads and he snapped away, merrily click-click-clicking. "It's strange," John said, as he rounded a pillar composed entirely of femurs. "No names. Six million people but not a single one has a name. There should be a list of them somewhere—do you think there is, in the hall of records? I once did a shot of The Wall in Washington, you know, the big one. All those people running their fingers alone as if it was Braille. But it was just names.

"There was this kid there—" *Snap snap,* he was snapping away quite urgently now. "—and I thought his grandfather must have died, and he's crying as if it just happened, as if it were a tombstone. But it wasn't. It wasn't anything like that. It was just a list of names, and he's crying and so I put my hand on his shoulder and I ask him why he's crying. You know what he says? He says his girlfriend just broke up with him." John shook his head in disbelief, but he stopped snapping very suddenly, and he clenched Becca's hand hard.

"I think I'd like to go now," Becca said. She could smell the hint of fresh air. She almost ran toward it. In fact, she did jolt forward, but John was still holding her hand and she was yanked back a pace.

"What's the rush?" he asked. And his eyes said, *please say this is great*. But he wasn't smiling. There was something wrong with his smile.

She tried that *ooh-aah* trick again, just let her mouth make a series of encouraging sounds that weren't quite words. He seemed to brighten up. What she was really thinking was that it was just bones. Rooms and rooms of them, skulls mounted on piles of tibias, giant circular ossuaries. Sometimes they would be artistically arranged—a line of skulls outlining a block of thighbones, with all the knobby ends pointed outwards. In one place, a giant stone cross was set in the middle. As if people didn't get the point. STOP! THIS IS THE EMPIRE OF DEATH! It was all a bit melodramatic, wasn't it? A thousand skulls would have been enough, but six million? Six million was overdoing it a bit. Six million was too many, they stopped being people at that point, they were just bits of debris, bits of things that had died.

"We can't go yet," John said softly, and there was something in his voice, something edging toward desperation. He tugged on her hand and it might have been playful, but maybe, just maybe, it wasn't. "What about that chapel, that was pretty good, wasn't it? And the light—the light didn't do it justice. I want to try again. I think I could make it work if I gave it another go."

Becca felt something inside her crawling. She didn't want to go. It was awful, the chapel was awful, and she just wanted to get out. But John tugged again on her hand, drawing her back, and he smiled that smile of his—the one that was mostly happy, but maybe just a little bit sad.

———————————

Becca was returning with coffee for her boss when she had her first, *real* conversation with John. They were both waiting for the elevator, standing awkwardly next to each other in the lobby of the building. His eyes flicked up and then away. She almost thought he didn't recognize her, but then they flicked back. A hint of a smile. Did he know her? She couldn't be sure. She tried smiling back, but he had already looked away. She bit her lip, waited, tried smiling again but now he was looking at his shoes, and then the floor display, and then he was pressing the button again impatiently.

"Coffee?" she asked. It was her boss's coffee—black, the way she liked it. He wouldn't like it though, that wasn't how he took his coffee.

At first, he didn't respond. Nothing. Eyes on the floor. Then, as if the words had taken a long time to penetrate, he turned to her and blinked once. "Yes, thanks," he said, and then that hint of a smile became an actual smile, a real one. Not as real as the one in the picture, not as full or as genuine or as happy as that one, but maybe it had a little of that in it. She handed him the coffee. She had no coffee to bring her boss now, but that was all right, she was doing good for the firm, keeping up morale. She dug into her pockets.

"Two sugars, right?" She produced them, and he smiled a little more, so she ripped the tops of the packages, both at the same time, and she dumped the sugar in. "Sorry," she said, "no spoons on me."

He took the coffee. The elevator door opened, and they both stepped inside. "You're Becca, aren't you?" he asked. "Beth's new intern."

Becca nodded. He sipped the coffee, smiled again, sipped again. Silence.

It was the sugar, Becca thought, a good thing I brought the sugar. He wouldn't like it black, and then we wouldn't be talking now. And she smiled back, and she surreptitiously patted the pocket of her jacket, crammed full of sugar packages.

But now John wasn't talking and the elevator was moving inexorably toward the top floor. Becca counted out the floors as they passed them—fourteen, fifteen, sixteen. John sipped. Becca fidgeted. She tried to look at him out of the corner of her eye, squinted so he couldn't see her doing it. Seventeen, eighteen. She was looking at his hand, his left hand, ringless, like there had never been a ring. Twenty.

"Where did she go?" She didn't mean to say it. John looked surprised at first, his mouth went through a little series of silent *ohs*, before it bunched up into a look of intense pain.

"I don't know," he said. His eyes dropped. "I really don't. They ask me sometimes, ask about the ring. I don't know. One day she was there, and then suddenly, she wasn't anymore. Pieces of her started to go missing. First it was an eye. Her hand. The whole left side of her body. No one noticed except me, but I could see her slipping away, a little bit at a time. And then she was gone. And then the ring was gone. And then . . . her things. The clothes in her drawer . . . her picture on my desk. . . ." he turned and he looked at her, but he wasn't really looking at her, he was looking past her, not seeing her. "I think I might be going mad."

Becca didn't say anything, he looked so sad right then, so terribly, terribly sad. She put her hand on his, touched him very, very lightly, so lightly she didn't know if he could feel it.

"You're not going mad," she said. "Shhhhh, it's alright. Don't worry, don't worry." Inside, though, she was thinking, she's gone, she's really gone, you never had a wife, John. You never knew her, you never loved her.

He looked up, very tentatively, met her eyes for the first time, smiled. The door opened with a cheery *bing* and he startled guiltily. Half-jumped out of the elevator. But then he paused, turned and put a hand across the door. "This coffee wasn't for me, was it? I haven't gotten you into trouble?"

"It's *your* coffee now," she said. "Just for you." And saying it she felt happy, just happy, and solid. Like he could see her at last. Like she was real to him.

"Right," he said. "Thanks." But as the doors closed again, she saw that look in his eyes, something speculative, something wondering a little bit—who was the girl in the elevator?—but a happy kind of wondering, a curious sort of wondering, a maybe-maybe sort full of hope and excitement. She saw it there, in the eyes, in the smile. And then elevator began to drop away underneath her with a feeling that might have been a little like love.

And now she felt anger, just the barest hint of anger that he should be sad, here, in Paris, the city of lovers, *la Ville-Lumière*. He was the one who had wanted all these fucking bones, these fucking dead Frenchman, what right did he have to be unhappy? He should be smiling, he should be smiling, and she should be smiling, like in the picture. But he wasn't. There was something missing from his face, some part of him that wasn't quite there, wasn't quite with her. He should have been smiling.

John was snapping away furiously now, and Becca wanted to go. She didn't want to be in this dank dark place any more, she wanted to be where there was light, where there were bottles of wine.

"There's supposed to be something here," he said, and he was staring at a place in the wall where an ancient skeleton had been composed on a little shelf. "A name. There's supposed to be a name here." Becca looked at John, looked at that handsome face, but the eyes were wrong, they were wide and staring. She wanted to be kissing John, but he was interested in all those bones, all those stupid, fucking bones. They weren't people anymore, they couldn't be. They couldn't talk, they couldn't fuck, they certainly couldn't love you anymore. Dead people couldn't love you. That was the point, why didn't he understand that? Dead people were gone, they were vanished forever.

John was muttering something now, and his breathing was hoarse. "I can't find any names, there must be names here, mustn't there? Who were all these people? Where did they come from? Where?"

"John," she said, "we're going now."

And he took a picture. And another picture. And another picture. So many goddamn pictures. And then he wasn't taking pictures anymore, he was putting away the camera, and Becca thought, thank god, at last, he's done with it. He doesn't need pictures anymore, he can just have me. But he was picking up the skull, he was staring at it.

"It's Laura," he whispered, and his face made a thousand silent, painful *ohs*. "I think it's Laura." He paused, and he was rubbing his ring finger then, and Becca stared at it, the band of light, untanned skin where that ring used to sit. In the washed-out light, he seemed to be a stranger. She didn't recognize him anymore, there were dark smudges across his face, the eyeholes deep and sunken. And full of something. Wonder. Love.

"She's here—she always said . . . Paris . . . she wanted to go to Paris. *La Ville-Lumière*. She wanted to make love in Montmartre. She wanted to stand at the top of the Eiffel Tower and see all those lights, all those little lights winking at her. She wanted to . . ."

And he was looking at Becca now, and he was holding the skull in his hand, and suddenly Becca could see it too, it was Laura, it had the same loving smile, and it was looking at him, and the word *SLUT* was written across it in large wobbly writing. And she was angry. You don't exist, she thought, you never existed. You weren't real. He never loved you.

"I remember. I remember her, she was there, and then she . . . Why are we here?" he asked, and he was staring, and his eyes were wide and dark as caverns. "Why are we in this *fucking* place? Why did you—?"

Becca found that she didn't want him to be there anymore, he wasn't *nice*, he wasn't kind, he wasn't the kind of man you ought never to leave. Because he was leaving her. She knew it, she could see it, she could feel the little pieces of herself disappearing. He was leaving her, and all for his wife, for his *dead* wife. She wasn't a person, she wasn't anything. There were six million dead people buried here, six million, and how many more? How many more everywhere? Throughout all of time? The dead are nothing, she wanted to scream at him, they aren't anything at all, just a little whiff of air, a thing that was there and then gone. She was nothing. She was a stone. She was a memory. She was band of white flesh wrapped around his finger.

"She's dead, John, she's just fucking dead!" And Becca felt it happening, felt that look in his eyes, felt the darkness of those caverns swallowing her up.

And he kissed the skull, he leaned over and he planted his lips on it, the warm flesh ones against cold, hard, gleaming bone. He didn't shiver. She thought he should be shivering, that he should be cold, that it would be awful to kiss a dead person but it wasn't. There was a look on his face. Happy. A smile that was a real smile, and the skull was smiling too. Nice little even rows of super-clean, white teeth.

Why are you doing this, John? she wanted to scream. Why are you doing this? Why can't you just love me, why am I not enough, why am I not real to you? All those skulls, all those skulls around her were laughing now, they were saying, "You mocked us but you are one of us. You are one of us, you are dead, you are among the dead and now we shall have you." The teeth. All those dark eye holes and smiles full of teeth.

And then John was looking at her again, really looking. Becca felt herself falling into pieces under John's terrible stare. And maybe it was a bit like love, that feeling of dropping away.

NO GHOSTS IN LONDON

This is a sad story, best beloved, one of the few stories you don't know, one of the few stories which I have kept to myself, locked up tight between cheek and tongue. Not a rainy-day story, no, not a bedtime story, but another kind of story: a sad story, as I said, but also a happy story, a story that is not all one thing at once and so, in the way of these things, a true story. And I have not told you one of those before. So hush up, and listen.

Gwendolyn had worked for the old manor house, Hardwick Hall, ever since her mum died. She knew all the stones in the manor house by heart, the ones kept rough and out of the reach of tourists, the ones smoothed by feet or hands, the uneven bits of the floor underneath the woven rush mat, the inward curves on the stairs; she knew the ghosts who had taken up residence in the abandoned upstairs rooms—dead sons and murdered lovers, a suicide or two, and the children who had died before reaching the age of ten. It was *her* home in many ways, the manor where her mum had worked. Her home. And though she longed to go off to university in the Great City of London, since childhood she had felt the Hall's relentless drawstrings tugging tight as chain-iron around her. The kind, best beloved, that all young people feel in a place that is very, very old.

There was duty, of course. The old duchess's bones creaked like a badly set floorboard when winter came to Derbyshire, and she was wary of strangers, wary of people since her brother's sons had died in the war, wary of everyone except for the sad-eyed, long-jowled bulldog, Montague, who would sit by her side and snuffle against her ancient brocade skirt as she sewed. The duchess's memory was moth-eaten with age, and the only faces that made sense to her were those that had been in her company for some time. As her mother had. As Gwendolyn had. And Gwendolyn found it easy to love the old woman, to love her pink-tongued companion. To love Hardwick Hall.

So there was love as well, which as we all know, best beloved, is as tight a drawstring as any. But love is not always happiness, particularly when you are young, and lovely, and just a bit lonely.

After she buried her mum in the spring in a ceremony that was sweet and sad and comforting with all the manor staff in attendance, Gwendolyn put on her mum's apron and she tended the gardens and organized the servants, keeping them straight, letting them know there was still a firm hand about the place. Yes, my love, this is one of the sad bits but, hush, it was not so very sad as it might have been, for Gwendolyn had been loved by her mother very much, and, in the way of these things, that matters.

So. Gwendolyn stayed, and she minded the manor and all was well for the most part. The servants came to respect her, as they had her mum, to mind what she told them. The only people who didn't attend to her properly were the ghosts. Oh, Gwendolyn would cajole, she would bribe, she would beg, she would order. But hers was a young face, and she was not a blood relation to them. She was a servant herself, and lacked, at that stage, a servant's proper knowledge of how to subtly, secretly, put the screws to her master. Her mum had known how it was done—but her mum had kept many secrets to herself, as all mothers do, sure in the knowledge that there would be time later to pass them on.

Damien, the crinkle-eyed cowherd who minded the animals of the estate and drove the big tractor, the kind of man who was father and grandfather rolled into one, insisted that such things could not be forced. "Ghosts are an unruly lot," he would say to her. "Can't shift too much around at once. They'll take a shine yet, bless."

Shyly, Gwendolyn asked, "Will she ever . . . ?"

But she did not finish and Damien looked away as men do when they are sad and do not want to show it. Then he took her hand very carefully, as if it were one of the fine porcelain figures the duchess kept in her study. "I do not think so, love. *Their* kind"—meaning the ghosts, of course—"they stay for fear, or for anger, or for loneliness. Your mum, bless, she had none of that in her bones and too much of the other stuff. She'd have found somewhere better to rest herself, never you fear."

Gwendolyn smiled a little, and she got on about the business of managing the place as best she could. But after a particularly bad day, when mad old William, the former count of Shrewsbury, had given her such a nasty shock that she had twisted her ankle on the uneven stairs, Gwendolyn decided enough was enough. It was one thing to have to deal with the tourists that filtered in every summer—they were strangers—but the ghosts were something closer to family. She missed her mum badly, but it was just too hard to shut herself away from a world glimpsed in strange accents and half-snatched conversations, a world enticing as any unknown thing is to a girl who lives among the dead, only to face the scorn and distemper of the closest thing to relatives she still had.

"I can't abide it," she confessed in a whisper to Damien as she cast her sad gaze over the roses clinging to the south wall of the garden where she had scattered her mother's ashes. "They never acted up like this for mum."

"Your mum, bless, she had more iron in her blood than the fifth cavalry had on their backs. Even those roses grow straighter and bloom brighter for fear of disappointing her."

"I wish she were here," Gwendolyn said.

"I know, love, I know."

And so Gwendolyn packed her belongings into an old steamer trunk her mum had bought but never used, and she bid the duchess goodbye in the afternoon, as the sun slanted through the window into the blue room and lit up the silk trimmings so that they shone. Montague lay curled in a corner, breathlessly twitching in sleep, his tongue lolling like the edge of a bright pink ribbon. The duchess plucked at the needlework, fingers mindlessly unpicking what she had done, her only sign of agitation as she smiled a soft smile and bid Gwendolyn go. Then she cast her sad, milky eyes downwards, and patted Montague on the head with a kind of familiarity and gentleness that Gwendolyn never saw in the hurried, boisterous jostling of the tourists.

Gwendolyn did not look away then, though she desperately wanted to, because when you love someone, best beloved, and you know you will not see them again then, in the way of these things, you have to look.

Gwendolyn gritted her teeth and she looked until she couldn't bear the weight of that ancient gaze any longer. Then she bent over, and kissed the old woman's forehead, skin as light as brown paper wrapping, so that she could feel the hard bone of the skull underneath.

Then Gwendolyn turned, and in her turning something heavy seemed to fall away from her: the afternoon sun slanting through the window seemed full of hope and promise and if, here, it fell on only the aged, the dying and

the dead and there, somewhere, it might also be falling upon things that glittered with their own newness. If she had been listening, Gwendolyn might have heard a whispered goodbye, and: "Please, my darling, do not come back." But with the sorry task of farewells done, Gwendolyn's mind was already ten miles ahead of her feet.

London was the place she had seen in that afternoon-sun vision, a city sharp with hope, glass and steel glittering above streets paved with crisp-wrappers and concrete. She loved the cramped and smelly Tube ride, the tangle of lines that ran beneath the city, the curved cramped space where she would be crowded against men in clean-cut jackets, some slumped over so their backs curved along with the frame, girls dressed in leather, or chiffon, sitting demurely or hurling insults at one another with complete abandon. She loved the cluttered streets, the brown brick walls and white-trimmed windows. Everything was pressed so closely together she could put out both arms and touch the walls on either side of her dormitory room.

There were no ghosts in London, best beloved, not where the living took up so much space. Her roommate, Cindy— you wouldn't like her, she was a lithe, long-legged girl from America who liked to wear heavy perfume and talk to her boyfriend in New York until ungodly hours of the morning—looked at her oddly when she spoke of them.

"We don't have anything like that back home," she'd say in a thick accent that seemed to misplace all the vowels and leave only the consonants in place. "In America, we like to get on with it, you know, lose the baggage."

Gwendolyn liked the idea of getting on with it. Losing the baggage. She liked living without ghosts. She was a city girl now, a Londoner, a girl from London, and she gave herself to the city, let the city transform her the way all cities transform the people who inhabit them. She started wearing heavy perfume and putting on thick, black mascara that promised to give her THE LONDON LOOK, make her eyelashes—formerly stubby and mouse-brown like mine, yes, just like that—long and curving with 14X the volume. Like a movie star, Gwendolyn thought, staring at the fringe of it, the way it curled up away from her eyes in an altogether pleasing manner. She got herself a boyfriend, learned something about snogging, got herself another and learned something about the things that come after snogging.

Gwendolyn wanted to be very like Cindy with her know-it-all attitude and her keen sense of how to get on with things. Soon enough the boyfriend back in New York had disappeared entirely, replaced by one from Oxford or Cambridge—she couldn't remember which, only that his college was one of the better ones, one of the *rich* ones. Cindy didn't shed a tear. "What's the point?" Cindy asked. "He's back home. No use crying over what's not here."

Gwendolyn liked that as well, and she said it over in her mind many times, "No use crying." This was some relief in and of itself, for the mascara made crying a sticky, abysmal business. No one in London cried. You couldn't pull off THE LONDON LOOK unless you kept your eyes bone dry. Soon Gwendolyn could pass rose bushes without ever thinking about the flowers on the south wall, the ones that grew straighter and brighter than any other in the garden. The roses in London were much smaller anyway, cramped into the gardens of townhouses or clinging to what light they could in the cracks between stones. They weren't proper roses, but sickly little things with barely any colour at all. No, it was very rarely now that Cindy would pull Gwendolyn aside, squinting, and tell her to fix up her face, the mascara was running.

The duchess paid for her education, discreetly of course, and Gwendolyn promised herself she would write in thanks, but she never did. She started with a major in French, but Cindy advised against that—"Don't trust the French here, do they?"—so she switched over to Psychology.

It wasn't until graduation (in Art History, not Psychology after all) several years later that Gwendolyn received a letter from the post. Cindy was preparing to move back to Chicago where she would be engaged to a fellow with an MBA from Harvard (not the Oxford fellow, after all) and had invited Gwendolyn to come with her and try out the Second City— for that's what they called Chicago in America. London had been Gwendolyn's first city, and if Cindy taught her anything it was that you could never stay with your first, could you? Not with cities. Not with men.

That sounded like a fine enough plan to Gwendolyn, and Chicago seemed like a fine enough place with its aboveground rail service and broad city sidewalks and gleaming steel towers, a place even newer than London. But then the letter came with its rich, velvety paper and the four stamped eglantine roses on the envelope. Gwendolyn felt her fingers shaking as she opened it.

It regretted to inform her of the passing of Lady Sirith of Hardwick Hall, twentieth Duchess of Shrewsbury, Patron of the Silver Garter, and a list of other titles that Gwendolyn only half-remembered. It was customary for a member of the family to sit in mourning at the manor and as she had no living family, the duchess requested that Gwendolyn do the necessary duties. Of course, continued the letter in a quite majestic manner, the terms of her bequest were *quite clear* and should Gwendolyn not arrive in three days' time, she would be required to pay back the sum spent on her education.

Cindy pooh-poohed and turned up her tiny mouth in a moue when Gwendolyn shared the news. "What an old bitch," she said, "threatening to make you pay all that money. It's just as well she's in the worm trough."

Gwendolyn nodded her head, but kept silent. The four roses had sparked a long-neglected sense of familial obligation in her, and she thought that maybe it was proper to visit her mum's grave one last time, to say a proper goodbye, before the government claimed the old manor for a fully renovated heritage centre.

Her bags were already packed, so she saw Cindy off to the airport and then rode the Tube (still cramped, still noisy, still flush with warm bodies crowding up against one another) to King's Cross Station where she boarded a train heading to Derbyshire.

Gwendolyn stared out the window, fidgeting sometimes, watching the rolling hills and quilted landscape with increasing apprehension, and asking all the kinds of questions young people ask when they go home again. Would Damien still be there, carrying toffee in his pocket for all those long years, just in case she returned? Would she still know the stones, the places to avoid on the stairs, the tricky bumps on the floor? Would the air smell the same, the sun cast its light just so, the tourists still flash their cameras and chatter on with noisy, Yankee excitement? But most of all, would the roses still grow straighter and brighter on the south wall than anywhere else in the garden? They were warm thoughts, sad thoughts, and when her mascara began to run, Gwendolyn wiped her face raw.

When she pulled into the station, Damien met her with a car from the estate. He looked nervous, picked at the dirt on his clothes with broad, flat fingers and smiled hastily, before averting his eyes away from her. He spoke a little on the ride to the manor house of inconsequential things, little threads that wound around Gwendolyn, picking out her absence, not with cruelty, but with a thousand stories resumed midway whose characters were no longer familiar.

"And the ghosts?" Gwendolyn asked at one point. Damien only looked at her queerly and pursed her lips. Finally, the car turned past the property fence, sped past the visitor car park, and arrived at the gates. "Your dress looks quite pretty." He smiled almost shyly. "New London fashion, I'd be guessing." Then he was tipping his hat ever so slightly, as if he couldn't decide if she were family or royalty, before disappearing entirely.

Gwendolyn walked the grounds like a nervous cat, feet delicately treading the path. She tiptoed past the lavender and lilac, remarked at the blush of poppies that had sprouted at odd intervals along the sides of the path, and finally turned the corner, past the old wrought-iron bench where honeymooners liked to get their picture taken, towards the south wall.

She was relieved to see that Damien had spent most of his efforts there. Even if the rest of the gardens looked a little shabbier, a little wilder than she had last seen them, the roses on the south wall still bloomed like giant, delicate clouds in hues that ranged from pink to orange-edged cream and yellow. They were beautiful, and looking at them, Gwendolyn felt tears welling up and she was glad the mascara was gone, that it couldn't make a dark muddle of her face.

And at last, Damien returned to take her to see the duchess.

The light was just starting to fade from the Blue Room, best beloved, leaving half- glimmers of turquoise and aquamarine like seashells on a beach. The air was warm from the afternoon sun, but there the duchess sat, unaffected, in her favourite seat, threadbare skin revealing the gnarls and whorls of ancient bones in her hands as she worked with a needle and thread at the stitching she always kept with her.

"My lady?" Gwendolyn asked softly, waiting at the door to be acknowledged as she'd been taught once, a long time ago, the proper forms of address feeling as odd as the unlearned French in her mouth.

The old woman's head nodded, and Gwendolyn approached, her feet already beginning to remember the soft give of the rush matting. But then those sad, milky eyes turned on her with a long, terrible stare and she said in a drawn-out, lisping voice that Gwendolyn barely recognized: "Who are you?"

I know, love, this is one of the sadder parts. So you may hold my hand if you wish, if that might make it easier for you to hear.

So. The duchess. She demanded of Damien in her lisping, stranger voice: "I don't know who this woman is. Why is she here?" The hands continued to work at the cloth, and Gwendolyn looked down to watch the threads unravelling, yes, just so, one by one, as she pulled at them, leaving only little holes in the silk where the needle had bound them in.

"My children lay unborn in a dead woman's womb, my brother's children unburied in the North Sea, at Normandy, on the banks. I asked for my blood, my bones, the children of my ancestors. *Who is this one?*"

And Damien replied: "It's Gwendolyn, my lady. I'm sorry."

At hearing her name, Gwendolyn turned behind her, but her gaze was blinded by a bolt of blue, the last light of the dying sun. She couldn't see the old cowherd's face.

"She is nothing. She wears strange clothes, speaks with a strange tongue. She is none of mine."

And, oh, best beloved, pick, pick, pick went her fingers until the cloth practically fell apart in her hands.

Gwendolyn felt something unravelling inside her, and though she knew it was *she* who had made herself the stranger, it hurt terribly to be recognized as such. She fled the room, stumbling past Damien and down the uneven stairs, half tripping, half leaping until her toes touched gravel, and beyond that, the soft grass of the gardens. And there, she stood, by the south wall, sobbing, while the roses quavered around her in the breeze.

She wasn't alone then, no, Damien stood beside her. "The dead are a hard lot," he said. His face looked sad. "They've been picking the place apart like vultures since you left."

But in that moment he was neither father nor grandfather enough to comfort her. "There aren't any ghosts in London," Gwendolyn whispered. And then: "I don't want any more ghosts."

"I know, love." He said softly, and his hands were as cold and chilly as any dead man's when he touched her.

Afterward: "You'll be leaving in the morning then?"

"Yes. But I must sit my vigil first. Blood or no blood."

Vultures, Damien had called them, best beloved, picking apart the seams of things. Gwendolyn saw it everywhere. The tables lay in pieces in the games room, the joints torn out, the curtains frayed to rags and trailing threads where they brushed the floor, the library littered with pages, paper from the new books—the history ones Duchess Hardwick collected from the Folio Society—and parchment from the very old ones, which had not been sent off to the Bodleian to pay the death duties over the last generations. The place smelt musty, and the flakes of gilt and paint glittered in the air.

This was what the ghosts had done. This was what ghosts *were*, my love—decay, ruination, things falling apart, coming undone, the terrible passage of time.

Gwendolyn felt an awful longing for the city, the ache that comes into the heart of all young people who leave and come home and wish they could leave again. But Gwendolyn could not leave. There was duty still to be done. The vigil.

And so, with a heavy heart, she took up the old duties once again—to clean, to mend, to care for—and Gwendolyn began to pick up the pages, to shuffle them back into the correct sequence, often squinting at the pencil folio notes in the corners made by visiting scholars to make sure she got it as correct as possible. She set the pages between the wooden boards in which they had originally been bound. She tried to forgive the ghosts for the destruction of her home and the bright, wondrous things she had loved as a child. She tried not to hate them.

It was only when she found the body of poor, dead Montague—flies crawling around the place where his stomach had been ripped open—that she began to recognize the queer feeling in the pit of her stomach as fear.

Ghosts could be something else, she remembered. They were not always kind.

Gwendolyn knelt beside the poor beast—hush now, darling, I know, I know, but it is how it happened in the story—and she stroked his once-silky coat, and said gentle things to him about loyalty and love. She unbuckled the collar from around his neck, and carried his body out to the garden to bury.

There was a spade lying by the south wall, where the roses grew straight and bright, as if one among them at least had known what ought to be done. She had not done much physical labour during her time in London, and her arms had forgotten much of their strength. By the end, her back ached, and dirt lined the insides of her fingernails. But, there, in front of her, was a hole approximately three feet by three feet. She feared digging deeper. She did not want to disturb the roses.

She laid Montague's limp body in the ground, and scattered the petals of four roses over top. It hurt her to pluck them, but she thought there ought to be something beautiful to mark the grave, even if he was just a dog.

The ghosts had gathered to watch. They wore silks and velvets, jewels in their hair and some of them had weapons buckled to their sides. They were beautiful and aristocratic, with faces that bore some resemblance to the duchess, but, their fingers—oh, my darling!—their fingers were *red*, and there was something wild in their eyes.

They parted, albeit angrily and with brooding looks, when she started on the path back into the manor, but part they did for she was sitting vigil and they knew she was not too be touched.

That night, Gwendolyn laboured at putting right all the things in the house. There was much she could not do, but she did as she could. And the ghosts watched. And they muttered. And when they did not mutter they stared at her with their grim eyes and their red, red fingers, until finally Gwendolyn felt something hot and bright flash through her, and it was anger.

"You did this, all of you! You loved this place, protected it for hundreds of years and then you tore it apart. Why? Why?"

At first, there was a long silence.

And then one answered: "We have no kin. We are alone, so very alone."

And another: "To pass the time."

And a third: "There was no one to tell us not to."

And, at last, the duchess spoke: "Because this is a place for the dead. We do not want strangers sleeping in the beds our children slept in, touching our things. I wish this place were dust, and we were dust in our graves, and all the forests of the world rotted down to skeleton leaves."

"You were a kinder person when you were alive," Gwendolyn replied at last.

"You were my closest-to-kin, and you left. It is not for you to judge."

Gwendolyn nodded slowly. Her hands were filthy from mending books, collecting strands of silk for repair, and from digging one lonely grave in the garden. They were servants' hands, calloused, scoured now of polish and perfection; and Gwendolyn knew they were her mother's hands, best beloved, hands that had been bound in service—and love— to this household. And Gwendolyn looked at her hands, and she looked at the hands of the ghosts—red, still, with Montague's blood—and she began to speak:

"In London, there are no ghosts."

Angry stares at that, and bloody fingers twitching. Gwendolyn did not care though. She hated their self-loathing, their spoiled faces, and the cold indifference that had settled into their expressions. Once, they had been a kind of family, familiar, comforting when her mum died. But these were different people, and Gwendolyn hated them. "In London, the dead are buried and gone in a fortnight, and the people ride the Tube every morning to work and every evening home, and they cannot breathe but for the press of bodies around them. In London they eat their dead. They burn them up in cigarettes and automobile crashes and pipe bombs. They screw them away with perfect strangers they despise the next day. They sniff the dead, snort them, inject them into veins. In London, they use up the dead. They feed their bodies to the city that neither loves them nor remembers them. I was happy there. In London. Where they carry around their ghosts inside, and the only harm they can do is to themselves."

And she looked at them, and her gaze was as terrible as theirs.

"I'm going home now."

That was what she said to them, best beloved, to all those dead sons, murdered lovers, and aged monarchs, and she turned away from them and she began to walk. Slowly, carefully, but proudly. Only when she stood last of all before the ghost of Duchess Hardwick—powerful, fierce as a lioness, the way the portraits showed her back before age had bent her spine back in on its self like an old coat hanger—did she stop.

"He loved you," Gwendolyn said. "He loved you without question, and you tore him apart." And there was no ghost for that little dog and Gwendolyn was glad of it. She met the duchess's eyes and they were hard and they were cold—the kind of eyes, best beloved, that command obedience and fear, the kind of eyes that order death, the kind of eyes that are death's ally—and she stared down those eyes until, at last, it was the duchess who turned away.

"Take us back to the city," she said. "Let the city devour us."

And Gwendolyn nodded.

The ghosts murmured, shook their gory fingers, but the duchess raised her hand and there was nothing more to be said, for she was, perhaps, the greatest of them and also, perhaps, the most terrible.

Then they began to file past Gwendolyn, one by one, the dead sons, the murdered lovers, faces that had comforted her at her mother's funeral, faces she had known from her childhood, faces that had loved her once, in their own way, and she had loved as well. Last came crinkle-eyed Damien, and his fingers were red too, but he kept them hidden in shame.

"Not you," she said, but he shook his head sadly.

"These grounds are no longer mine to keep," he told her. Gently. In the voices of a father, and a grandfather. "And I would like to see the city."

"You wouldn't like it," Gwendolyn said softly. "It's a cruel place for the dead."

"Aye," he said. "Most places are." He made a move to join the others, but stopped. "Care for your mother's grave, love. It is a hard thing to be dead and alone."

Then Gwendolyn really did cry, and they were large, proper tears, the kind you can only cry when family is around. And she sobbed until her nose was red, and her face was a roadmap of dust trails.

The ghosts took the morning train back to London, and as it snaked its way amongst the hills and clumped villages of the English countryside, Gwendolyn found them on their best behaviour. They chatted amiably about the city in their days, meeting Queen Elizabeth and that firebrand Mary, Queen of Scots. How it might have changed, what they had heard about the smog. They seemed happy almost. Excited. Like children going to the fair.

Gwendolyn listened a little, but mostly she sat with Damien and told him all about her life at university. She left out the parts about snogging, because, my darling, that is the way of these things, and besides she thought that maybe he knew all about what growing up meant.

Finally, best beloved—and I know you must be tired, my girl, you have held on for such a long time and you have listened well—they alighted at King's Cross, and one by one the dead sons, and the murdered lovers, and the aged duchess disappeared into the press of people boarding the Tube for work. It would be quick, Gwendolyn knew. The city was a cold, indifferent place. It had eaten all of its own ghosts long ago, and would be hungry for more.

Only Damien remained. Gwendolyn smiled, shy again, afraid, sad. "Will you go too?" she asked.

"Aye, love. It's long past time I did something with these old bones. I've followed that lot around so long, I'll be half-mad without them."

"You could stay," she said.

"I shan't, though. Your heart only has room for one ghost, Gwen, love, and you must keep her safe from the city, and from us."

Gwendolyn nodded, and she reached out to touch him, to offer a final gesture of goodbye—but it was too late, too late as all goodbyes are. Particularly the ones that matter. And when he vanished, it was amongst a group of giggling school girls come to the city for the weekend to celebrate their A-levels.

She knew she was supposed to be sad, but the funny thing was, in the end, she wasn't anymore. The sadness was gone with the ghosts—for that, my best beloved, is the way of things. It has always been the way of things. The dead cannot stay. They are decay, ruination. Things falling apart. They cannot stay, my bright, beautiful girl—my Gwendolyn. My best beloved. But I will tell you a secret, a secret only I know—the secret that makes this a happy story, after all, and not a sad one, or a scary one, or even a hurtful one. As Gwendolyn left King's Cross, she felt a kind of weight settling in her chest, a good weight like a rosebush anchoring into her stomach and sprouting beautiful blossoms, pink, orange-tipped, yellow, into the dark spaces inside her.

It is time, best beloved. I have held you and I have loved you and but my fingers are cold and dead: you cannot hang on to me forever. You are young, as *that* Gwendolyn was, as her mother was before her, and you are destined for places that sparkle with their own newness. Those places would devour me. What is warm and bright for the living is hateful to the dead. It is the way of things. Always. Even thus. Look once, my love, my little girl, because when you love someone, and you know you will not see them again, then you *must* look. And then carry me with you. Inside. Where I can take root and grow. Where my hands will stay clean.

[heart]

PIECES OF BROKEN THINGS

When Carolina Herschmire went out of the house on that warm day in September, her husband of twelve years, David, took all the things she had left behind—old CDs, her favourite pink argyle sweater, picture frames purchased together, a single lolling-tongue sneaker—and buried them in the backyard by the garden. He dug the hole with an old spade, and as he shovelled each layer of dirt aside, he thought back on his life with Carolina. There were good times, mostly, as he remembered them. They'd fought as any couple fought—over work, over money—but he'd always taken heart in the fact that the fights, framed as they were by the banalities of life in the city, had always been about their love for one another. Loneliness. Separation anxiety. The fear of disappointing the other, the fear of the other not being happy with a smallish, shared house with thin walls. They were fights about loving too much, not loving too little.

And so David had been caught off guard when Carolina—Carol, he had called her sometimes, when she was bossy, or 'Lina when she was sweet—said her love was gone, that there was nothing left. He did not know what to do. He was used to the moods that her love took, the way it could be as strong, and swift and absolutely present one moment and then an elusive thing the next. It was not how David loved, never with that surety, that flood of passion that she could show, but then again, never did he have those moments of absence, the blank holes when his love disappeared altogether. He thought this might be one such time. And so David offered to share. He took out a piece of his love—wriggling from exposure to the cold—and held it in front of her. But Carolina—Carol, this time, he thought—kissed him very lightly, very chastely, on the cheek and closed his hand, pushed the love back into his chest where it continued to squirm and wriggle uncomfortably. She said that it was all right, she hadn't run out so much as she'd decided to get rid of it, she didn't want love anymore. Love, she said, love was messy and incomprehensible and she, almost forty now, almost the big four-zero, didn't want messy and incomprehensible.

She had, she told him a little bashfully, replaced her heart with the only thing she could get to fit—a tiny clock the pawn shop owner had handy. She showed it to David. She undid the front of her cream silk blouse, and David got a glimpse of a little ormolu face with two prim hands nestled in the little hollow between her breasts. He loved her breasts. They were petite, like teacups, and they fit perfectly in the palm of his hand. A day ago, had she undone her blouse, he would have thought it was the prelude to something a little more exciting, it would have been a Good Thing in his books. But the sight of the clock chilled him to the core, and he felt something inside his own heart go *pop-whir*—

he knew there would be no more Good Things coming, knew with absolute certainty that it was over.

"It was all they had," she said, just a little shyly now, but David realized it wasn't shyness about him, about what he thought of all of this. It was a kind of shyness with herself. She touched the clock, just once, and it made a kind of a little *bing*. When she looked up, her eyes were shiny like new pebbles, but there weren't tears in them. She wouldn't be staying, she said. Without love it felt odd to see David, he looked so different from the days when she had first met him in high school, older, he wasn't the same person. And she already had one clock in her chest—another reminder of all that time slipping away, that time that was all hers, that she didn't have to share it anymore—it would be too much to bear.

"Please, Carol," he whispered.

"I never liked it when you called me that," she said.

So David made a pot of coffee. He wasn't used to doing it, Carolina always made the coffee, but she was leaving and David didn't know what to do about it. She said she was going to stay with her mother. While she began to collect her things, he fiddled with the filter and watched it percolate with a steady fascination. As the coffee drip-dripped out, he thought about the slowly ticking clock where his wife's heart had been, and felt for his own heart, tried to feel the beat of it, tried to check if it was still going. The coffee dripped. It was the only noise. He wondered if he was dead, if he was heartbroken, if she had maybe, accidentally, gotten rid of his heart instead of hers. She was always doing things like that. Taking his socks, his favourite books, his reading glasses. But then he felt a light thump-thump, and he breathed a sigh of relief, only it wasn't quite relief. It was something else.

On the morning after Carolina left him, David woke up in an empty bed with missing things around him, things he remembered used to be there. Inside him, he thought, would be another hole, another empty place where all the love for Carolina had been. But he was surprised to discover that it was still all there, wriggling around inside him. It was strange—his love had become a gentle thing over time, a comfortable thing he wore like an old sweater or stubble on Saturdays. If he had been asked, he would have said he was very much in love, that he never looked at other women, that he was quite happy. But the love he felt now was different—it wasn't *that* love, it was something hammering at his ribcage, something strong and desperate to be satisfied.

He tried to make the morning coffee, but his hands shook and the coffee grounds spilled across the counter. He could hear his heart still beating firmly away. He didn't know what to do. He looked at the argyle sweater that Carolina had left behind, and his heart gave a little jerk. But it didn't stop. It just sped up, faster and faster away. He saw the picture frames she had left behind, saw *her* picture in the frame, smiling with something that used to be love, he was sure of it, and that was just like rubbing flint and steel together. His heart began to gallop along so fast he thought it might just burst from his chest. He couldn't look at anything else. It was too much—all this love bouncing around his ribcage and nothing to do with it.

So he closed his eyes and he very carefully wrapped up the picture frames in the morning newspaper so that he couldn't see them anymore. Then he went to the pantry and he got out a load of disposable plastic bags, the kind that Carolina used to save from the grocery store. He was relieved to find that his heart only sped up by a beat or so at the thought of those grocery bags. One beat, that wasn't so bad, that would be all right. He took the bags, and he began to place things inside them, all the things left behind. He couldn't look at them properly—that would just get his heart going even more. So he tried to squint his eyes so they looked like other things—things that hadn't belonged to Carolina. He was squinting so hard he bumped into the kitchen cupboards and stubbed his toe viciously. The pain helped. The pain seemed to overtake the love all at once.

After that, he learned. He would squint, and then he would try to remember what things of Carolina's might have been left in the house, to collect them without seeing them. But he found he couldn't even think of them, that he had to sort of squint his mind around them, trying to pick out innocuous things from his memories to focus his attention on, anything in the background, anything that wasn't actually *her*.

It took a long time, and David stubbed quite a few toes. He broke a lamp and found that he didn't care. It was hard to muster an emotion as simple as caring when there was all that love; his head was full of it, his heart was full of it. So he took the bags to the backyard and he began to dig, fervently, desperately, lovingly—sinking the spade into the earth that she had been planning to build a garden out of this year (or maybe next, if there was time for it). She seemed to be everywhere, and it wasn't just in the things, she was in the earth, she was the earth, and he was digging, ripping into her face with the spade, digging as hard and as fast as he possibly could until it wasn't her anymore, it was just a hole in the ground—unfamiliar as any kind of absence.

When he looked at the hole, he felt a little of the love shudder out of him. It was just a tiny bit of love, but it flopped in the dirt by his feet for a moment like a fish. His heart slowed, just a few beats, but it slowed. He wiped his forehead, which had beaded with sweat at the hard labour, and he put the bags in the hole. As he laid them down—bags of trinkets picked up on vacation, broken earrings, receipts from the hair dresser—the love fell out of him bit by bit. Sometimes it squirmed on the earth, sometimes it lay there like a dead thing. But he put it in the hole along with all the other things, and as the love lay there glistening wetly, it didn't seem like so much after all. David's heart was slow now, and he could barely make out the sound of thumping, he had to pound at his chest several times with his fist to make sure the blood kept moving. But it was all right. It was better.

That night, David poured himself a glass of scotch—three fingers, more than he normally had, but there was no one there to stop him. He sat down in front of the television, and he flicked it on. He watched a police procedural. He'd seen it before, he knew right from the start that it was the creepy convenience store worker who had done it, but then it was always the creepy convenience store worker. He wanted to make a joke about that, but there was no one to listen. He watched another. He didn't know why. He didn't particularly like police procedurals, but he liked the sound of voices in the apartment, the sudden violence of gunshots and sirens. When he got tired of the television, he listened to the couple who lived in the other half of the shared complex through the thin walls. They fought incessantly. They always kept Carolina up. They were in love, he decided. You only yelled that much when you were in love.

Eventually, it was four in the morning and even his quarrelsome neighbours went to sleep. He climbed the stairs to the bedroom. The house was eerily silent. He slumped onto the mattress, waiting for exhaustion to claim him. Nothing ticked. There was no noise. There was no movement. Utter stillness. David twitched, reached out his hand to the space beside him where he was accustomed to feeling Carolina's tiny body stirring, fragile as a hummingbird, but there was nothing—absence, loneliness, a hole in a thing that should not have been empty.

David dreamed that Carolina had died in her sleep, and his arm was wrapped around a cold, stiff corpse covered in grave-dirt. But there was an odd sort of comfort to it, even if she was dead, she was still there, and that was better than nothing. He felt her clammy cold hand in his and was relieved at its presence. He touched her stomach, her face, her breasts as chilly as cups of tea left out too long. None of it was right. None of it was her. He thought he should feel sad, but he didn't. He held the hand and he tugged the dead body closer to him and he breathed in the dead-earth smell, the scent of earthworms and insects, the corn-dry hair of her head tickling his nostril, and he dreamed and he dreamed and he dreamed it would never end. But then it did end, and that mouldering smell stayed in his nostrils, the smell of damp earth, but also the smell of *her*—Carolina— and then something really was tickling him, but it was soft, and it felt so much like Carolina except it wasn't dead. David knew it wasn't dead, because it was *moving*. He didn't open his eyes, he kept them jammed shut. What if he opened in his eyes and it was Carolina, and then he couldn't stop the love again? He couldn't bury her, he knew he couldn't make it stop a second time. So his eyes stayed shut. But something moved against him, a lump in the bed, it brushed his leg, his thigh, and then he *did* open his eyes.

It wasn't Carolina. He knew it could not be Carolina, but it smelled like her, and it was soft and pink and just the feeling of having something in that space beside him dampened the shock of what he saw: not Carolina, but it wore Carolina's cashmere sweater, Carolina's discarded earrings, her tongue-lolling lonely sneaker. It did not speak, but it moved beside him again, settling into the nook made by the curvature of his body. A mass of broken, forgotten things packed in with dirt. It was beautiful, David thought, drowsily, not quite believing, not quite caring. He let his arms settle around it. It wasn't warm as Carolina had been, and there were odd edges to it, corners, a sharpness Carolina had never had. But in that moment it was close enough—it was something—and so he slept.

On the morning of the second day after Carolina left him, David woke to find dirt in the bed, under his fingernails, crushed into his skin, but David didn't mind. It felt good. He went downstairs, he made coffee. His hands were very still, precise. When he drank it, it tasted as good as Carolina's used to in the morning—his heart gave a little *ping*, just a little one, and David smiled. He spent the day the way he usually spent his days: he went to work, he made important business phone calls, he said "good morning" to colleagues. When Carolina didn't call him at lunch as she usually did, his heart gave another little *ping*—this one a bit more intense, and he worried that the love was coming back, but it was all right, it wasn't too much. He went and chatted to the copper-haired secretary who stapled things for him and brought his coffee. Her name was Annie. He had never quite managed to remember that. The conversation was awkward getting started, but it turned out that she had watched the same police procedural the night before, so they had a bit of a laugh about it. Wasn't television shitty these days? Wasn't it hard to find good programming? She gave him a list of things she was watching. He hadn't been watching anything in particular—Carolina had found TV crass, had preferred reading the paper in the evening and doing the crossword together—so he named a number of things he'd seen adverts for but had never bothered watching. At the end of the day, he offered an appropriately weary "good evening" to his colleagues and he even waved to Annie as he left.

When he got home, he made his own dinner—*ping, ping*, he was sweating a bit now—and then turned to the paper. He started in on the crossword puzzle and there was a very palpable lurch from his chest. Too much, he thought, it was too much. He took the newspaper and he stumbled out to the backyard where he began to dig. He didn't use the shovel this time: the earth was loose and easy to scrape aside with his hands. It had a warm loamy smell to it, like springtime, and thinking about that eased the franticness of his racing heart. When the work was done, he looked down on the bundle of things he had left, and he saw the pink argyle sweater poking out from the bags. He touched it, once. And then he saw the lone sneaker at the foot of the grave, the rubber sole lolling away. Seeing it there, a single discarded thing, his love came out of his mouth all at once in a rush like vomit, and he caught it in the newspaper with a violent grab. He wrapped it up gently, and laid it in the hole.

That night David did not sleep. He drank extra coffee, and he read as late as he could into the night—past the hours when Annie's television shows played, past the noise and the fighting from next door. When his eyelids started to drift downward, he pinched his arm. And again. And again. And when he dreamed, he dreamed he was dead and he had been laid at the bottom of a deep, deep hole, walls of earth cathedralling around him into the sky. And when Carolina came, he didn't recognize her, she was so old and it was only when she slipped open her blouse and he saw the gold ormolu face gleaming in the moonlight that he knew it was her. She said to him that it was all right, the clock had stopped ticking and they had time now, they could be together. But he didn't want to be with her. She frightened him she was so different. There were all of these pieces of her that he didn't recognize anymore—whatever she said, she was a ticking thing, and when she spoke her words ticked out of her. When she touched his chest it was cold and chilly, and the smell of dirt was the smell of the grave. It wasn't a light touch or a gentle one, there was something insistent about it, and then she was opening up the chest and she was taking all the love out of him.

He woke with a start, body frozen up in a cold sweat, muscles aching and he wanted to call out to Carolina that he'd had a nightmare. But then he remembered the nightmare, and he was suddenly afraid that if he looked over, he would see that she had come back. But, no, there was something beside him on the bed. He could smell loam and earth, and this time he reached out, and in the space where Carolina used to sleep there was a warm, dark thing that smelled like springtime. He breathed out. It was all right. He held it in his arms, his face pressed up against the pink argyle sweater that no longer quite smelled like Carolina, but that was all right too. And it pressed its picture-frame arms around him, its broken-sunglasses arms, its discarded-stockings arms. David felt warm and happy, and he could feel the love inside it, his love, but that was all right too.

On the morning of the third day after Carolina left him, David found dirt tracks on the carpet—one perfect shoeprint and one long, dark smear beside it. On the stairs, the waffle-print of her sneaker. In the kitchen, one clear set of tracks to the backyard and a sinuous slur of dirt trailing behind. David considered the tracks, but he couldn't quite bring himself to clean them up. He found himself at work remembering the feel of the warm argyle sweater, the weight of those arms around him so very much like Carolina's. He thought about Annie's arms—she waved to him as he came in—but, no, Annie's arms were tiny and thin and covered with freckles. She smelled like candy and he imagined she probably listened to loud music in the evenings and didn't need reading glasses.

At lunchtime, David jumped when Annie put a call through. He didn't imagine his phone would ever ring again at lunchtime; it was just one more thing that had been cut out of the fabric of his life. His heart gave a little jolt, but only a very small one. It had learned now. He picked up the phone very tentatively, and said hello. He waited. He waited a little longer. Nothing. He looked through his window at Annie, but she just gave a little shrug and then a little smile. There was still nothing on the other end. But then—it wasn't just nothing. He heard a tiny noise, a scratching sound. Like the creaking of plastic, like the rustle of wool. And this time— he was amazed—his heart did speed up a tiny bit.

"Is it you?" he asked, and he heard nothing in reply. Nothing but the scratching, the rustling. "Carolina?" It wasn't, he knew it wasn't, but he found he didn't want it to be. "Don't go back there," David said. "Don't go back into the hole. You don't have to. It's okay. I love you." There was nothing on the other line. "I love you. You don't have to sleep in the hole. I'm sorry. I'm so sorry. Please don't go back there."

The line disconnected.

That night, David did not go home. He took the car down Banks Avenue, into the north end of town where Carolina's mother lived, and he parked it three blocks away. He waited. When it was late enough, when all the lights in the windows had gone out, then he fetched the key out from under the mat where her mother kept it. Silently, he slid the door open. Silently, he crept up the stairs. He knew where Carolina slept. He had been here for countless Christmases and birthdays and barbecues over the years, and he thought that it might kill him, being in a place that was so solidly Carolina, where photographs of her as a child dotted the walls, the place where she had grown up, where the bric-a-brac of all her life had come to rest. But it didn't. They were just thing now, cells sloughed off like skin, and there wasn't any love in them after all. His heart was slow and gentle, and it was only when he saw, outside the door to her bedroom, a discarded shoe—the frayed laces and the scuffed sole—that his heart gave a little lurch.

David opened the door carefully so as not to wake her. He knew how lightly she slept, how a bad movie might upset her and then she would ask him to hold her and stroke her hair until the memory of it was gone. How she might wake in the night to a noise, a backfiring car, a midnight screaming match next door, and she would clutch his arm, "David, David," she would say, and he would hold her again.

He stepped lightly into the room, past the lonely shoe, and there she was in her old bed, covered in a lilac duvet. He could make out the curve of her shoulder, her body so thin and tiny in the giant bed. He suddenly felt very unsure about why he had come. Carolina—'Lina, he thought—looked very peaceful, and he could barely make out the slow tick-ticking of the clock in her chest.

He made to move toward her, to touch her, perhaps, and see how chilly she would feel under his hand, how cold she would be without a heart. But the floorboards creaked, and her eyelids fluttered very briefly. The blankets rustled as she moved, as her arm crept out into the open space beside her and then gradually retreated to the pillows. Her mouth twitched, and David couldn't make out whether it was a smile or something else.

He left her bedroom as silently as he could. The walls were thick here, there were no neighbours, she wouldn't be used to noise. When he closed the door, a final sliver of light remained, a tiny crack between the door and the frame deliberately preserved so that the lock wouldn't catch. The noise, you see.

He stood on the landing. The house seemed so small now, so much smaller than he had remembered it being when he had first met 'Lina. He barely recognized it, and when he looked at the pictures on the walls, he had to squint because he didn't have his glasses. He realized they weren't 'Lina after all, they were just an array of nieces and sisters and cousins, they never had been 'Lina. But the shoe. He bent down and he picked up the shoe, and he remembered all the times she had laced it up, had worn it through until it was broken and it didn't fit her anymore. But she had loved it so much she hadn't wanted to throw it out. She had wanted to carry it with her, here, she couldn't get rid of it, long past the point she should have.

It was all right. It was all right then. David's heart was calm and full and the love settled deep in his chest like a sleeping kitten. He tucked the shoe under his arm, and he left.

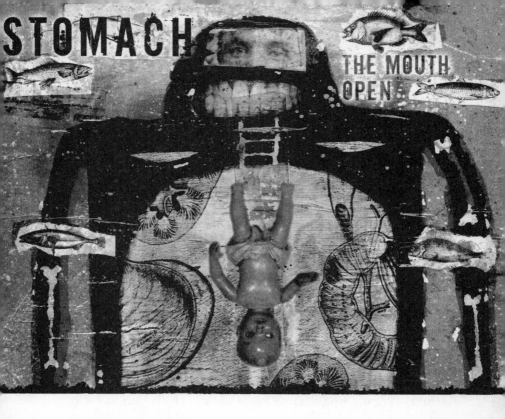

[stomach]

THE MOUTH, OPEN

"It's rude," Jonah's brother-in-law, Petar, whispered beforehand, "to turn down food. We've found the trick is to leave a little room at the end of the first helping so you can take some more when my aunt asks you."

At the time, Jonah had agreed, but when ten o'clock rolled around, after the plane trip to Zagreb and the ensuing drive, the thirty-year-old programmer found that he was starving. Petar's aunt served up a pot of peppers stuffed with rice and pork, mashed potatoes, thick crusty bread, baked string beans, and another bowl full of potatoes fried with mushrooms. Jonah began to salivate, and try as he might to follow Petar's advice, he found his plate heaped higher and higher with food. He couldn't help it. He never could.

"Aunt Katica may look stern," Petar had told him, "but she'll love you. You're family after all, what with Deborah and I." When he said that, he leaned over and kissed Deborah—Jonah's super-beauty of a little sister—on the cheek. She smiled, and wriggled her body again at Petar in a way Jonah didn't entirely approve of. "She's just very old fashioned, you know, caught in the old ways. Her sons died when the Serbs bombed Dubrovnik back in the War of Independence. She takes good care of us now. And she'll feed you until you're fit to burst."

Jonah had been doubtful about the trip, and about his reception with this new family he was supposed to be part of. He wasn't terribly close to Deborah. He had showed up to her wedding late, and missed most of the major festivities before and after. And, so when he arrived in Petar's family home, back in the old country that Deborah had told him so much about, when they started piling food in front of him, despite the doctor's warning, despite his avowal to drop thirty pounds, and despite Petar's advice, he began to eat.

Travelling made him nervous, Petar's family made him nervous, and when he was nervous he wanted to eat. After all, eating meant that you didn't have to talk.

He shovelled forkful after forkful into his mouth, long after Petar and Deborah had stopped, while Petar's cousins chatted to each other in Croatian. They were big, burly men, all of them, with bulky biceps and skin burnt to an attractive red-gold. Jonah, on the other hand, felt pudgy and fish-belly white. He went to the gym when he could, but sitting in front of a computer all day did nothing for either his complexion or his physique. So his own wife had told him before she packed her bags to leave him for her fitness instructor.

"You've let yourself go, honey," Sarah said, eyes big with concern. "I can't watch you doing this to yourself anymore. I don't want to see who you are becoming."

Doing what? He had wanted to ask. Working twelve to fourteen hours a day organising trade routes for shipping companies, implementing database systems, waking at six in the morning to answer his Blackberry all so that she could have a beautiful apartment in the nice part of town and spend hours at the high-end FemChic gym in Yorkville?

But Jonah had not said that. He had said nothing when Sarah left, and so here he was, joining his little sister, her husband and his Herculean cousins in an apartment in Dubrovnik.

"What you need is to get away," Deborah had told him, patting his hand with that awkward breed of affection and contempt that only family can get away with. "Come with Dam and I. He won't mind. And his family is our family now."

They certainly didn't look like *his*—Jonah's—family. The younger Malinaric men had large foreheads and faces that seemed moulded from clay. They had welcomed Jonah solemnly, drank a shot of *šljivovica* with him, and then ignored him completely in favour of Petar, the prodigal son, and his beautiful bride.

Mashed potatoes it was then, mixed with tomatoes and onions, and a second piece of bread that he could stuff in his face, so that when, at last, all the bronze, golem-faces turned to him, he could shrug and mumble apologetically.

"You don't have to eat so much," Deborah leaned over to whisper discreetly. "Really, you can just say no. They'll understand. You aren't from here."

Jonah wanted to point out that neither was she, but Deborah, being Deborah, had left a smattering of meat and vegetables on her plate just to prove that she had really, really tried and that she was definitely good and full.

Jonah instantly put down the piece of bread he'd been about to finish off. "Okay, Sis," he whispered. "Thanks."

But when she turned away, he quickly popped the stub into his mouth and chewed as fast as he could. Petar shot him a look, a friendly are-you-having-a-good-time smile, but Jonah caught the quick eye-flick to his belly, bulging out from beneath his navy t-shirt.

Only the aging Aunt Katica, a buttery-looking woman with sagging skin and sharp, bird-like eyes, looked on in approval. When at last Jonah's plate was clear, she tapped a wooden spoon against her chin twice, and smiled at him. It was a strange smile, but the only genuine smile he had received since he arrived.

Deborah and Petar wanted to go with the cousins to a nightclub and they insisted that Jonah tag along as well.

"The women here are beautiful," Petar said. "My parents were shocked that I found a Canadian girl as pretty as the girls in Dubrovnik."

"Prettier," Deborah added. "And Canadians age well. It's the cold. Keeps us well-preserved."

They kissed then, a long post-honeymoon but pre-anniversary kind of kiss that involved a lot of tongue. Afterwards, they bobbed along, hand in hand, like two buoys floating in the ocean. Jonah felt a pang as he watched them. Sarah would have fit right in here. All the Croatian girls had surprisingly perfect bodies. It was the kind of place where everyone felt comfortable wearing bikini-tops. The cousins had each managed to find themselves identical counterparts: tanned, well-built girls with dark curling hair and sombre faces.

The nightclub was dark and dingy, just like every other nightclub Jonah had ever attended. They played American music, and served Croatian beer—"*Pivo*," Petar informed him, "the only Croatian word you need to know." The beer came in half-litre bottles, and tasted gritty but not unpleasant.

The music was hypnotic, and Jonah was still exhausted from jet lag. His belly felt too full, and the beer was very strong. These were people who liked to drink. Liked to drink and fight, Jonah remembered. It hadn't been that long since the civil war had ended. You could see bullet holes, Petar had said, on the doors in some of the smaller cities where they hadn't yet rebuilt. And there were villages bombed by the Serbs during World War II that still lay empty and deserted.

It was a place for strong beer and quiet faces. When Jonah looked around, there seemed to be something angry and feral to the dancing.

"The Croatian women are very beautiful, yes?" one of the cousins said.

Jonah muttered a reply he hoped was polite, but he didn't really want to talk to this hulking behemoth of a man—family, Deborah had said. Not his family. Hers.

"Is okay. Very beautiful. You dance now?" Jonah shook his head emphatically. "Is okay," the cousin repeated, smiling.

A moment later, Jonah was alone again.

Disorientated and a little drunk, Jonah took a taxi home alone, hours, he suspected, before the others would be getting in, drunk and grinning, arms hugging companionably around oversized shoulders. When he slipped through the front door, Aunt Katica was there at the little kitchen table, clutching a hand-rolled cigarette.

She beckoned him to the table, and though he was tired, Jonah did not refuse.

The smell of tobacco was heavy. Wordlessly, she poured a small cupful of *šljivovica* from a plastic water bottle in the fridge. The air conditioner buzzed angrily, but it was still hot in the room. Jonah sipped the liquor, enjoying the sweet, burning sensation it left in his throat.

"You did not like the club?" the old woman asked him. Her English was surprisingly good, though the syllables still sounded heavy and guttural in her mouth. She didn't have the high-pitched voices of the cousins' girlfriends. Hers was harsher; her mouth scowled when she spoke English.

"It was very nice," Jonah lied. "I'm just tired after the flight, is all."

She grunted in reply, and poured him more liquor. Jonah felt lightheaded. The smoke scratched the inside of his lungs. It had been a while since he'd smoked, something he'd given up when he and Sarah had started dating.

"Is okay," she said. "You are good boy. You will do well in this country."

He coughed as he swallowed the *šljivovica*. She stood, eyeing him, and cracked a window open. A breeze wafted into the room, stealing some of the heavy, circling smoke.

"I'm not staying long," Jonah replied.

The old woman took a long drag from her cigarette. Jonah found himself studying her in the paper-yellow light. Her skin was brown and doughy, a thousand lines creased into the soft folds of it. She hadn't gone to fat like so many of the other old women in the country, brought up the old way. In fact, Jonah had yet to see her eat. She had simply brought plate after plate to the table, and then observed as the family sat down to dine.

"It was a woman, yes?" she said after some time. "A woman from your country?"

Jonah nodded, feeling uncomfortable. "She's gone now."

She took another drag, and Jonah wondered where all the smoke had gone, whether it was pooling in her lungs. Finally, she exhaled a small cloud. "We have many ghosts here," she said with a soft snarl. "The young people can be foolish in their forgetfulness."

"It must be hard."

"Yes. Very hard in Croatia, for a long time."

She extinguished the last of the cigarette in an ash tray, and then rose to shut the window again. Jonah watched the red ember die to ash, while Aunt Katica looked on in thoughtful silence.

That night, Jonah dreamed that he was hungry. A woman sat on the other side of a table, but there was so much food piled between them that he couldn't see her face properly. He began to eat and eat and eat. Dumplings, cabbage rolls, roasted chicken legs, breaded pork chops. His stomach pressed against the table, curving overtop and spilling onto the plate. The more he ate, the closer he felt to seeing that figure on the other side. Soon, he knew, soon.

Finally, as Jonah felt his stomach begin to burst, he heard a voice, Sarah's: "I can't watch you doing this to yourself." But when he saw who was on the other side, she wasn't alone. Aunt Katica sat next to her, sucking on her cigarette, eyes burning like red-hot embers as she watched him.

"You must eat," she said. "Is good."

And she pushed Sarah onto the plate.

Jonah couldn't help it. He was so hungry. He took one of her pale, manicured hands and he popped it into his mouth, crunching down on the fingers. Soon he had eaten his way to her elbow, but Sarah only looked on with those sad eyes of hers. "This won't make me love you any more," she said. And then she gave him a languorous wink, and he imagined her rubbing up against the man at the club.

He could feel his skin tingling, could feel her pressed up against his insides as if she was wearing him like a second skin.

"This won't make us closer," she said, her words rippling out from his lungs, through his windpipe.

Aunt Katica nodded, tapped a wooden spoon to her chin, and smiled.

———

Deborah and Petar were late waking the next morning, and they grinned foolishly to each other at the breakfast table.

"I'm not used to drinking like that," Deborah said. "You Croats must have cast-iron stomachs."

"It's taken practice. At least we excel at something."

"In Croatia," said one of the cousins, "we say we are very good at fighting. Not so good at peace."

Aunt Katica gave him a dark look as she set down a pot of hot coffee. Jonah helped himself to a cupful, serving it out with a long, rounded spoon as he listened to the banter. He felt guilty he hadn't stayed. They all seemed closer now without him. Deborah laughed easily with the cousins, making quick and clumsy jokes in their language.

They poured another round of *šljivovica*—"It's how we start the day over here," Petar winked—but Jonah was somehow left out. He didn't mind. The coffee was sweeter than he expected, and when he had finished it, he poked the dark silt at the bottom and licked the grounds off his finger.

Deborah gave him a look, and he tucked his hands back under the table, as the others all downed their liquor.

They ate thick slices of bread, spicy salami and cheese, along with a heaping spoonful of scrambled eggs. The cousins seemed in fine form, nudging each other in the ribs, their appetites unaffected by the apparent debauchery of last night. Deborah looked a little paler, and only nibbled at the food. Aunt Katica stared disapprovingly at her, and Jonah found himself doing the same thing.

Food was a gift. Food was hospitality. Food meant you were family.

He hadn't felt like he had family in a long time. Deborah was great, but the two of them were nothing alike. She was tiny, trim, the kind of woman who went for a ten-kilometre run first thing in the morning. After their parents' divorce, the family had become fragmented, with holidays so unbearably tense that Jonah had been happy to ditch them in favour of a low-key morning with Sarah, and dinner with her teeming, multitudinous assortment of cousins, nieces and nephews. But they had never been his family.

Here, though—here he felt a warmth creeping into his stomach, and at one point, Aunt Katica came and rested her hands on his shoulders. They were icy cold, but the touch was kind, a gesture of affection.

"It's the dragon's own weather outside," Petar muttered. "I wanted to show you the beach today. I guess we can go to the market instead. The Old City."

"*Pijaca*," said one of the cousins. "Is very nice."

It took some time to get moving, but eventually they boarded the tram into town. Even early in the morning, underneath a cover of grey clouds, the sun beat down on Jonah something fierce.

They passed through the ancient gateway into the Old City. Despite the sun, and the heat, and the sweat, even Jonah was impressed. The ancient fortifications still stood intact after all these years—after a vicious earthquake that had almost levelled the city, and after invasions by Venetians, Turks, later by Napoleon.

The walls towered over Jonah. There were already a number of people up there, tourists for the most part, remarking at the colour of the ocean, taking pictures of the Adriatic. Jonah felt exhausted from last night as it was. Jet lag tugged at his eyelids, and he felt as if he had eaten a cannonball for breakfast, the weight of it sagging from his stomach. But up sprinted Deborah with her trim runner's legs, the flesh smooth and expensively tanned. Jonah followed, taking one step at a time. He didn't like heights much. But when he reached the top, the view really was spectacular. On one side, he could see a patchwork of red clay rooftop tiles jostling one another for space. There were so many different shades: the old tiles, grey where they had cracked and sun-bleached where they hadn't; a variety of reds, oranges, browns of the newer tiles. In some places, he could make out the bright, coloured tiles where the rooftops had been patched. After the war, he thought. The too-even colours had a bright flesh-over-a-scar gloss.

It reminded Jonah of the way their apartment in Toronto had looked, the week after Sarah had left. She had let herself in while he was at work to collect all of her things. When he'd returned at the end of the day, exhausted from troubleshooting the glitches in the system he had been working on for the last month, he had found empty craters in the dust on bookshelves and tables where a lamp or vase had stood, nails sticking out of the wall.

She'd left a note:

Dear Jonah, sorry to collect my things while you were away, but it didn't feel right to see you. Not yet.

I know this is all my fault.
I left the key in the ashtray on the kitchen table.

Sarah

Perhaps all loss felt like that, empty places where you knew something special, something important, had stood.

Traversing the walls took a good hour. Jonah sweated through most of it with a fairly good temper. Deborah and Petar often asked him to take cute-couple pictures of them kissing. Each time, Petar would open his mouth, like a fish, to suck on Deborah's top lip. They fit together like two gears turning, mouths clicking together, camera clicking to capture the shot.

Finally, they found themselves in a large plaza filled on the one side with two-person tables where tourists reclined, drinking pale beer out of enormous glass mugs. On the other side, the square was filled with stalls perched under rectangular, blue and white striped umbrellas. The bustle of people was ferocious and Jonah was almost immediately swept away from his group by the crowd. There were enormous watermelons bulging out of crates, tomatoes, cucumbers, limes, olives, eggplants, bunches of bananas, and strings of garlic hanging from the rafters.

He made his way to a huge statue with large, bronze panels on it that stood in the centre of the square. The panel before him depicted a dragon and a winged lion bowing before a woman on a throne. It was beautiful, and imposing, a relic of the ancient spirit of Dubrovnik exerting itself against its would-be enemies. *Libertas*, Jonah remembered, was the motto of this town. It had never let itself be conquered, not by the Venetians who ruled the rest of Croatia nor the Turks, their ancient enemy.

But Jonah's gaze soon swept back to the lines of burdened stalls. Where had the others gone? He tried to shade his eyes and get a better look.

"Try, yes?" called out a slender woman selling giant wheels of cheese. She shaved a piece off a crescent and offered it to him. Jonah, without thinking, put it into his mouth. "You try, yes? Try all!" She cut off more from something darker, an orange-yellow with a red skin to it. He took it. And the next piece, and the next. He tried to put his hands up apologetically.

"No more, no more," he pleaded, and disentangled himself from the booth, offering twenty *kuna* to satisfy the woman.

Where were Deborah and Petar? He thought he spotted Petar's head towering over the crowd, and he tried to wade through the crowd to rejoin them.

Someone tugged at his arm.

It was a small child, shirtless, nut-brown from head to toe like all the Croats. His eyes looked up with an eager expression on his face. In his hands, he clutched a thick slice of watermelon, which he held out before Jonah. He did not resist when the fruit was pushed into his hands. He bit down, felt the juice running over his chin.

Then there was a girl, fifteen or sixteen maybe, in a knotted white dress. She came up to him shyly. He still held the green rind of the watermelon in his hand, so she leaned in close and pushed some kind of sweet pastry into his mouth.

"No," he whispered. "I don't need it." But she simply smiled and fed him another. He dropped the shell of the watermelon.

There was another hand. Something dark with a thick, aromatic juice was pushed toward him. And then a red sliver of tomato.

Jonah had barely closed his mouth, barely chewed. His stomach felt tight against his shorts. It bulged out under his shirt. He tried to protest, but there were so many hands, so many offerings. He couldn't stop. He felt his mouth unhinge like a snake's, as meat and cheese slid down his gullet almost effortlessly.

"*Alklha*," he heard them whisper. "*Alklha*." He didn't know what the word meant, but it didn't seem to matter. The marketplace came alive before him, a thousand tanned hands and smiling faces. He was fit to bursting, but his hunger was deep, so deep. It was as if he had never eaten in his entire life. Jonah could feel a fire beginning to burn in the pit of his stomach, a fierce joy, protectiveness, something like love even, for these people and their gifts. *I love you*, he wanted to say. *I love you all.*

The chatter grew louder. There was quite a crowd of people now, all those dark, brown eyes staring up at him with hopeful, expectant faces.

It was then that the nut-brown boy—the one who had first offered him the watermelon—was pushed to the front of the crowd. His eyes were bright, shining, his skin smooth and youthful, long-limbed. He would be a handsome boy one day, barrel-chested like the cousins. He slipped his short child's fingers into Jonah's mouth. They tasted sweet, sweeter than anything Jonah had ever tasted before. The boy pushed further, and soon it was his whole arm, and then a leg, and then both legs, so that the boy was sitting on the edge of Jonah's jaw, half in, half out. He didn't seem scared. In fact, he seemed happy, excited. Jonah couldn't speak. His throat began to work, constricting in tight circles that caught hold of the feet and dragged them deeper into his throat.

And then the people were pushing, pushing the boy further into him. Jonah squeezed his eyes shut, caught somewhere between the fear and hunger, the moment dreamlike in its intensity.

The boy's head disappeared, and then, at last, the final hand slithered between his lips.

Jonah felt heavy now, terribly heavy.

The crowd was dissipating, all those happy, faces blending back into the dull morass of hot, sticky tourists and bored vendors. The bright white and blue of the tents were blinding. Jonah found himself slumped on a bench, half in the shade, his stomach sagging pitifully over the belt of his shorts. He felt queasy. His vision blurred. The sun was too hot, and he could feel prickles of sweat running down his neck.

Deborah and Petar appeared, as if out of thin air. Deborah sat down on the bench beside him, while Petar peered off, his hands shading his eyes. The cousins ringed them like an entourage.

"You don't look well," she said, her voice laced with concern. "Maybe you should go lie down?"

Jonah nodded his head, moaned something low.

Deborah put her hand on his wet, sticky back. The gesture was so intimate, so familiar, that for a brief moment Jonah felt tears at the edges of his vision.

"One of the cousins can take you home," Deborah said softly. "Petar wants to show me the harbour. It's supposed to be beautiful. Do you want to come . . . ?"

Jonah shook his head. There was an intense pain in his abdomen. He felt hot and sleepy, fevered. He closed his eyes, and when he opened them, a cousin had propped him up under one arm, and they were walking toward the tram.

"Sorry about this," Jonah muttered. "I hate to spoil your day."

He looked up, and the cousin was smiling a tight, sharp smile. Jonah recognised him as the one from the bar, the one who had sent him fleeing back to the apartment. At that moment, he didn't care though. He didn't think he could make it back on his own. Another wave of pain overtook him, and he almost doubled over with it.

"Is okay," the cousin said. "*Alklha*. We wait for you."

The air in the apartment was thick with the growing heat of the afternoon. Jonah was sweating profusely now, his shirt almost soaked through. At one point, he half-dreamed he saw Sarah in the kitchen, but when he blinked his eyes, it was Aunt Katica, clucking sympathetically, while she poured a glass of cold tap water for him. She wore a green printed dress, and for a moment, Jonah was glad it was her there and not Sarah. When he had got the flu, she had locked him in their shared bedroom with an electric kettle, a small jar of honey, and a box of Twinings teabags. Not much of a caregiver.

But when Aunt Katica put her hand to his brow, he felt something blissfully cold slither down his spine. "You rest now," she said firmly. "Grow strong."

The bedroom felt smaller today. Jonah's belly heaped like a mountain under the cover. The walls were so close on either side that he felt he could reach out and touch them.

Sleep was difficult coming, but when it did, he saw Aunt Katica staring down at him from an enormous height. Her cigarette tip glowed in the darkness like a third eye, and Jonah found himself enwreathed in delicious smoke. He breathed it in, feeling it travel through his veins, bringing a rich wave of shuddering heat to the tips of his body.

Aunt Katica drew closer, and her eyes flashed red. The folds of her skin now were a burnished bronze, gleaming in the light of the cigarette. She took his hand in hers and pressed it against her cheek. There was no give. Jonah felt something hot and metallic underneath his fingertips, like a penny that had been out in the sun too long. But he didn't want to stop touching it. He hadn't felt desire for anyone since Sarah had left. He had thought his capacity for it burnt out of him. But Aunt Katica's age sloughed off her like a second skin: her flesh was smooth, taut, her breasts were firm and perfect, thighs slim and tapered. She tugged him closer, and his erection was stiffer than it had ever been in his entire life, his penis engorged, terribly sensitive. Her smooth, metallic fingers touched it gently, and he almost came right then. But she grasped him firmly, and her fingers were very hot.

"Is good, yes? You grow big?" she whispered and suddenly there was no air in his lungs for speaking. His white flesh shuddered against her. She leaned in close to kiss him, her tongue darting in and out of his mouth. Their tongues met for a moment, his large and fleshy, hers soft, sharp, forked at the end like a snake's. But, god, that was even more erotic. She kissed his neck, his chest, flicking across his nipples as if she was tasting them.

He tangled his hands in her hair, overwhelmed by their combined scent. She smelled dry, like the desert.

She moved against him now, rubbing his erection between her legs until he was gasping with pleasure, with the pain of wanting her so much.

She guided him into her then, and he just about dissolved into the hot, liquid warmth of her. He thrust once. Again. He could see the weight of his stomach bouncing with the effort, but he didn't mind. He seemed to be growing thicker, not with fat, but with muscle, his body expanding, expanding. Suddenly she was a tiny thing next to him. He thrust and he thrust, each stroke engorging him further as if his entire body had grown priapic. Then, at last, release came.

His muscles contracted, painfully, ecstatically, all at once.

—————

When he woke, Deborah was sitting by the side of the bed. She had a small, strange smile on her face.

"Do you want to come down to dinner?" she asked. "Aunt Katica said you've been sleeping all afternoon. Feel any better?"

"I—I think so," he replied. Jonah found he did feel better. The queasiness and the pain in his stomach had all but disappeared. He looked over at his sister, small and petite, next to the bulking mass of him. His body wobbled as if it had grown an extra set of skin.

"Are you doing okay here?" She flicked aside a fly that had settled on the sheets. "You don't seem yourself. Is it—?"

"It's not Sarah," he finished.

She nodded, her smile sympathetic, not really hearing him. "We thought you were going to get married, Mom, Dad, all of us. I really liked her."

There was something soft and accusing in her tone. Like it had been Jonah who had screwed it all up.

"I know, Sis."

"We want you to be happy." Jonah wondered who the *we* was. His parents? They hadn't called after the break up. Petar? He hardly knew the man. "Look, I know Mom and

Dad were shit. Arguing all the time. And I know you're still angry at them—"

"I'm not—" he protested.

"—but it's not always like that. Petar and I, we—"

Jonah wasn't listening. He shut his eyes and let the hum of the air conditioner buzz around him. *I didn't want her to go*, he thought. *I wanted her to stay. I wanted her to love me.* He thought about Petar and Deborah kissing, their mouths open, trying to devour each other. His stomach rumbled.

"Family's important," she was saying. "That's why I brought you here. I wanted you to see what Petar's family is like. They're all so close. It's different. It can be different.

"You don't want to end up alone." Again, that strange smile.

"I know, Sis," he repeated. He patted her hand gently, though he wasn't sure if he was comforting her or the other way round. He wanted to tell her about what had happened in the square, but looking at her just then, the gulf between them seemed so wide, unbridgeable.

She quirked her lips, tossed her hair back with a sweep of her muscular arms. "So, dinner then?"

He nodded, and heaved himself out of the bed.

There were new faces at the dinner table: the girlfriends were there alongside the cousins, but also several older men and woman, some grey-haired, some burly, some dough-faced with creases in the folds of their flesh from age. But they all had the same sloping foreheads, the same dark eyes. Jonah wasn't sure how they all managed to fit in the apartment. He felt bulky beside them, and try as he might to take up less space when he was seated at the dining table, he still felt his flesh crowding those beside him. He tucked his elbows in, but there seemed nowhere that he could put himself.

Aunt Katica stood in the corner, directing an armada of pots and vessels to the table. They drank, all of them, small glasses full of *šljìvovica*. One, two, three shots they knocked back in quick succession. Jonah's eyes watered and his stomach burned with the liquor. He noticed, though, that Deborah had not touched hers this evening. "*Živjeli!*" they shouted, as each glass went down.

The chatter buzzed around Jonah. He couldn't make out the slurred Croatia syllables. It all sounded so strange and yet comfortable. The woman beside him—she looked familiar somehow—wore a white knotted dress that stood out against the dark burnished brown of her skin. She smiled genially at him, and clinked her glass against his.

"You are the brother, yes?" she asked. Jonah nodded. "Good, good. Welcome!"

Her leg brushed against his.

And then Petar was hushing everyone. The murmurs died down, and all eyes turned toward him.

"Deborah and I are so glad everyone could be here tonight." Deborah stood beside him. He snaked an arm around her, pulling her closer. "Because we have an announcement to make."

Jonah stared at his sister, saw the way her hand fluttered against her belly delicately, almost protectively. Her eyes were downcast as if, for once, she didn't enjoy all the attention. For a brief moment, Jonah almost felt sorry for her. Her glass of *šljìvovica* still remained untouched. Jonah felt a stab of panic.

"I'm pregnant," she said, her voice shy, uncertain. Her eyes darted up to meet Jonah's. They were wide, blue, maybe a little bit happy, maybe a little bit scared. Petar tugged on her. She turned her face toward him, and then they were kissing with that open-mouthed, fishy kiss of theirs. Her body relaxed into him.

The cousins burst into a happy chatter, some banging forks against plates, some raising glasses. The *šljìvovica* went round again. And again.

Jonah drank to steady himself. The woman beside him murmured something into his ear and patted him on the back. "We are family now, yes? It is good luck, this baby."

But Jonah was only half listening. He searched the crowd, looking for a face, and then he found it: Aunt Katica was nodding approvingly, but not at Deborah. She was looking directly at him with eyes that burned through the haze of the alcohol. For a moment, as she drew a cigarette to her lips, he thought her skin flashed gold and metallic. Heat swept through him.

And then they were all rising from the table, the cousins and their girlfriends, the woman in the white dress, Petar, Deborah. They were spilling out into the night, into the streets, a sea of white teeth set in dark faces. Jonah felt drunk. He was unsteady on his feet, but someone put an arm out to help him. The air was cooler now that the sun had set. Jonah breathed it in, tasting the salt of it on his tongue. Someone jostled him. They were moving now, sweeping past white buildings roofed in red clay tiles. The ground was uneven beneath his feet, but he kept up with them. The alcohol sang in his blood.

Pregnant. She was pregnant.

He felt large and clumsy, but this time, somehow part of the crowd. It felt good. A new child. That was something to celebrate.

Plum liquor poured down his throat, as the woman in white offered him a slug from a plastic bottle.

"We are family. Is good!" she shouted.

The streets seemed to contract around him, and he had to suck in his belly to pass through the narrow corridors, elbows pushing at him, hands pulling him along. His legs and arms felt enormous. He could have been floating, a giant blimp above them, thick sausage-like fingers, legs thick as pillars.

Down, down, they went, along the city walls, until they stood on a pier, the whole riotous lot of them. Jonah could hardly see, but he could smell the tang of the Adriatic, could hear the crash of the waves against the rock. He stumbled, and fell hard against the wooden boards of the dock. The ocean leapt up in a spray between the planks, cool against his skin. There were hands on his shoulders now. He couldn't quite get up. His body felt too round. He couldn't get his legs under him. The hands pinched into his flesh like claws, and Jonah looked up to see Aunt Katica standing over him, but her face was different now, like in the dream. Her skin was metallic, and her fingers were long, with sharp nails that tug into him. Those eyes burned, and when she exhaled, a small plume of smoke formed.

And then the woman, the one who had been sitting next to him, leaned down, her lips brushing lightly against his. His mouth formed a surprised "o" and before he could think, before he could react, she had reached both hands into his mouth, and pried his lips apart, crawling in, all the way, disappearing down his throat.

He tried to struggle, but his limbs felt so heavy. Aunt Katica's nails dug into his shoulders. His mouth was opening again, and then one of the cousins climbed in, and then another, and then another: the old men, the young, all those Slavic faces disappearing inside him.

"They come soon," Aunt Katica whispered in his ears, looking across the Adriatic, beyond the borders of Croatia. "The young, they are foolish, they forget. But we do not forget. The serpent will always rise again, and it will eat our children, our grandfathers.

"We cannot forget this. You understand, yes?"

Jonah squirmed, but he could not escape. They had to crawl over him now; his body was mountainous. He had long since split the seams of his clothes, and he lay naked on the dock, as the line of cousins and uncles and aunts grabbed hold of the thick folds of his skin, pulling themselves atop him.

"You are family, yes? You help. You protect us, the child. Your sister's child." He couldn't see Deborah or Petar. Did not know if they had been left behind somewhere along the way. There was a fire burning his belly now. The child, yes, the child must be safe.

"Our blood is your blood." Aunt Katica whispered. Her tongue flicked out, forked, to tickle his ear. "Is good now."

And then she twisted her grip, and he was rolling off the pier into the Adriatic. Inside him, there was an inferno, and the air hissed and twisted into strands of steam that braided above him. He was heavy, so very heavy. The waves lapped over his face and he sank, Aunt Katica's words whispering in his brain.

The water felt cool against the heat of his skin, and he did not struggle. He could feel all the cousins inside him, the thick muscles of their bodies, their quiet strength seeping into him. There was a fierce joy to it, as if all the empty parts of himself had suddenly been filled with presence. He opened his mouth, and the water rushed inside.

Somewhere he could hear Sarah's voice: *I don't want to see who you are becoming.*

Her face was turning away from his, and his heart felt empty, bombed out, each word dropping with an explosive force that shattered memories of the two of them together, dreams of the future he had once thought they might share.

His tears mingled with the salt of the ocean, his skin felt hot and molten, moving and sliding, until the water burst in. Then it cooled and grew hard. The shape of it was strange and unfamiliar. His blood sang with a thousand new voices that drowned out the destruction Sarah had wrought. They were with him. He *was* them, could feel the ache in his bones, bones like the mountains that ringed the country, protective, imposing. He rubbed up against the coastal rock, and felt a screeching kind of pleasure as the sharpness of it made channels in his skin for the water to seep through.

He took it all inside of him, drank in the jewelled water of the Adriatic.

His muscles began to respond again, and he stretched, feeling all those bodies, not as a weight, but as a wonderful fullness. He lifted his head, and water streamed off it.

There stood Aunt Katica on the pier, flame-eyed, beautiful in her grimness, but smiling, smiling down on him.

"Yes," she said with a sibilant hiss. "You grow big now. Beautiful, beautiful boy."

He opened his mouth, and a tendril of smoke drifted out to wreath around her like a coronet. Then he tensed, corded the thick, ropey tendons, the great bulk of him, and lifted himself out of the water. His body was long and sinuous, gleaming in the light of the moon, and he curled his body around her. She touched her hand against his massive, sloped forehead. Her nails traced along his snout, and around the bunching muscles of his jaws.

They would come again, he thought, remembering the patchwork rooftops where the bombs had fallen. A flicker of anger burned through him, inferno-hot, and with it something like joy. They would come again.

It is good, he thought. He was hungry.

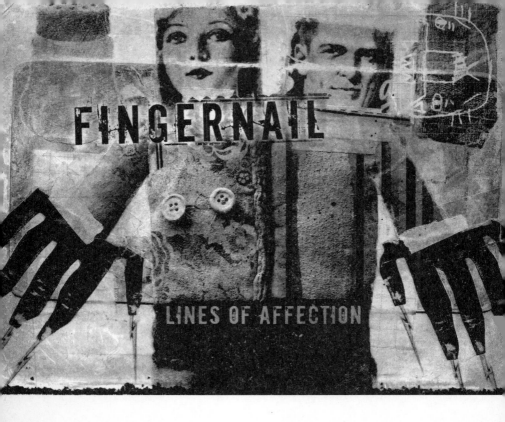

LINES OF AFFECTION

The first time he stepped through the threshold of the door into their tiny two-bedroom apartment, Marissa felt the tiny hairs on the back of her neck stiffen like cilia. It wasn't the way he smiled at her, or even the way his right hand brushed lightly against her mummy's back as he passed her, suitcase in hand, easy-breezy gait like he owned the place. Marissa had seen those before. Those were fine, normal even. It was the way she felt her body start to tingle, like the whole floor had become charged with static. His fingers seemed to give off tiny blue sparks when they touched her mum, and her mummy, in turn, shivered in pleasure.

Marissa's body shivered too, until she told it to stop.

Marissa knew her mummy very well. She had to when they lived in such close proximity. But she had never seen her like this: eyes glassy, fingers twitching like she wanted to touch something—him, probably, just to rub herself all over him like a cat.

It was new, and it disgusted her.

"Marissa, darling, I want you to meet someone," her mummy cooed.

Marissa did not move.

"You can just put that over—Marissa, this is Sampson, the one I told you about?—no, don't worry, I'll just hang it up."

The stranger was taking off his jacket, and Marissa watched with a strange kind of fascination. It was a normal jacket, the kind men had been wearing to the office for years, but on him it was transformed. It whispered like silk, slid off his arms making beautiful noises until—there—it was off, and only a jacket once again. Underneath was a tan dress shirt with tiny buttons, dark as mahogany. She wanted to rub her fingers along them, to slip the little nubs through the thread-lined slits and—pop!—there it would go, one, two, three, all the buttons through, and that shirt slipping off after the jacket. She wanted to . . . she wanted to . . .

Marissa shrunk away through the doorway.

Her mummy was already turning away from her, distracted. Her mouth hung open in mid-sentence. Marissa couldn't remember what she'd been saying. Then her mouth closed, and her mummy touched the stranger's wrist.

"I'll just let you fetch dinner yourself, shall I, sweetie pie?" her mummy murmured. "I've got to—we need to . . ."

She didn't finish the sentence. Her mummy turned her head, and met the stranger's eyes. She smiled and electricity seemed to wind around the two of them like a Tesla coil.

Marissa said nothing.

In a moment, the two of them had slipped up the stairs.

Marissa stood in the doorway, clutching the frame until her knuckles were white, and she could feel the shape of it imprinting itself in her flesh.

Upstairs, she could hear the sound of a door closing, and then, after a few minutes, the sounds she hated hearing most.

"Marissa, honey, pass us the salt, would you? There's a good girl."

They were sitting at the dinner table, the three of them, Marissa, her mummy and the stranger. It might have looked like a proper family, had someone stumbled in from the street. A sleek silver fox of a man, his beautiful wife and daughter. Except it wasn't quite right. Marissa was sitting on one side, by herself, while her mummy and the stranger shared the other. The table felt lopsided, all the weight shifting over to them like an overbalanced teeter-totter. She nudged the salt carelessly, half expecting it to slide the rest of the way under the combined force of geometry and gravity. It didn't. She nudged it again until it was close enough that the stranger, with his perfectly clean, half-moon fingernails—beautiful those, she thought—could snatch it from the table.

Marissa moved a potato around her plate.

"How was school?"

"All right."

"Did you learn anything interesting?"

"Yes."

"Did you . . ." And there it was again, her mummy turned idiot as the stranger did something with his hand. He didn't speak, no, just touched her, briefly, like he was picking a stray hair off her shoulder. Her body arched, and she let out a little moan. Her fork clattered to the table.

What was she *doing*?

Marissa stared at the stranger's face with all the menace she could muster. *You don't belong here*, she yelled at him in her mind. *This is our house and our dinner table and our salt, and you don't belong here!* She thought if she yelled it loud enough in her mind, he must be able to hear. But he wasn't looking at her. His eyes were watching the place he had touched, watching the expression on her mummy's face. And then he smiled, ever so softly, the way a cat purrs.

Get out get out get out, she shouted in her head. But her lips were frozen, and all she could say was: "Can I please be excused from the table?"

Once upon a time, Marissa had a proper family. If she squeezed her eyes hard enough, she could still remember her dad. He wasn't a handsome man, not really, and she felt a little bit guilty thinking that, but his face was a bit squashed, like a melon or something that had fallen out of the bin at the grocery store. It wasn't a bad face. Mostly it was kind and it liked to smile.

Marissa remembered her dad taking her to a fair once in the centre of town, where they had a Ferris wheel and cotton candy, and she got to ride a donkey for an extra ten minutes because her dad had slipped the handler a note.

Her dad had been a nice man, she remembered. Most of the time.

He'd have moods sometimes—dark, brooding, bruised moods when his face was slightly more squashed than usual and he didn't smile at all.

He would say things like: "Marissa, daddy loves you but you must go play in your room now." And then: "Marissa, go play somewhere else, kid." And finally: "Just get the fuck out!"

Marissa knew her dad loved her, and so she padded silently up the stairs to her bedroom to draw. When she was younger, she always kept a box of pencil crayons and paper in the little desk next to her bed so that she could draw nice pictures of her dad, where his face was perfectly round and not squashed at all. Sometimes she'd draw pictures of her mummy too, but they never quite looked right. And she never drew pictures of them together, because then her dad's face seemed even stranger, even more squashed, and her mummy wouldn't smile properly and then she, Marissa—the drawing of her—wouldn't fit properly between them. She'd have to tear up the whole picture and start again.

Marissa went to stay with her dad for the weekend, and as she packed up her suitcase, the one with the cartoon cat on it, she felt the lightest touch of relief feathering down her spine. The house had been uneven, like it was set badly on stilts, since the stranger came home and her feet didn't feel quite right as she walked through the hallway.

When her mummy dropped her off with a quick peck on the cheek, Marissa managed to smile and say, "I love you." She wanted to say more, but she was twelve, and she didn't really know what else to say. As the silver Mazda drove off, and she stood on the stoop, hand hovering over the doorbell, she turned and thought for a moment about calling her mummy back. She wanted to, badly. But instead, she pressed the doorbell and waited through the chime, and the shuffling noises and footsteps.

When her dad opened the door, Marissa felt a little pulse of happiness, the barest one, because he was smiling and his face looked mostly normal.

But then Marissa saw that someone was with him. She was gorgeous, all long legs that glittered darkly in black stockings beneath a sleek black pencil skirt that whispered as it moved.

"Marissa, sweetie pie," he said, "I'd like you to meet someone. Sorry, your mummy didn't call beforehand—she normally does—and I nearly forgot it was the weekend at all." And then: "This is Delilah."

Marissa glared at the stranger, and her perfect, pointed breasts beneath their creamy, silk blouse, and her lips that seemed to draw up like a bow. Her hair, her hair was the worst of it, because it was so long and gorgeous that it seemed like silk too. Marissa wanted to touch it, to stroke it, but her dad was already doing that even though *she was right there!*

Marissa wanted to scream at him. At them both. *You're my parents,* she said in her head, *and I don't care if you don't love each other anymore, just not . . .*

But it was too late. Her dad closed the door, and Marissa had to squeeze past him with her tiny kitty suitcase, past both of them. There was an electric shudder as her elbow bumped against the stranger. Her arm felt numb, but the rest of her felt on fire.

In her room, Marissa began to draw, but all she could draw were long legs, and black suits, and hair and half-moon fingernails—all those bits of body parts that didn't seem to fit together properly. She stared at the picture, adding in lines to connect the pieces.

It wasn't beautiful at all, she thought. It looked like some kind of monster.

Across the hallway, even though the house was bigger, Marissa could hear noises, and she tried to imagine him smiling, his squashed face next to that perfect one, that one with a perfect nose, and perfect eyelashes, and a mouth drawn on it like a bow.

And then Marissa began to cry.

For breakfast, Marissa had a bowl of cereal. Her dad hadn't come down yet. He liked to sleep in late on the weekends. But then *she* was there, the stranger, walking elegantly in her black stockings to the breadbox where she took out one piece of bread, and buttered it, and sat down at the table.

Marissa tried to ignore her. The stranger didn't eat her bread. She just stared at it like she didn't know what to do next. There was too much butter on it, Marissa thought. And she's already wearing lipstick. You can't eat buttered bread with lipstick.

Finally, the stranger picked up the piece of bread and dropped it into the garbage bin.

———————

That night when Marissa fell asleep, she had a terrible dream, and she woke up with her muscles shaking and weary, her whole body covered in sweat, the blankets wrapped around her legs like knots.

And there was the stranger, staring at her from the doorway. Her eyes were very bright, and she was staring at Marissa the way she had stared at that piece of bread, not knowing what to do with it, but hungry, oh yes, very hungry. Marissa shrank into the covers, and a moment later her dad was there too, peering in through the doorway.

"Is everything alright, jellybean?" he called. "We heard something from the other room."

She nodded her head warily, and began to untangle the blankets and set the bed right.

"I think I want to go home," Marissa said after a moment. "I'm sick. I want mummy."

Her dad looked nervous then, but he nodded his head. "I'll call her, tell her to pick you up." He disappeared from the doorway, and Marissa closed her eyes in relief, tears already forming behind her eyelids. When she opened her eyes, though, the stranger was at the foot of the bed. She sat down, tentatively, and Marissa could see, still, that she was wearing black stockings and that cream-coloured, silk blouse.

The stranger didn't say anything, but simply put out a hand. Marissa, unthinking, put out hers in return, and they touched, their two fingers, just the barest of touches. She has the same fingernails, Marissa thought, and she wasn't surprised. She wanted those fingers to touch her a little more. She edged closer, dragging herself across the feather duvet.

"I want you," she said. "I don't feel sick at all."

The stranger smiled, though her lips weren't kind, but Marissa felt happy anyway, sitting on the bed, touching the stranger's hand. She wondered if that's how her dad felt, and her mummy. The stranger nodded slightly. She took away her hand. For a moment, Marissa was sad, until the stranger began to stroke her hair. Lightly at first, and then her longer fingers begin to wind their way through like the teeth of a comb. Marissa wished her hair were longer, that it ran all the way down her back, and that she could feel like this forever, those fingers running through her hair.

But then her dad came into the room, and the stranger took away her hand, even though he seemed to smile more, to approve of the filial affection. "I'm going to drive you over," he said. "I'll just get your things."

Marissa looked longingly at the stranger, and she looked back too, and Marissa pretended she saw kindness there though she knew it might just been a trick of the light.

"Daddy," she said in the car. "Do you still love mummy?"

"Of course, I do."

Marissa remembered, then, that he was a mostly nice man, and mostly nice men must mostly love their wives, even if they were ex-wives.

But mostly wasn't everything.

Her mummy put her to bed again, cooed over here and poured her a glass of water first. But the house felt odd, and so Marissa knew that the stranger was still there. She drank her water, promised her mummy that she was feeling *much* better, and it would be all right to turn off the light.

But Marissa didn't fall asleep. She didn't want to. She just waited, staring out her window and connecting the lines the bare tree branches made into different shapes. Finally, she had waited long enough, and she tiptoed out of the room and into the hallway.

She had to move slowly. She knew all the places where the floorboards creaked and even with the carpet to pad her way, she wanted to be noiseless, like a ghost.

She opened the door to her mummy's bedroom, just a crack, and there was one hump in the covers, just one body. And *he* was standing next to the window, smoking a cigarette, the white plumes drifting out into the night air. He turned when the door opened, and he looked at her. She looked at him back. And then she shut the door, very softly, and went downstairs to wait.

Marissa was unsurprised when the stranger appeared in the living room some time later. He sat down on the couch next to her, and she felt the cushions dip with his weight, the world tilting just a little bit so that gravity pulled her toward him. He didn't move, when she touched his hand, not at first, just waited to see what she would do next.

"Do you love my mummy?" Marissa asked, though she didn't quite know why. The stranger said nothing, but his tongue flicked over his lips like he was tasting the air. She wanted him to smile, but he didn't.

"Would you love me?" She paused and then continued, "If we were a family?"

The buttons of his shirt were brass nubs, and Marissa fingers tugged at them gently. His shirt whispered as it slid away. His body, underneath, was cool to the touch.

Finally, he did move, and his arms circled around her, and they were hot like the coils of an electric stove, burning against her skin. She didn't move, but she let herself feel the heat, felt something rising with her.

She thought about her dad then, yelling at her to get the fuck out of the room, and she let her head come to rest against the stranger's shoulder. The heat was so intense she could feel herself growing woozy with it, lightheaded.

"I think maybe I could love you."

When his fingers stroked her arm, lightly at first, she felt the hair begin to rise like cilia, stiffening, pucker marks forming on the surface of her skin. Marissa wanted to rub herself all over him, like a cat, like her mother had. She opened her mouth to speak, but there was a kind of mist rising out of her. She thought, maybe he hadn't been smoking in the room after all. She hadn't smelled smoke, in the bedroom, and he didn't smell like smoke now.

No, strangely, he smelled of nothing at all, and his face was perfect, so perfect, and she traced a finger across the line of his jaw, making the picture right in her head.

Fine, she thought, as the white stuff curled out from her mouth, *you can have it. You can have me.*

He opened his mouth, bent closer, and Marissa felt ready for him to kiss her. This was it, wasn't it? The burning was so hot inside. But he didn't kiss her. His mouth hovered inches away, and he caught the stuff coming out of her, like steam, she was so hot, boiling up.

Marissa let him do it.

"I love you," she whispered, as her breath puffed out in a thin white mist. "And maybe they do too. Mostly. But you need to go somewhere else now." And then, as she felt her body shuddering, emptying of everything that was left inside, she scowled horribly: "Just get the fuck out."

The next morning, Marissa sat at the table and spooned mouthfuls of Rice Krispies into her mouth. She waited, ears pricked. Nothing. Then she rinsed her bowl and placed it in the drying rack very carefully before tiptoeing up the stairs, down the hallway to her mother's room. When she peered through the doorway, opening it ever so slightly, there was only one lump in the bed. The window was open.

Her mummy rose late, as she always did on Sundays. They didn't go to church. Marissa scribbled away at her homework, tackled some tricky math problems, and waited for her mummy to come down.

Her mummy slept later than normal, but she finally did come down, wrapped in a terrycloth bathrobe and looking a little green around the gills. Marissa offered to get her breakfast, but she declined. Her fingers tapped against the kitchen table.

"I've got something to tell you, Marissa."

Marissa sat down. It was just the two of them.

"Your father and I . . . we've been seeing each other again."

"No, you haven't," Marissa said.

"What?"

"You haven't," Marissa repeated. "That's not right at all."

"Oh, my darling girl," her mummy cooed, and wrapped her in a warm towel embrace, "oh, jellybean. I hope you're not upset."

"I'm not upset."

The hug felt more fragile now, but finally Marissa sighed, and relaxed into it, let herself be hugged, and even reached up to squeeze, once, her mummy's hand.

"It'll be just like before," her mummy whispered. Marissa wanted to smile, but already she was trying to draw lines in her head, trying to make room for herself between them, herself and the new one, the one just beginning.

"I love you, mummy," she whispered back, and tried a little bit harder to feel something.

[wing]

In the High Places
of the World

A fact: during Soledad's birth, a dove crashed into large, glass window of the delivery room of the Hospital do Coração de Messejana, snapping its neck instantly. They had thought the baby dead in the womb, and her mother, grey-faced with the pain of pushing, saw only the flurry of feathers, saw it slantwise through eyes that had long since ceased to register details. Soledad's father was not in the room. He paced outside, a cigar clenched between his teeth and in his hand, a very chipped enamel lighter hovering, spitting out a flame, then snapping shut before it could catch. He had been given the cigar by a friend, had never smoked but liked the idea of it, the root-smoke taste of the thing turning to pulp in his mouth.

The doctor in charge saw the bird, and in that moment his eyes flicked away from the trembling mound of flesh of the mother. He was not an inattentive man, but his eyes slipped for that brief moment, and so he was startled when he turned back to realize that he now held in his hands a wailing girl. He did not look back to the window as he performed his duties: cleaning, weighing and inspecting her. But when the child's mother kissed her three times on the face and announced, with joy, that she would be named Soledad, he nodded with approval and recorded the bird's death on his patient's medical history. He did not know what such a thing would mean, only that it surely meant something, and it would be good to remember.

When Soledad was presented to her father, he squinted with something that might have been surprise, maybe joy, perhaps even love, and then promptly let loose upon the cigar. He found, however, that cigar smoke was an entirely different beast than he had been led to expect, and he choked noisily at the burning in his lungs. This was another sort of sign, but the doctor in charge did not notice it, and so it slipped from the minds of all involved. Signs are like that sometimes.

Another fact: In 1957, Lucio Costa envisioned the city of Brasilia in the shape of a giant bird. Some say on the day in question when the first inkling of this settled in his skull that a giant kite landed upon his shoulders and whispered a secret in his ear. Others say that his wife kept many caged birds: saffron finches, the beautiful blue azulão, green-winged saltators and, rarer still, a host of bicudos and curiós. It might have been these who sang to him in the great dark night with their vision of the new city.

But having considered these preliminary remarks, let us now consider how the later situation was born, took shape and resolved itself: Brasilia was built in forty-one months, from 1956 to April 21, 1960. On the day Brasilia was inaugurated, Soledad turned six years old. Little about her life, to that point, had been special. Little was worthy of the tiny scribbled note in the margins of her file about a dead bird and what it might mean.

It seemed to mean very little indeed. Except this: on that very day upon which, by happenstance, the girl had been born six years previously, Soledad learned she could fly.

Jeremy, Simon Hatch wrote in his notebook at the end of an eighteen-hour flight from Los Angeles to Brasilia, fifty years after the city's inauguration, and two days later than his publisher had planned. *Jeremy, what have I done? Why am I here? I hate flying.*

Simon had made a career of writing—a career that had, his publisher noted, suffered serious setbacks over the last six months. And so, before his chest began to squeeze with the double anxiety that writing and flying seemed to bring on now, he wrote: *I have spent the last day stuck between a child of twelve years (female, black hair, bob-cut) and a somewhat hairier man (native?). The latter is a great beast who smells of cigarette smoke and old meat. But the girl, the girl is worse.*

Simon considered the girl. The girl considered him back with wide, unblinking eyes. He wondered who she belonged to. Where were her parents? It wouldn't be safe to travel in Brazil alone. He had read in the guidebook a number of somewhat worrying reminders that although the city of Brasilia was beautiful, Americans ought not to travel alone through its wide thoroughfares, to avoid carrying expensive electronics, or making eye contact with strangers who might easily identify them as tourists.

As he mopped his brow with a handkerchief, Simon realized that he was still looking at the girl directly in the eyes, still making eye contact despite being warned against it by the guidebook. He mopped for a moment longer, and then did it again, and then he almost offered her the handkerchief except, of course, she seemed unnaturally untouched by the heat.

Somehow their gaze had survived all that mopping entirely.

She'll have to blink now, Simon thought, *she'll blink and then I'll just look away.*

She didn't blink. He didn't avert his eyes. He couldn't stop staring.

The moment stretched out until Simon could feel his eyes tearing up. *Just blink*, he thought, *blink, goddamn you. Blink!*

Just as he thought his eyeballs would dry out and crack, the stewardess fortuitously drove her cart over the toe of the tobacco-smoked man in the aisle seat, who let fly a meaty elbow into Simon's midsection. Simon gasped, but the pain and the whoosh of air from his lungs were worth it. He blinked and blinked until hot tears ran down his face, and the man beside him looked at the weepy-faced American and snorted, "*Bicha*," with a tone of utter contempt.

Simon wiped his grateful eyes, and swore to keep them locked on the tray table in front of him.

Bicha.

He didn't know what it meant. By morning he would remember it only as "bitch" and that's how it would stay lodged in his memory. He had been called a little bitch, and the child next to him had definitely been a criminal, rifling through his belongings whenever he got up to stretch.

Jeremy, why didn't you come with me? You should have come with me. It would have been manageable here, with you.

But even as he wrote this, Simon remembered that Jeremy was dead, and the grief seized him all over again like a hard rock in his chest.

In that moment, as they began to circle for landing, the illuminated city below a perfect shadow of the plane with its wide, angled wings and narrow body, Simon was happy for even the contemptuous glare of the man next to him, even the too-eager gaze of the little girl. He was happy for anything that let him know that someone, a stranger even, was beside him.

On her third birthday, Soledad's father left to build the great city of Brasilia. Soledad did not remember a tearful farewell, only her mother's sadness the next day and her own not-quite-sadness. Her mother afterward told her that she was too young, and that was why she did not remember. But the older Soledad knew that this was not quite the case. She remembered her father. She remembered loving her father, but she also remembered, very keenly, not loving her father.

They received a letter several weeks later. Soledad's mother clutched her tight, and made her sit close while she read. Back then, they lived in Ceará, in the northwest of the country. It had taken Soledad's father eighteen days to reach Cidade Libre, they read, where he began work as a labourer, a *candango*.

Soledad's mother wept then, but her face was very proud and she clutched the letter close to her heart. "Your father," Soledad's mother said, "he is a good man. It is as I have always said, a good man."

Her mother had said no such thing. Soledad remembered her saying many other things, but not that.

"He loves you very much," her mother said. "He is building a wondrous city for you to live in, and so you must be very brave and you must never cry that he is gone."

Soledad nodded. She had not cried at all since her father left, though her mother had cried a great deal.

But outside the parakeets were beginning to sing. Soledad wanted to listen. She did not want this fierce woman gripping her wrists. She did not want to sit still while her mother read the letter one more time, and so, she began to cry after all, for she was only a little girl.

Her mother, with her own tears running down her face, looked down at Soledad with approval even though she had said they must be tearless in their love: as if this had been a thing lacking from her strange, stone-eyed daughter. She hugged her very quickly and said, "You will see. It will be a beautiful city, and when we live there we shall be very happy."

Upon landing, Simon was met at the airport by a translator sent by the Cultura Inglesa, Beatriz—a grim, unblinking woman who could have been the mother of the girl on the plane. She had a silver-grey jacket slung over her shoulder and a sign reading SIMMON in large blocky letters. When Simon hurried up to her, sticky with travel sweat, she offered him a cool greeting and, having confirmed that he was the expected guest, motioned for him to follow her. When Simon pointed out that it was one "m" and not two, she merely shrugged and flicked him a glance.

They rode in relative silence through the city's Monumental Axis, past the Plaza of Three Powers, the Planalto Palace, and the twin skyscrapers of the Congress.

The air-conditioning hummed a ragged staccato. Behind the windows Brasilia seemed noiseless and barren. It made Simon nervous, he didn't like silence.

Simon gazed out at the city, at its almost irritatingly insistent architecture. Words. Words he understood. Words had a kind of power to them: they were electric, moving, open, liberating. You moved through words. Words were something you could live in. But not these. Not these . . . symbols. There was no life to them. What were buildings like these? How did they speak?

Simon tried to write in his notebook, but Beatriz kept looking at him with the same unblinking stare the little girl had.

He tried looking out again. Gave up. Stared at the reflection of himself into the dark, tinted windows.

He wondered if the tinting might be because of who he was, as a gesture of respect for such a prestigious author.

When he voiced this opinion, Beatriz shook her head, and explained that there were many carjackings in Brazil, that the windows hid the people in the car from those on the street.

"Yes," Simon said, "but does it help much?"

Beatriz shrugged again.

"They just use axes to break the glass."

Simon didn't speak for the rest of the journey.

When the car pulled round the Sonesta Hotel, Beatriz got out first and opened the door for Simon. She spoke in sharply fluent Portuguese to the hotel clerk, settled Simon's bags, and handed him a folder with his itinerary.

"You will speak tomorrow, yes? They are all very excited. They like your books very much."

"Oh yes?" Simon fidgeted with the folder.

"The reviews, they are very good." Her eyes flicked up and down. "They say you are a voice for your generation. They say you capture the spirit of America. Your writing, it is . . . exuberant. They say it . . ." She stumbled. "*Como se diz? In English?*" She shook her head. "Ah yes, they say it takes you over. It is fresh. It inspires."

"Well," Simon said. "That's very kind. Thank you."

"They say we need the Americans. That it will be good for our culture."

A longer pause this time.

"They will not have read your books. They are in English, *sim*? Do not embarrass them by asking. It is Brazil they want to know about, this great country of ours. Keep your remarks on the book short."

There were many letters in the intervening years from Soledad's father that spoke of the great hardship: long hours worked clearing the forest to carve out the city's wide-paved central axis, jokes told to keep themselves from dying of boredom or homesickness. Soledad never laughed at these jokes. She did not understand them.

But eventually, after many tear-filled farewells in Ceará, after a long ride in the back of a truck, huddled together with a shared blanket and their belongings piled around them with her mother whispering how happy they would be, on Soledad's sixth birthday they arrived in the city of Brasilia, which her father had built for them to live in.

They were lucky, Soledad learned. Many of the *candangos* could not afford to live in the city itself and had to take up residence in the satellite towns where the housing was cheaper. But Soledad's father had been particularly good with his hands, and had a loud, booming voice. He had done well for himself, and they were allowed to move into one of the shining new superblocks in the wings of the giant bird.

That first reunion involved a great deal of weeping, and Soledad's mother told her this time that she *must* cry to show her father she had missed him and that she appreciated the sacrifices he had made on her behalf, to build for her this bright, beautiful city.

When they met, Soledad's father crouched down to meet her gaze, to wish her happy birthday. She smiled as she had been told and she pinched her palm until the tears flowed. Her father smiled too, and embraced her. The smoky scent of him muffled her crying as the blanket had done for her mother's.

"Happy birthday," she whispered into his ear. "Happy birthday to the city."

"You are a good child," he said. "Now go play so that I may be alone with your mother."

Soledad was very happy then. She spent many hours exploring her new home, but much to her disappointment she discovered that each block, as beautiful as it was, was exactly the same as the others. Each very empty of people.

Later, her father would tell her that the blocks had yet to be filled, and they would have new neighbours very soon, but as it was Soledad began to feel quite scared. There had been many people in Ceará, more once her father left, once her mother took to inviting cousins and aunts and uncles for company. Soledad wondered where the people were, and why no one had come to live in this beautiful new city her father had built.

She climbed to the very top of her superblock to see if she could spot someone. But no. There were merely row on row of superblocks, each identical, each empty.

She leaned out farther until there was barely a bit of concrete between her and the wide chasm of space. She strained her eyes but it seemed as if there was not a single person in the entire city.

"It is a city of ghosts," she said to herself, and then she wondered if she too were a ghost, if perhaps she had never been born at all. The idea of this was both frightening and comforting.

Just then the wind began to pick up and a particularly strong gust tugged at her dress, and shoved her quite suddenly off the edge of the roof. There was only a moment of fear as her heart thudded in her chest, and the shock of the roof's absence registered. Only a moment. Then Soledad knew that she truly was a ghost, for she spread her arms and the wind caught underneath them and it lifted her up, up into the sky.

"Happy birthday, city," she whispered as she rose higher and higher, the air soft as down on her skin. "Happy birthday, Soledad," the city whispered back.

Simon was relieved to find the Sonesta Hotel luxuriously American. Plush pillows. A suite in which he could have held dinner parties. A view of the skyline, but not quite the skylines he knew: New York, Seattle, Los Angeles, Atlanta. It looked like the view from a thousand hotel rooms he'd stayed in, but the oppressive heat smudged the city lights, making them indistinct. Strange.

He flipped through the package Beatriz had left him: programs written in English, schedules with worrying Portuguese marginalia he couldn't decipher.

Rather than worrying at his dictionary, Simon opened up his notebook.

Jeremy, he began to write. *You would like Brazil very much. The people here are beautiful.* He thought of Beatriz, the almost mannish curve of her jaw. Those unblinking eyes. *Most of them, anyway.*

He wanted to write more, but when he reached for the words, they drifted away from him, as they always did now.

Six months and not a chapter finished.

Six months and the advance on the next novel already burned on medical bills for a treatment that hadn't worked.

He'd have to take more speaking engagements if he wanted to keep the house.

Simon felt the early signs of a panic attack, the tightness in his chest. He put down the pen. Went to raid the minibar. Why not? The Cultura Inglesa was buying.

He settled on a tiny but perfectly sculpted bottle of vodka when a loud noise like the sound of a baseball on a brick wall almost startled him into dropping it.

Simon's eyes snapped to the window. A flurry of silver-grey movement. Something against the glass.

His seat retained a sticky impression of his body as he got up, went to the window. There was only the ghost of an image, a snow angel amalgam of cracks where the bird had impacted. He would have to call down to the front desk to let them know. The glass would be weaker now. If someone leaned up against it, put too much pressure in the wrong place . . .

The vodka cooled his anxiety, and loosened the ache in his chest. He took a breath, and stared out at the foreign skyline. Relief, or the beginnings of it.

Something caught his eye. On the building next to him, there were black graffiti strokes on the cool grey façade of the Hotel Minerva. They had a jagged look. Unnerving. Angry. A shape almost like the imprint of the bird on glass with a word nestled inside the toothed strokes of the wings. A word he couldn't read. Portuguese?

God, it was high up, impossibly high. It was a mystery how it had got there.

He took another gulp of the vodka. Felt his mind muddying like the skyline. And so it was he wondered, only briefly, what might be worth risking a thirty-storey fall to write.

In the year after the inauguration, Soledad would press her face against the window to count the brown-haired heads of the *candangos* as they came from the coast to live in the new city of Brasilia. Sometimes, her mother would shoo her away. She would mutter about fingerprints on the glass, how long it would take to clean, but she never cleaned them. Soledad could see all the marks accumulating on the glass like pebbles rolled smooth by the ocean.

Soledad saw more than that: the whites of her mother's eyes, the fear. She wasn't used to heights, was always worried the glass wouldn't hold. She always kept a broom's width between herself and the edges of room.

I can fly, Soledad wanted to tell her mother. *I will never fall. I am a bird, a windmill.*

But Soledad never spoke these things. She never opened the window although she longed to hear the singing of the birds outside, to clear the apartment of the floating corona of cigar smoke that trailed after her father. Wanted to wave to the *candangos*, her neighbours, as they arrived.

"Put down your hand," Soledad's father would snap at her. "They will not be our neighbours. They are lazy, they are rich, they came too late. Did they build this city with their bare hands? No. Did they topple trees and live without the company of their wives and daughters? This city is not for them."

Sometimes, if she did not listen, he would yank her away quite suddenly and Soledad would cough at the acrid stench of the smoke.

Then, she would take to the roof of the building, and she would let the breeze lift her up gently. She did not fly during the day, but sometimes she would leap into the air and hover for just a moment longer than she ought to, letting her lungs balloon with oxygen until the concrete of the roof edge fell away and all she could see was the city itself—*her* city, her beautiful city.

"Ah," she would whisper to herself. "You are so beautiful, Brasilia. Even if there is nothing else, he has built you and you are the loveliest thing in the world."

Some nights, she would open the window by her bed and she would welcome in the great dark night, let it settle around her like a blanket and she would let it whisper her to sleep.

Other nights, when she was restless, when the air in her room was thick and smudged, she would climb up onto the bed, and she would let the wind take her out into the darkness. She would soar over the city high up where the people could not see her, where the world became the unbroken shell of an egg, perfectly smooth, perfectly round. From the air, it could be so beautiful, and her heart would open wide to that glorious bird shape below her.

That night, Simon dreamed of Jeremy.

In the dream, Simon stared out the window of his hotel. Stared at the black silhouette on the wall. As he stared, there was a noise. Not the thump of bones hitting glass. Softer than that. Wings. The beating of wings in flight.

Jeremy's wings.

In the dream, Jeremy's body had slimmed skeletal, bones sharp under his skin, hollowed out by the chemo. An off-green hospital gown fluttered, barely substantial, and from his shoulders were two great, hulking shapes. Not wings exactly. The bones of wings, blanketed in Jeremy's thick, dark hair. It came out in soft clumps as the wings moved in the air. Floated gently like flakes of finger-drift snow.

"I know you hate flying alone, funny face," Jeremy murmured. The hair-wings beat a slow, lazy rhythm.

The dream stayed with Simon into his waking hours.

It stayed with him through breakfast with the head of the Universidade de Brasilia.

It stayed with him during a signing early in the afternoon.

It stayed with him as he was ushered into a gallery where earnest television interviewers asked him question after question about the influence of American writing upon Brazil, and what directions he thought they might pursue to achieve international significance.

He had prepared sound-bite answers as his publicist

instructed him, but after he had delivered these, the mic didn't waver, and the unblinking eyes of the interviewer seemed to demand that he keep talking. "You are the voice of your country," they said, "tell us how. Tell us how to make them listen."

All Simon could hear, though, was the slow beating of wings.

He stumbled. Caught Beatriz's eye. Her head was glacier still, tilted, listening. Waiting for him to speak.

"Art," he mumbled, "shared art. We need it. It's an increasingly globalized landscape where art . . ."

The wings beat, and his chest began to tighten the way it did when he tried to put words on paper. *Christ*, he pleaded. *Not now. Not with the cameras. Please don't let this go up on YouTube.*

The silence lingered. Stretched. Broke into a murmur.

Beatriz's mouth became a thin, angry line.

The drive back was torturous. Beatriz didn't even look at him. She went over her papers. She made inscrutable notes in Portuguese on her copy of the next day's schedule. Simon tried to meet her eye. He wanted her to say something. Anything. When they arrived at the hotel, she opened the door for him as she always did, and waited for him to get out.

"Today was not good," Beatriz said at last.

"Sorry," Simon muttered. "I'm sorry. It's. Well. I'm sorry."

"They are angry. They want to know who this is they have brought to their country, this man who does not know what art is."

"This is Brazil," he pleaded. Simon could feel the tickle of those soft clumps of hair on the back of his neck. "What do you want me to say to you? How much does it really matter?"

Something rippled across Beatriz's face. At first he didn't know what it was, only that it made her ugly. Then he realized why he didn't know it.

Anger.

No one had shown him anger in six months. Pity, yes. Sadness, yes. Worry. Concern. But not anger.

He thought she was going to slap him. But she didn't slap him. Her eyes narrowed.

"We know what art is," she said. "In Brazil, we know what art is."

Her eyes flicked up, but not at him. Up toward the chicken-scratch silhouette of a bird intersected with black lines. A name, maybe. Or a word.

"That—" She paused, her mouth twisting. Were the Brazilians beautiful? Had he ever really thought that? He couldn't imagine this face as ever being beautiful, it was so full of anger. "That is *pichação*. Wall writings. Not so common here, *sim*? You find it in Rio de Janeiro, Sao Paulo, where the young people are less happy."

"I thought everyone was happy here."

He knew it was a lie as soon as he said it. Weak. He saw himself suddenly the way Beatriz did, the way the girl in the plane had. A pale-skinned *gringo*. A stranger. Condescending. Smug. Was that what the cameras saw?

"What? We Brazilians with our suntans? Our perfect beaches? Our perfect happiness? *Fweh*. They say everyone in America is happy, yes? That is the dream of your country? No one here is happy." She gave him a look that might have been disgust. "The city is beautiful. But it is not made for the children. So they write their names on it, in the shape of the city. A giant bird. *Pichação*."

"What does it say? The writing?" Simon asked.

The sun was just setting behind the crest of the building, sending down blinding showers of light. He squinted as he tried to find the markings again. The jagged silhouette. The toothed wings.

"It is nothing. Just a name. A name inside the city."

Night lowered its blanket across the city, adumbrating the writing in darkness. Simon looked at Beatriz again. Unlovely Beatriz with her hair dark and coarse tied so tightly to her skull. Her face had lost its knife-sharp edge. This should have made her prettier. It didn't.

There was a gentle rumbling sound nearby: the car engine. The driver tapped the window, and Beatriz looked away.

Gestured to him curtly. "You should sleep now. Tomorrow will be harder."

Simon nodded, not trusting his voice. He took his bag out of the car, slung it over his shoulder and began to move toward the hotel door. But he stopped. Turned. There was something about the writing that didn't make sense. Something absurd about it, some kind of impossibility tugging with fish-hooks at the edges of his mind.

"How do they do it? How do they get up there?"

Beatriz hadn't moved. "The *pichadores* are very brave. They must go as high as possible if it is to remain. So the city cleaners cannot reach it."

"But surely it is dangerous? They must fall?"

"*Com certeza*," she said. "Of course, some of them fall."

Simon waited a beat, but there was nothing more forthcoming. He shook his head.

Most nights, Soledad would go out through her window, and let the great dark night carry her into the city. But as she grew older, she found herself heavier and heavier, her growing body clumsy and leaden on the wind. And so she learned the trick of it: she would strip herself naked of the simple cotton nightgown she wore to bed, and then she would strip off her skin as well, all the heavy, new-grown bits of her and she would lay them in a neat pile underneath the covers of the bed. Then, made light and smooth without her skin on, she would fly easier: a ghost, a ghost of the beautiful city.

One day when the city had grown silent and drowsy, when Soledad returned to her room, she discovered her mother sitting on the bed, cradling the cotton nightgown and her skin as well, like a baby in her arm. They looked upon each other, mother and daughter. "I do not know you, Soledad," she said. "You have become a stranger to me."

"I am who I have always been, mother."

"Do you love me, Soledad?"

"Of course."

"You are happy, here, in this house?"

"Of course."

"You must be grateful, Soledad. So much has been given for you."

Soledad thought upon this. "I will give you my skin," she said. "I do not need it. It makes me heavy, and I cannot fly so easily."

"No, Soledad. You must wear your skin. You must keep it close around you like a blanket. You must make the *feijoada*, and find a husband."

"It is so heavy," Soledad whispered. "Why must I find a husband? My husband is the city. My husband is the moon. My husband is the great dark night."

"Those are not husbands, Soledad," said her mother. "You must do this if you love me." And Soledad put on her skin, and the next day it was bigger and heavier than it had ever been. When Soledad went to the kitchen to prepare the daily meal, she saw her mother and her mother saw her, and her mother smiled, watching her cut and scrape and stir. Watching her sweep the floor with the soft-haired broom. Keeping from the edges of the room where the windows looked out onto the beautiful city.

Beatriz was wrong.

A full night's sleep in the icebox air-conditioning of the hotel cooled Simon's skin. Hardened it into a super-thin shell of protective plastic. He matched the Brazilian intelligentsia stare for stare. Didn't feel anything. He felt the panic easing. Glibness returned. He smiled for the cameras, shook hands, never mentioned his books, spoke only of the great voice of Brazil, how it deserved an audience, how it needed to be heard.

"Memory," he told them, "art is memory, and the city of Brasilia, it has to remember if it is to make art."

Then he smiled. It was a confident smile. What Jeremy

used to call his bastard smile. And seeing that bastard smile, the crowds smiled too. They applauded. They gave him their hearts.

Simon felt as if a great weight had been lifted from him.

The buzz of the day carried over into the evening and then past midnight when the air had gone dusky and flat like cola left out too long. Still, Simon felt buoyant. Triumphant. Generous with his wit. He was a bright sun circled by a handful of satellite planets: dark-haired, dark-eyed artists, grumbling, fawning, earnest as sin or giggly with dope and booze.

"It's a disaster," said Gabriel, a Somebody among the Brazilians—all delicate beauty and aristocratic despair. "The worst city ever. Lucio Costa was a crank, an eccentric."

"It's not so bad," Simon told him, gamely, kindly. He winked at Julia—some sort of glassblower? or a potter?—who kept trying to find a way to make him properly Brazilian by weaving a fuchsia flower into his hair. Luan, her sister, helped. Pretended to help.

"No, no," said Gabriel. "Oh God. It is very bad. It's not even *Brazilian*. That's the problem. It's not our art, it was not built for us."

Luan's fingers were combing his hair, tying in flowers. Her breath tickled his ear. She was whispering that he was very *fofo*. That seemed to be a good thing in her estimation.

But there was Gabriel still—beautiful and dark-haired. A good-looking man. Long eyelashes. A beautiful man's mouth. Smug and desperate at the same time.

He pointed an emphatic finger in Simon's face. "Brasilia was built for the automobile in a society where no one can afford automobiles. It is a failure. The city is a failure." He said this very triumphantly.

"Tell me," Gabriel said, "tell me this city is a failure. Surely you think it is a failure?"

"Let me tell you, *fofinho*," Luan whispered, "what they say about Brazilian women." And she did, and Simon tried to keep a poker face while Gabriel's triumphant finger blurred and doubled in front of his nose.

"It's very modern," he managed in reply.

"Aha!" Gabriel cried in ecstatic response. "There you have it. Very modern. But who wants to live in a city designed like a modern art exhibit? Who, my friend, *wants* modern? We want *memory*. It is like you said. Art is memory, and this city, *fweh*! This city remembers nothing. You know what they say about Lucio Costa? They say he died like a little bird. A little bird. *É mesmo*? It is crazy!"

Now Julia was finished with the flower. She draped her arms around his neck, cat-like, but neither Gabriel nor his sister seemed to notice or care. Simon began to lose track of which limbs and appendages belonged to which artist.

All at once, it was too much.

He made his excuses while he found the men's room. Inside it was empty and the air was blessedly cool, free of smoke and the city's humidity. He splashed water on his face.

The door swung open lazily: it was Gabriel. Beautiful, long-lashed Gabriel.

"Ah, here you are," he said. His voice too loud in the small space. "The sisters, they worry. Americans are their favourites. They are happy when the tourists come. The tourists buy many things. Americans, they like Brazil, do they not?" He took position at the urinal and unzipped, comfortable, unabashed.

Simon turned away. Cupped more water in hands.

"But it is not the sisters, is it, my American friend? No. You would not like the sisters."

A creeping heat gumshoed up Simon's body. He kept his eyes locked on the mirrored reflection of himself. The water slid off the curve of his chin. He could hear the steady noise of Gabriel urinating.

"I wonder, what is it that you come to Brazil for? Escape, maybe? Or is it just that you are looking for something? Something beautiful? Something to remember Brasilia?"

The words were a tangle in Simon's throat. He wanted to run. He didn't want to run. He could feel the heat ballooning his cock, and he coughed. Doused his face with water again.

"I have embarrassed you?"

There was the sound of a zipper, and then that beautiful face appeared in the mirror reflection beside Simon's own.

"You are like a little bird, and I have put you to flight. Do not be embarrassed, my friend. We are artists, you and I."

Then Simon was alone again with only his erection and the scent of something musky and male in the space like a shadow where Gabriel had stood, very close, beside him. He suddenly very much wanted to be back in the car with its gloriously tinted windows. Happy in the knowledge that none of these people could likely afford one to follow him.

He fled back into the night air. Found Beatriz quickly, thank God, and seeing his panic she took his arm and led him away. Made the appropriate signals to the group that they were finished, the night was at an end, her charge had very important things to do in the morning that required him to sleep.

"They are foolish, those people," Beatriz said as she steered him, weak-legged, from the courtyard. "Do not mind them."

"I don't," Simon said. Tried to say. "They're just artists. They're all like that, artists. It doesn't matter."

He settled heavily in the car, and wiped pink petals from his jacket. His body was sticky with sweat, made suddenly frigid by the air-conditioning.

"God, it's like this everywhere, isn't it? It never changes." He shook his head. "I could write the story of Brasilia and it would be easy: in 1957, Lucio Costa envisioned the city of Brasilia in the shape of a giant bird. But Lucio Costa—he couldn't see his way into it. A bird is a lousy metaphor for a city."

Simon mopped sweat from his forehead. Put his hand to his lip. Tasted the salt of it, and the faint ichor of damp cigarette smoke still clinging to his fingers. Imagined briefly, vividly, what it might be like to have Gabriel lick it off him.

That damned erection again.

There was quiet for a time. Simon was surprised to find his face was wet. Tears. God, he hated crying.

"Damnit," he said at last. Beatriz's eyes flicked to him.

He looked away. Cursed more softly. "Just goddamn it, okay? Leave me alone, would you? Just. I don't know. Stop staring."

Her eyes flicked away from him.

This is it, he thought. *Here I am, the voice of my generation. What the hell is that supposed to mean? Who* says *that about a person?*

"Look, I'm sorry," he said at last. "It's just. You look at that writing—the, what, the wall writing—you look at those kids and you think they are terribly brave because they believe so strongly, they want their art so badly." This time it was Simon staring. Simon growing angry. Angry or something like anger. "Some of them fall. Of course some of them fall. But the thing is. The thing is that we *want* them to fall. That's the fucking truth of it. We want them to fall. We want them to fall. Why the hell shouldn't they fall?"

He stared through the tinted glass out at the city, the grand promenades, the carefully orchestrated and arranged city blocks, planned perfectly. Planned to be what? A plane? A bird? Something with vast wings of bone shedding chemo hair as it flew?

Beatriz touched his hand. He looked away from the window, met her eyes. They were not wide and unblinking. There were lines of something—pain, perhaps—around them and her face was soft, softer than he had seen it, but her hand was strong: the veins thick and ropelike under the papery skin.

"Come with me," she said.

———————

Soledad's body grew thicker and heavier until her mother brought her to see the doctor, and the doctor said that Soledad had something inside of her.

"It is a bird, mother," Soledad wanted to say. "There is a bird living inside my ribcage, and it sings to me in the great dark night. It teaches me to fly."

"It is a baby," said the doctor. And Soledad's mother smiled very fiercely.

"No, no, *mamãe*," Soledad said. "I am afraid. I am afraid of it. How will I fly without my little bird?"

Beatriz took him away from the Esplanade—away from the Cathedral and the statues, away from the civic buildings and theatres and hotels. They passed row after row of clean, white buildings, each identical. And then she led him to the top of one, identical to all the others. It looked older. Worn but clean.

The air was cold. It sucked and pulled at the thin linen shirt Simon had worn to the party. He didn't like heights. Never had. Didn't like the way they made you feel like something else. The way that the empty space suddenly seemed like a living thing drawing you closer to it until you could just step off over the edge.

See if you hung in space. See if you plummeted.

But across that living thing, the vast summoning chasm, across it, on the building opposite, were strata of angular black lines punctuated with windows and balconies.

"My mother lived here many years ago. It was not so good back then. It was hard for my family. Wide streets, they are also good for tanks. They are good for armies. This has not always been a happy country. We do not always live easily with our neighbours."

She sniffed, and the sound was almost lost in the whistling breath of the night.

"My grandmother used to tell me about her: that when my mother was born, there was a bird, and the bird was always trapped inside of her. She died when I was very young, but I remember her. Happy. And not happy."

Darkness falling. The sky a peculiar shade of grey somewhere between pewter and gunmetal, darkening. Lights came on in the windows across the gap. Bodies outlined against the light. Silhouettes moved. Arms black and crooked.

"I have seen them," Beatriz murmured. "The boys, the poor ones who climb. I have seen them drop from the sky."

They were very close to the edge. Too close. He could see the shape of a bird, jagged, black against the white superblock. And in it a name. He thought he could read it. *Soledad*, it said. *I am alone*, it said.

"I don't understand. Aren't they afraid of falling?"

"Afraid?" Her eyes were very wide, very dark. "*Com certeza*. Of course they are afraid. Of course they might fall. But this is how we know we are not alone in the city."

"Come away from the window," said Soledad's mother. "The child is crying for you."

"But I do not want a child," she said. "Let it be a bird for me. Let it be the great dark night."

"No," said her mother. "I had a bird inside me once. I named her Soledad, because she was so beautiful and I was so lonely. But no one should be as lonely as you are, *anjinho*. There are so many ways to live in the high places of the world. The baby is beautiful."

Soledad did not turn; she dreamed she was free of her skin out there over the city.

This is how Simon learned to fly:

He hung in the air as the wind whipped around him. Beatriz, peculiarly graceful, beside him. Muscles strained. Pulled and slacked. Her form, incandescent. Alive. Beautiful in a way that only pure movement could be beautiful. The kind of movement that seemed to throw off sparks. She was at home with the bright city laid out beneath her. She was at home in the air.

The rope pulled tight against Simon's paunching stomach, grabbed up between his legs, cradled his crotch. It hardly felt secure, hardly felt safe, but that was the point, wasn't it? It shuddered, held as he swung out after her.

His fingers rubbed raw against the concrete of the wall,

but he planted his feet. The solvent smell of the paint burned and twitched in his nostrils, but the wind tore it away from him. Left him feeling clean and empty. He flicked his wrist and now there was a wing. Jagged. Toothed feathers cutting the concrete. And another wing. The sleek shape of its breast, body, flanks, tarsus.

He breathed deeply the cool, crisp, acetylene air.

Here, with the edge of a three-inch ledge digging a groove into the soft instep of his foot. Here, with one hand desperately tamping down on the nozzle, while the other blindly felt out and stabilized each step. Here, in that shiver of adrenaline, something burst free. Simon felt the city opening up beneath him, the beautiful city. A moving, beating thing.

And then, as the paint blossomed, pooled and dripped in sticky lines, as Simon slashed at the wall in frenzied strokes—a name, a name in the centre of a dark-winged bird—he felt Jeremy moving too. The hard stone at the centre of him.

It was easy then. Easy in a way that only truly terrifying things are easy.

Simon opened himself up. The wind whistled madly around him. One hand clutched at the skin of the building, Beatriz beside him, helping him, the other hand carving out those letters. Putting a word to things. Claiming something, but also letting something go.

Simon was frightened, of course he was. The fear was alive in him, and his heart hammered like a trapped bird. But then, it wasn't his heart hammering, it was Jeremy, Jeremy hammering inside him.

With a word, he let him free.

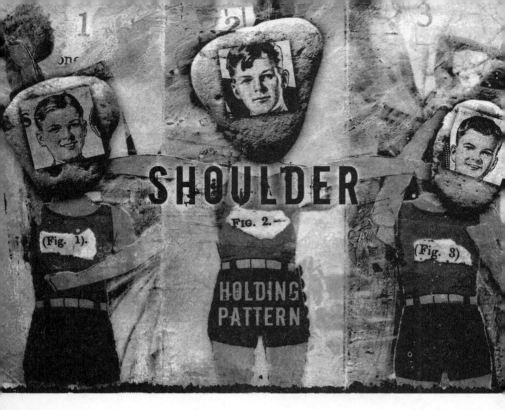

[shoulder]

HOLDING PATTERN

They say it started with the angels and the saints in Saint Peter's Basilica: Maderno's façade with Christ, John the Baptist and eleven of the apostles (the eponymous Peter was somewhere to the left of the stairs, away from the pack, but no less effective, the rumour went, no less inspiring). And to be fair, that's where it *should* have started. There would have been something proper about that, as if it were God who had done it. But believe what you want.

It started with the statue of Paul on the road to Damascus in Soho Square. You know the one. No? We used to pass by there when you were young, when we had that little place in the West End, but I suppose the statue wasn't there yet. Most people didn't notice it, they certainly didn't visit it the way they would visit the Charles I statue in Trafalgar Square or Frampton's Pan in Kensington Gardens. It never rated highly in the tourist brochures if it was given a look at all. Life-sized and cast in bronze, the horse rearing up and a surprised Paul with one hand thrown over his face to block out the blinding light of God. A decent enough statue, I suppose, as far as these things go. The kind of thing you might spot in half of London's public parks.

But there had always been something about the face, and if you ask me, that's what got the whole mess started, that's what I say: Paul's expression should have been terrified, and that's what the sculptor had gone for, terror, mingled with something else, but it hadn't quite come off. Paul looked startled, certainly, but the hand shielding his face, the angle was just a bit wrong, just a bit off, and so it seemed more like he was falling into a faint. When you spotted the thing you couldn't *help* but mimic it, that look of surprise, the sweep of the arm over the forehead. We used to see tourists doing it in Soho Square. You don't anymore of course, you wouldn't *now*. But back then, there would be flocks of tourists, great red-faced, sweating men, wives armed with guidebooks and vacant stares, and children, bored mostly. They'd all perk up when they saw the statue. They'd crowd around in groups of two or three and take turns, bulging their eyes, sticking out their tongues, bodies bending like broken coat hangers into a half-faint. Oh, some of the parents would squeal with joy. The mothers would applaud their little darlings, the fathers would beam with approval: "Look at my boy," their eyes would say, "look at him go, clever kid."

I don't know who the first kid was, probably a Tommy or a Tucker or a Timothy trying to show off, maybe he was part of a tour group and his friends, other boys of a similar age, say, thirteen, all egging him on. And he would have screwed up his eyes, that boy, let's call him Tucker, he would have tried to get the look just right. He would have studied the angles of the arms beforehand, you know how kids your age are, always wanting to show off. And he would do it, he would get that face perfect, the arms held out stiffly, comically above his head, a phantom horse squeezed between his knees.

And then it would have stuck.

At first it might have felt like a cramp, the way muscles lock up when you've been out in the cold too long. But then the boy would try harder, try to unscrew his face, but he would find his eyebrows frozen, his mouth locked in that very funny, perfectly sculpted *oh* of surprise. Perhaps the crowd is moving on now, perhaps they've gotten bored, it was a good trick, really, but the kids are antsy—kids your age always are, hey?—it was the kind of thing funny for a moment, or funny in a photograph, years down the line when his mother wants to show off the album to a new girlfriend but even then, even then it's only funny until the page flips. But Tucker doesn't move. He just stands there. And on the other side of the square there is another kid doing it too, another boy Tucker's age, and he's just nailed the look, got it to a tee, but *his* parents are starting to roll their eyes now, and they are trying to usher him along, but now *he* won't move. At last, Tucker's dad grabs his arm and tries to haul him away, but he can't do it. His son, at thirteen, hardly a scrap of flesh on his tent-pole arms, is now heavy as stone, heavy as time. Frozen. Still as that statue.

That's where it happened first.

The angels, the saints, they all came after. Those were the expected places and, to be fair, that's where it *should* have started. If I'm honest. In Rio de Janeiro they say there's a crowd of them settled around that giant statue of Christ the Redeemer now, his arms spread out a hundred feet up in benediction over the city. But they look like seagulls in the photos, or people pretending to be seagulls, all of them with their arms stretched out like wings, their heads lolling just so, just the way that Christ lolls his head a hundred feet above them. They can't move. Their jackets flutter in the breeze. Sometimes a scarf comes undone and you can see it floating away, off the edge of the plinth, like a banner above the Corcovado Mountain. The place has become the hunting ground of pickpockets, they say; no one moves a muscle to stop them. No one can. Not anymore.

But it wasn't *just* the saints, no, you couldn't say that it was something about God. It was all the statues of the world. In Paris, they've had to close the gates to the Musée Rodin. There are thirty-seven people trapped there at last count: sixteen hunched over, hands curled backwards like commas to support their chins, eyes downcast in inner turmoil; a group of five posed as the Burghers of Calais; and the lovers, oh, the lovers, pairs of them twisted, contorted, hands seizing or spurning, faces turned away or else locked together in passionate embrace. The lovers, I've heard, are the biggest problem; they still line up outside the gate, they climb the walls of the garden, even after the warnings, even after the closures. Every day the security guards discover more of them, teenagers, barely fifteen, re-enacting *The Kiss*, newlyweds, and the desperate ones, the ones afraid of having lost that spark in their marriage years ago.

We went to Paris for our honeymoon, your dad and I, oh, a good fifteen years ago now. Back when he had a full head of hair and he still worked for the bank, all those dark suits and expensive ties, he looked so *posh*, so important! Before you were born. Before he gave up on suits and I got the stretch marks and the grey hairs, back when the skin didn't hang off me like old laundry. Oh, I was a looker back then, there's no doubt about it! We couldn't keep our hands off each other, your father and I.

The curators, the ones at the Musée Rodin, they don't know what to do with all the bodies. All thirty-seven of them. They've taken to leaving out the young ones, the pretty ones—the kind of statues your dad and I would have been, I reckon—but the older couples, the ones who are not, if I'm honest, in the best possible condition for all that contorting and kissing, those ones have been put in the basement. The paper said there is an art collector in Germany who has offered twenty thousand euros for a pair of honeymooners. They're considering the offer. The austerity measures have hit the arts hard. Even in France.

Nobody knows what it is like, whether they can feel anything, whether it hurts. Some say it must be agony, but I don't think so, not really. It isn't the standing still that hurts, is it, love? Well, you don't know yet. You wouldn't.

It is harder to get access to the sites now. Statues have been pulled down in public squares, gardens have been scoured of cherubim, fountains smashed. The Mayor of New York has called for giant tarpaulins to be suspended from helicopters to shroud Lady Liberty. Her victims have filled up Ellis Island. They've stopped the ferry from running, but it hasn't done any good. Not one bit of good. They mimic each other, all those people; they pose like the statues of statues, and the statues of those statues, and when they get it exactly right, when they get it just *so*, then—then it still happens, and they are frozen in place forever.

They want it to happen, that's what I think. They want to be like that. They do it on purpose now. You can see them on the subway, in coffee shops, the people standing absolutely still, trying not to move a muscle. They want it.

But who can blame them, darling? Sometimes you find that moment in your life, that perfect moment, and you want it to stick. To really stick.

I remember sitting in Montmartre, oh, years ago now, and we were eating croissants at a table in one of those open cafes, and he was sweet then, your father was, and I took his hand ever so gently. I had been afraid he would be cross, you never can tell with your father how he'll react to things. He doesn't like surprises, doesn't like changes. He never has. But I told him the news, that I was pregnant, that we were going to have a baby! And then I waited, just waited to see. He sat there for a moment, licking crumbs off his fingers and I thought maybe he hadn't heard me or maybe it had all been in my head, maybe I hadn't told him at all. Then he took my hand, and he didn't say a word, he just smiled. And it was perfect. It was perfect then, and maybe, if I could have kept it that way forever, then I would have. Oh, I don't know, it's silly. But I might have.

Perhaps they'll all wake up, they'll shake out those tired, stiff limbs of theirs and they will realize it was all a dream, it was all of them pretending, it was all that wanting to stay in one place, to be one thing forever, all that dreaming and wishing crystallized.

Last night I had a dream. I dreamed that your father took me out into the garden, to that little patch of lobelias, the ones I put in two years ago, and he told me to hold still, to hold my arms just so and then I could stay like that, I could stay there forever, amongst the lobelias, in our little garden. And I wanted to. I wanted to so badly, but my muscles get tired so quickly now and they wouldn't hold, and he kept moving bits of me. "It's not supposed to be like that," he would say. "You have to get it right, you have to get it *perfect*. And then you can stay."

Don't worry, darling, it wasn't a sad dream. That's the thing, that's the thing about it. I was happy.

I love him, you know. It hasn't always been like that between us—there have been rough patches, everyone has rough patches, of course, when you grow old together, when you grow out of one thing and into another, but I've always loved him. He gets scared sometimes, when he sees me looking out the window. I know he does. I know he asked you to keep an eye on me, to make sure I don't wander into the garden. He's afraid, you see, he's just afraid. Poor man. He doesn't like change, but then, who does? Even Paul needed a thunderbolt before he got the message.

In that dream, though, it wasn't so bad, it wasn't so hard. I could learn to do it, I know I could. I could learn to hold myself like that. Just the way he wanted. Until the stillness settled in. And the quiet.

[knuckle]

THE BOOK OF JUDGEMENT

Let us say that she was sitting at needlework when he came for her; that her fingers were still deft, that they moved without a stumble as the thread tucked in and out; or perhaps it is better if she were at the pianoforte, playing, and she *did* stumble, her fingers slipping on a jarring note. It might have been something by Handel or Haydn or Dibdin or Samuel Webbe; or, were she venturing further afield, she might have attempted Corelli or Cramer. But, no, despite what they say, *I* know better, and she had no especial taste for the pianoforte; she did not care for it though all the world said she did; *I* know she did not, I *know* it.

And so it could not have been that she was at the pianoforte when the stranger came, but let us say she was, let us not unsettle the sensibilities of those who claim intimate knowledge of her practices, let us say she was there, bent just so, rapt in the rhythm of Handel, then, (for I admit I am partial to Handel even if Jane was not) and let it be a jest between us against my detractors if it were not as I have described it exactly.

When the stranger entered, he may have startled her, so that the "March" in *Judas Maccabeus* was insensibly altered, and her chin might have nodded up at the unexpected sound of the door, and perhaps a slight gasp even escaped her lips when she saw him; this Hun invading the centre of her quiet domesticity. Some might describe him as tall, and that would be a perfectly adequate description; he *was* tall. But to say that is not to capture the sense of magnitude he brought with him, the grandeur. I have been told that some hear a rushing noise like a cataract when they first look upon him, the sound of pounding blood, and it may be this that she heard, her heartbeat accompanying the forever-marred Handel. I cannot say. And to say he was handsome, again, might be seen as somehow a lessening, and such falsehoods, such tendencies toward understatement are inappropriate in a chronicle such as this, which requires the strictest veracity in all things; his hair was soft as lamb's wool, curled gently over his forehead; black, most likely; he had dark, piercing eyes, possessed of intelligence and keenness, and sensuous lips of the kind true lovers, or lawyers, possess. Perhaps, she had some subtle premonition when she first saw him; perhaps she heard a note like a bell, tolling, as some saints do. But there was almost certainly something; *that*, at least, is not in question.

And so her pen might have fallen from nerveless fingers, yes, it was a pen after all, and so it was the writing desk at which she sat and not the pianoforte. And he will have said to her, "Fear not, madam, that I should disturb you at this late hour, for I have come with tidings." And she will have been shocked, but that stubborn grace to which she was born will have steeled her resolve, and she will have said, "Indeed, sir." And he will have said, "You are to die." And she will have said, "That is known. For is it not that every woman on God's earth is appointed an hour of death?" And he, with a terrible smile, though not terribly meant, of course, but frightening, nonetheless, to a mortal, will have said, "Yes, Miss Austen. That is so."

Since the beginning of Time, there has existed in Heaven a perfect record of all deeds, an accounting of each man and woman upon which they will be judged, a great Book written with words of gold, watched over by Saint Peter, the holiest and most trusted of the Apostles. All this I revealed to the astonished Miss Austen, her face flushed to a beautiful pink, like the first blossom of a rose; all this I revealed and something more: that I, myself, had been chosen as the Author of that Book. Certainly, she was wonderstruck that such a task had been entrusted to one so beautiful and terrible, though, of course, not willingly terrible, never willingly terrible to her. Certainly, she will have felt as if her story were perfectly safe, that each notation should accord perfectly with how it had been performed in History, that the accounting should be true and her immortal soul safe.

And I assured her, eagerly, that this was so; that there had never been a keener observer of her manners than I; that none had been so attuned to her every thought, the reveries, the little meanderings of her brain, than the one who stood before her. And she might have nodded, just a little, but at this point I will have noticed that the wonderment she felt, the jarring to her soul had jarred her hand as well, and a thin pool of ink might have been gathering on the pages before her. Gallantly, I might have said something to draw attention to this, "Madam, the ink is running." And she will have said, "Why should ink matter when an Angel of the Lord stands before me?" and I will have said, "Because it is all that matters. Was not the universe brought into being with a Word?" And she will have said, "Yes, perhaps." And I will have laughed gently, "Then you must attend to words, to your little creations, lest some force of evil enter into the world." Perhaps this was not a very kind joke.

———————

The other angels had little in the way of poetic sensibility; they were wise, yes, and terrible, certainly that, but none of them, at their hearts, were aesthetes. They were messengers, servants, builders, killers even—you might say that there was a certain creative flair in, for example, that little episode with Lot's wife, but you have to realize that even Azrael was a little embarrassed about it, he didn't know what had come over him, and the others, they wouldn't trust him with anything apocalyptic for centuries. You see, they wanted wisdom; they wanted terror; but poetry, that was a thing for mortals, that was a way of imagining the world not how it was but how it could be; and as the world was exactly how God had ordered it in his Infinite Wisdom and Infinite Knowledge, it was, therefore, Infinitely Perfect. Why sadness, you might ask? Why death? Why pillars of salt and punishment? Why manna in the wilderness and the twelve plagues of Egypt and the forbidden fruit if not for the sheer *poetry* of it? I asked Azrael once, but he only looked at me with those eyes that had seen the passing of eons, that had basked in the radiance of a most perfect love and had delivered thousands upon thousands of mortals from one world to the next—eyes that did not want questions, only thousands put to the sword, not even a fiery sword, just a simple iron sword with two sides honed for cutting down mortals like wheat—and he said, "I don't *know* why I did it, mate. I don't."

———————

Jane did not like jokes. That was very clear to me; she might have, in youth, enjoyed the odd frivolity, but in old age her mind had hardened into a shell around her frail body, and she did not smile.

"Am I to die, then?" she will have said, and I will have said, "Yes. I have said as much."

"But when?" she will have asked me. "When?"

But I could not tell her, I could not tell. To do so would make me anathema, and besides, I was not there as a messenger, nor as a servant, nor even as a killer—I was there to record. And it would be then that I heard a knock at the door, and in will have come a great clod of a man wearing his bulk upon him as if it were an expensive suit, tailored to fit, a plain-looking man, aggressive in conversation and almost completely tactless, with a quite unappealing stutter. And he will have said, "You have r-r-r-ruined the Handel." Stricken, she will have apologized though I am sure she did not wish to. "Indeed," he will have said, "again please." And he will have left the room as abruptly as he had entered.

"Mister Harris Bigg-Wither," I will have stated, and even then words were written, somewhere, in shining gold on pages white as snow. *A great clod of a man* . . .

"My husband."

"I know."

"He proposed after his time in Oxford."

"I know."

"Marriage might offer many practical advantages. A permanent home for Cassandra, assistance for my brothers in their careers. . . ."

"I know, Miss Austen," I might have whispered, and, somewhere, the words *many practical advantages* . . .

"Do not call me that."

———————————

God, it is said, sees all things at once; for Him there is no such thing as Time, for indeed, He exists outside of Time and for Him all things are immediate, all things perpetual. God has no understanding of narrative; how can He? For narrative is the pleasing arrangement of one incident after another, the compelling build of drama and the proper, appropriate resolution when all things have occurred, as they must, in a certain order.

In Heaven, it is said, there sits the Book of Judgement and each mortal is recorded there so that upon the day of death, Saint Peter might open the book and find ascribed there a full recounting of their deeds. But it is not said, that albeit the words are of the finest gold and they shine like the light of Heaven itself, albeit the parchment is of the finest white vellum, as smooth as newborn flesh, as white as newfallen snow, when one reads from the Book of Judgement it is a fast and simple thing: *Missus Clara Crawford lived a good life and is deserving of reward*; or *Mister Timothy Branton was good for many years but fell under the influence of evil friends.*

And I read from the Book and I examined the lives of those I had been sent to watch over, and each of them seemed like such a tiny thing, so tiny, and I would turn the page and ask, "But where are they, the little loves and betrayals, the tests and mishaps and abandonments and reversals?" and Peter, with an infinitely loving look, with the weight of ages sitting upon his poor, beetled brow, would say, "Just leave it, already. We don't have time for plot."

Miss Austen played very nicely this second time, and the G major was sweet and pleasing to the ear, her transition to the "Duet" flawless. I said nothing. I simply watched her at the pianoforte, watched the elegant curve of her neck bowing toward the keys, the litheness of her fingers, the way her eyes would close for a moment as she played and then flutter open furiously. She was a beautiful woman, this Miss Austen, or as she preferred, Missus Bigg-Wither, and as one who has seen the many specimens of Creation, I can say with some authority that here was a remarkable creature, here was a creature of virtue and kindness, deserving in every way of the especial attention of one such as myself.

When the piece came to an end, she sat for a moment, utterly composed, and I thought she would speak but she did not, not immediately, she listened as if to some phantom music of her own; but that was not it, it was not some inner symphony she attended to, no, but the creak of the house, the sound of footsteps in the hall. There was none. She relaxed.

"Are you here to haunt me?"

"No," I said, "this is not one of your Gothic tales, with wild-haired men and buried secrets."

"I do not have time for stories."

"No," I said. "Not any longer."

"Why do you look at me like that?"

"Like what?" I replied, startled.

"As if you were a child, and I a much sought after sweet that had suddenly turned sour in your mouth."

I regarded her in silence for a time; her body shuddered with the effort of playing, and I found myself listening too, for the sound of footsteps, for the sound of something beside her breath coming in and out of her lungs in ragged little bursts. There was light streaming in from an open window and it touched her hair, burnished it to gold.

"I think you are very beautiful," I said.

"You must not say such things."

"But I am bound to truth in all things." *She was very beautiful. . . .*

"I am not," Miss Austen replied, and she turned her head so that the light slid off her hair, touched her lips, her eyes. "Truth is a not a thing for a woman, or novelists, to be concerned with; it is only the appearance of truth that touches us, for a thing feigned becomes true enough given only sufficient time and inclination for the masquerade."

"It is different for an angel."

"Yes," she said softly. "I would very much like to imagine it is."

Let us say, now, that her husband, Mister Bigg-Wither, never entered the room; let us say that we sat, the two of us listening, for some time, and we heard only birdsong or, perhaps, the pianoforte, but no footsteps in the hall.

———————————

At the beginning of the War—and even I do not remember, good record-keeper, good servant that I am, which it was— Azrael was thrilled.

"It will be good to see action again," he said, "just to try my hand at it again. A sword is an easy thing to lose touch with, a sword requires practice, effort, and I," he confessed, "have not done much of either." Azrael went to the Peninsula where the French were massacring the British and the British were massacring the French, and as I visited Miss Austen, so did he watch the course of the War creep across those other lands; when I saw him, he was gleaming, resplendent, and there was a thrill to his voice when he spoke, as if the crack of cannons had infused him with a thunderous rapture. Azrael was happy with the simple tasks of warfare.

"Let them do as they will," he would say to us, "it's all the same. French. English. Not a Joan of Arc to look out for among them, not a vision to dispense with. Just mind the cavalry and keep out the way. Easy work." He smiled then, happy to have something to do, happy to be of service. But the next time he didn't bother with bringing his sword. "All muskets now, isn't it? Not like the old days. Muskets and cannons. Good things, cannons, I'm not complaining, but it's all a bit imprecise, isn't it? They just fire and, hey, maybe it'll hit, maybe it won't. But never let it be said that I'm complaining, I like a good war, a war is a good thing."

But he looked sad, somehow, and after that he confided to me, "I don't know what I'm doing there. I just don't know. There aren't any orders. I just watch, now, it's all just watching. I don't know what it's supposed to mean. Shouldn't I be trying to inspire them? Shouldn't one side have a moral right over the other?"

"It means that history is advancing, and Creation is more infinitely complex than we can possibly imagine," I said.

"I stride about the battlefield," he said, "and I watch the cannons go off, and the charge, and then I sort through the dead, and when I come across one, someone writes down his name and puts a little tick beside the box. And they respect me, the ones from Records, they absolutely respect me, you can see it in their eyes. But all they want to know is did that one manage to hit anything? Because if he did, that's it then, isn't it? The little bastards know which box to tick."

When Jane's beauty left her, she still had the pianoforte, and her skill at it was extreme, sublime. Her fingers were precise if arthritic; and when she played it was as if a tremor rippled through me, as if she were revealing some hidden part of the divine plan, some especial function of grace that I had never been privy to. And I would listen to her, sometimes, and we would speak, sometimes.

"I do not understand why you have come," she would say to me.

"It is my purpose to discover your secrets, that I might see the truth of you and write it in Heaven."

"There is no truth to me that you have not seen," she would say, "for I have no pretensions to that sort of elegance which consists in tormenting a respectable man, and as such I have laid bare for you whatever you ask."

"Ah," I would exclaim, "what I search for is the parts of yourself that you do not yet, and may never, understand; for that is where the true character of a woman is written, not in what she knows she can reveal and does however willingly, but in what she is unaware of, even in herself."

"Then you assume I do not know myself."

"No mortal can."

"And yet I have made a study of it, these long, lonely years, a perfect study so that I could paint a likeness of myself for your Book that, I have no doubt, would be suitable to your purposes."

"What would you say?"

"That I am a woman."

"That would not be enough."

"It was enough for Eve," she would say, "and it is enough for my husband."

"It is not enough for you."

It is said that in Heaven there is an order to things, and we angels understand it perfectly, that we lack the requisite means to question, those of us who stayed, that is, who did not fall in the War. And so I did not question when Azrael came to me, no longer resplendent, the crack of cannon fire gone from his voice.

"They've taken me off Warfare," he said, and his voice was melodious and sad. "They say that I do not understand the New Order, that I am a cog in a perfectly ordered machine but, perhaps, it is the wrong machine, not the machine of Warfare. I don't even know what that means," he confessed, "but one of them, one of the dying ones, asked for a sign. And so I appeared to him, I let him see that God's love was infinite and that he was safe, and that flesh was just a little thing, just a very little thing, and he had a place in the cosmic order. That God was merciful.

"Did you know that they have a Book? And in that Book are the names of the angels—everyone one of us? And it says, *Azrael—a good servant for many years*. For many years, what does that mean? Am I not eternal? Am I not free of flesh and beyond the scope of Time? *For many years*. And one of them found me. He said to me, 'Azrael, you are made to serve.' And I was. I am. I live to serve, service is the very truth of what I am, that's what I told him. 'Good,' the little bugger said."

Jane never lost her beauty; let it not be said by anyone that she lost her beauty, for Beauty is an eternal thing, like Truth, and there can be no changing it once it is possessed.

And I said this to Azrael, as he stood by me, I said, "Is she not beautiful, is she not possessed of some higher substance? Does she not deserve something more than that clod of a husband? What a noble mind, what a keen observer of the human condition, what a record-keeper of all that transpires in the hearts of those who surround her."

And he said, "I was made to serve just like you. This is what they have asked of me, it's not cannons, it's not thunder and death, but it's what they asked me to do."

"Let me speak with her."

Let us say that she was sitting at her desk when he came for her; let it not have been the pianoforte where she had laboured, for hours, for the love of a husband who did not love her in return. Let us say that there was no husband. Let us say that she was only passably good at the pianoforte, and that she had, instead, a keen fascination with words, with writing out the hearts of men and women upon the page. Let us call her, not Missus Bigg-Wither, as she herself might have done, but Miss Austen, alone, yes, but beautiful and keen-witted and happy.

Perhaps she would have heard a tolling of a bell, as some do, and she would have turned to see a stranger standing before her, tall, resplendent, with hair as soft as lamb's wool. Perhaps there would have been a rushing noise in her ears, the sound of a great cataract, more deafening, perhaps, than the crack of a cannon.

And he will have said to her, "Fear not, madam, that I should disturb you at this late hour, for I have come with tidings."

And she will have been shocked, but that stubborn grace to which she was born will have steeled her resolve, and she will have said, "Indeed, sir." And he will have said, "You are to die." And she will have said, "That is known. For is it not that every woman on God's earth is appointed an hour of death?" And he, with a terrible smile, though not terribly meant, of course, but frightening, nonetheless, to a mortal, will have said, "Yes, Miss Austen. That is so."

Afterwards, I would say to Azrael, "Why pillars of salt and punishment? Why manna in the wilderness and the twelve plagues of Egypt? Why sadness? Why death?"

And he would shrug, looking uncomfortable. "I don't know, mate."

They say, in Heaven, that there is a Book, and in it are written all the names of the universe, that an accounting can be made of each. They say that beside the name of Azrael it is written, *He was a good servant.* And I know it to be true. And there will be another name, Harris Bigg-Wither, and there will be a very brief account, and there will be another name, Jane Austen, and it will say, *She was very beautiful and died too early. Let her fondness for words have never stinted, let her books last for generations, let them be written as truth in the hearts and souls of the generations to come; let her never have feared the footsteps on the hall, let her have known much love, let her have disliked the pianoforte.* I do not know if it is a kindness, these things I have written. But it *is* a record. Of a sort.

They say, in Heaven, that Time is infinite and all things happen at once, that there is no order to events; that there is no such thing as music for all notes sound together and the listener cannot differentiate; music is temporal; music is of the flesh; it is mortal. In Heaven, they say, there is no grandsweeping narrative, for God stands outside the possibility of such things; that He sees all things, the loves, the triumphs, the betrayals and reversals in a single moment, an eternity that renders as chaos for his servants what is perfect order for him. They say that His forgiveness is absolute, his His love is absolute, His observance is absolute. They say this, my many detractors. Let it be a jest between us; let it be the first betrayal; let it be a mark, spilled ink, in that perfect chronicle of His that I should believe otherwise, that I should doubt, that this doubt should run through to the very depths of me.

In Heaven, there is a book, and in that book, there is a name: *Lucifer, called Lightbearer, a good servant, once, turned rebel.*

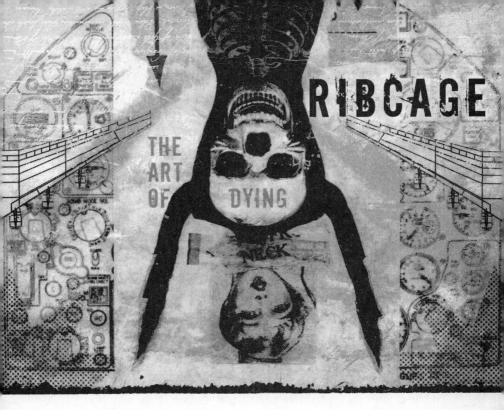

[ribcage]

THE ART OF DYING

I have only slipped away into the next room.
I am I and you are you.
Whatever we were to each other,
that we still are.

—Henry Scott Holland, "What is Death?"

I.

Sitting in the coffee shop, staring at the steady stream of students cruising along Bloor Street, Clarissa knows that in ten days she will be dead.

She always knows when she will die, can tick away the seconds on her finger like a clock winding down.

She can feel the bustling crowd around her, ten days from now, the dark lights of the subway and the sound of guitar music from somewhere in the distance. Young women carry logoed bags, yoga mats, strollers with small children that look like blurry photographs of themselves. Men talk on cell phones, read newspapers, stare at the women. It is a Thursday, and Clarissa has never liked Thursdays. People are in too much of a hurry to get to the weekend.

Clarissa imagines herself standing a little over the yellow safety line. She looks down, studies the dull gleam of the rails at the bottom of the drop in front her. There are signs nearby warning people not to charge the doors when the bell chimes. People always ignore them.

Distant rumbling. The elbows are hard at her back. She wants to sink back into the crowd. Instead, she leans forward to catch the first sight of lights in the tunnel, bursting out of the darkness.

A whoosh of displaced air, a high-pitched squeal of brakes as the driver slows for the turn to enter the station.

The chatter behind Clarissa hums, but it is impossible to make out what anyone is saying. If she turned around to look, it would be like staring at a muted TV, like people caught naked without words to hide behind. But her eyes are fixed on the approaching lights.

Then it happens.

Behind her, elbows and shoulders bristle in hedgehog anticipation. The muscles of the crowd tense. Someone calls out behind her, but she doesn't turn.

Clarissa is staring at the lights, watching them grow large as an opening eye. Her pupils dilate. The train is almost here.

Now Clarissa feels the impatience around her. She is impatient too. When the warm bodies finally shove her forward, she wonders why it has taken so long to happen. She teeters, eyes locked with the growing eye of the train.

But there are still ten days, and right now her fingers shake with a different kind of anticipation.

Paul was supposed to be here five minutes ago.

When the door to the coffee shop swings open to reveal him—casual jeans, a button-down dress shirt, apologetic smile—she can't help but smile back. She doesn't want to smile. Doesn't want to be here. She wants to be in her apartment where she has been packing away this body's possessions so as not to be a burden to her family when they come to clear it out. Her brother, Jamie, is the oldest and would be expected to take charge of her effects. But he's a sensitive guy, always reading, even now that he's done school. She doesn't want him to suffer.

Clarissa, unexpectedly, has forgotten the art of dying and so she is here waiting for Paul.

"You're late," she says.

"Not *that* late." His answer is well-timed, funny, and Clarissa is worried that she may be in love with him.

II.

Consciousness.

Her body is soft, moving lithely, sweat-locked beneath a linen sheet. She can feel it rubbing against her back like sandpaper, and then hitched like a coarse rope around her hips as she leans back, into him.

The body beneath her thrusts, sending a column of electricity up her spine. For a moment there are stars in front of her eyes, as the blood pulses. She can feel him within her, moving. It always starts like this.

A thought: *I am happy.*

This time her mouth jerks open and the muscles in her forehead tense. Her cheeks are hollow. Sound reverberates in them, the quick beats of her breath.

She is leaning back, and his body lurches upward.

She is in love. His hands are beautiful against her, fingers beautifully smooth as if he had no fingerprints.

It is often at this moment that Clarissa awakes. That thought—*I am happy*—and the next one: *I will die.* But Clarissa is still nothing more than the whisper of consciousness. She is watching this scene, here-but-not, peering through the cracked doorway of this other body.

The hips beneath her lift up one last time, and the blanket slips away entirely. She is lifted free, spasming blissfully, that tiny niggle of doubt disintegrating in the rush.

I am happy, thinks the self that owns the body. *I am happy. And I will never die.*

The doorway closes. Clarissa feels consciousness sliding sideways away from her.

Then, nothing.

III.

The next time Clarissa wakes, she feels the heavy weight of a bookbag slung across her shoulders. She remembers: Lorna Crozier, P. K. Page, *The History of Criticism.* She is late for class, standing on the curb at Queen's Park. The grass smells musty, and there is more mud than life here. Winter has only begun to thaw, and the scent of it tickles inside her nose, all those things falling apart and being put back together again.

She has made this crossing many times. Everyone has. The City of Toronto never built a crosswalk at this particular juncture, but rather moved it twenty metres along the crescent. No one waits for that light. The most direct path is to cross here, racing the traffic.

But it is easy. She's done it for months. Just watch the lights two blocks away and you can catch the beat of the traffic flow, find your place to slip through.

Today she is distracted. She is thinking about the taste of him, the scratch of the new lace bra rubbing her the wrong way since she put it on this morning. It's a beautiful piece of work, all shiny black, the kind you see in movies. She knows he will like it. She is wearing it for him.

And then she steps out.

The cyclist swerves, nearly knocks into her with the front tire, but instead a flailing leg catches her in the thigh.

The bike is off-kilter now, and the cyclist struggles to get his balance, his foot on the pedal, the wheels straightened. That's when he hits the curb. Already there is a car racing past her, honking. She gasps and takes a step back.

The surge of adrenaline brings Clarissa to life. Her eyes blink in that girl's head. The cyclist is lying in the mostly mud of the park, and the back wheel is spinning.

Clarissa sees it happening again. The bike speeding into her, her body crumpling or spinning, like that back wheel, out into the street.

Air is suddenly difficult to find.

"I am going to die," a piece of her says, the I-am-in-love girl who had put on the beautiful lingerie this morning, had picked it out from the Victoria's Secret catalogue, and who now feels the rawness of the skin circling her chest.

Inside is a different kind of rawness. Clarissa can see, although the girl, the other girl, cannot: the train racing towards her. It is two months away, but they both know it is coming, something, death. "I am a piece of your death," she whispers. And then: "Don't be afraid. Please."

And that is why Clarissa is here. She knows how to die, like the other girl does not.

Already, she feels synapses firing, the network of tissues responding to her thoughts, her impulses. The other girl is something fluttering in the corner of her ribcage. Clarissa calms her. Their shared heartbeat steadies. Clarissa recedes with the cool wash of restored composure. The other girl fills her lungs, bears the abusive shouts of the cyclist, mud-covered, starting to turn over his twisted bike.

Air. Breath. The door is closing for Clarissa, the last sliver of consciousness knifing away. This time, something remains. Inside the girl is a hard kernel of knowledge, the kind that makes her skin bleed sweat, and brings a kind of tightness to her throat.

She is going to die.

Clarissa waits.

IV.

On Tuesday, as Clarissa wraps glasses and bowls in newspaper, she stares outside the window. A plane descends slowly toward Pearson Airport. The arrow-straight line of its flight pattern is beautiful. Sometimes chaos looks orderly from a distance, she thinks. From here, it is impossible to tell if the plane is making a controlled descent or tumbling through space, having lost power. You couldn't tell, from down here, if the engines were working, the pilot calm, the passengers sleepy, or relieved, or anxious to be on the ground.

She thinks about chaos, and flight lines, and the inescapable force of gravity. In that moment, she bitterly wants it to be over. Even if it hurts.

This waiting is terrifying and she wishes it would just stop. Stop and be done.

This is a new thought for her. She has never been scared, the other times.

The phone rings and she picks it up.

"Amanda, is that you?"

She breathes in, says nothing. Amanda. That was the other self's name.

"Mandy, I've been calling you for days. Why won't you just talk to me?" A pause. He is upset. "Did I—did I do something wrong?"

Clarissa recognizes the voice. It the man whom she— Amanda—was in love with, months ago, perhaps even days ago. Richard. His name was Richard.

Another disruption to the pattern. Normally, she would feel the residual emotion. She would care more, want to comfort him. To prepare him for what is to come. The other girl flutters in her mind, beating against the inside of her ribcage like a fly against glass.

"Shhh," she says. And she realizes she has spoken aloud.

"Mandy? Mandy, are you there?" The voice is strained. "Just say something! You're really scaring me. Everyone.

Jamie said you're packing up your apartment. Does that mean . . . do you want to move in, after all?"

She puts the receiver gently back on the phone.

The room is still now. Somewhere, kilometres away, the plane is on the ground and people are gathering their belongings.

She puts a hand to her cheeks and finds unexpected tears there. She closes her eyes, counts to ten in a slow exhale, and turns back to the cupboard.

V.

Clarissa takes Paul's jacket, and places it neatly on one of the few hangers in the otherwise bare cupboard.

"Are you moving?" he asks as he surveys the place: a beautiful two-bedroom apartment right on the edge of Forest Hill. Mandy loved this place, the huge bay windows in the solarium, the tiny stained glass lily pad in the door, the way her feet moved drunkenly across the uneven, renovated floors. Sometimes, Clarissa sees it through her eyes. Normally, it is much easier but the contact is weak, broken.

That is why Paul is here tonight. It should have been the man who had called her, voice panicky with concern, but it is not.

Tonight it is allowed to be someone else.

"Not me," she replies. "A friend. I'm just helping her pack."

"She won't mind me being here?"

She smiles awkwardly, doesn't answer, and takes a step toward him.

His hands are gentle as they take hers. She closes her eyes, breathes him in until her lungs reach their full capacity, ballooning in her chest. Their lips meet. He tastes sweet.

Clarissa feels happy, like her lungs are filled with helium and she is rising off the floor until her head knocks gently against the ceiling.

"You're beautiful," he whispers after, a tiny smile. And then he cocks his head. "But you look sad."

"Moving pains," she says. She kisses him again and steers him toward the couch. She packed up the bedroom two days ago and has been camping out in the living room with a blanket and a pillow. She wants to take up as little space as possible in this other person's house.

They make love, surrounded by stacked boxes labelled in steady handwriting.

Something is knocking against her ribcage, but Clarissa does not allow herself to feel it. Instead, she feels Paul, his steady strength, the salty taste of his sweat in her mouth. He knows what he is doing, and Clarissa feels lightheaded as he urges her body towards climax.

I am happy, she thinks. *I am in love.* And then: *I will die.*

The knocking recedes.

VI.

On Wednesday, Clarissa opens the door to find Jamie. His clothes are characteristically wrinkled from a day at the office. He can never keep himself as tidy as he wants. He offers a half-shrug apology, embarrassed to be interrupting her unannounced.

"Sorry for just dropping in. It's been a couple of days, and Dad was wondering if you were going to be at the restaurant on Friday. You haven't been picking up the phone." His eyes re-punctuate the sentence with a question mark.

Clarissa half-shrugs back, genetics taking over seamlessly. She doesn't let him inside.

"I've been really busy with all these papers. But I'll do what I can to make it."

"Listen, can I come in? I've been meaning to talk to you . . ." He puts his hand on the door to push it open.

"It's not a good time right now."

"Jesus, Mandy, do you have someone over there? Richard says you won't talk to him."

"I don't want to talk to him."

"Did the two of you have a fight?"

"Well . . ." She bites her lip without knowing it. Mandy's gesture. "It's complicated. I'm worried about him. What might happen."

"So you're, what, protecting him? By not speaking to him?"

"It's not that." Clarissa doesn't want the conversation to continue. Her body is already starting to slip from her control. "I love him," she blurts out. "He wants to get married, and I want to marry him, really, Jamie, I want to marry him, but I can't. I know I can't."

She doesn't know who is speaking anymore. "I want to move in with him. He just asked me. And I've got the key"— it had been sitting by the phone, waiting to be packed; Clarissa had almost forgotten it—"but something isn't right. I don't know how to explain."

Her hand slid off the door, and Jamie's weight sent it open.

"It's okay. It's okay to be scared." He puts his arms around her, and all Clarissa can think is *Paul, Paul, Paul* while another woman sobs into his chest.

"I'm not *scared* of moving in with him," she whispers. "I'm scared of . . ."

She does not finish the sentence. Jamie doesn't notice. Clarissa can feel Amanda receding back now that the wash of emotions has begun to drain away, but she is angry. She does not want this body, this death.

Take it, she thinks. *I don't want to live your life for you.*

I can't, Amanda says. *I don't know how. Do it for me. I'm afraid.*

It is a child's voice.

Synapses fire. Clarissa can smell Jamie's sweat, the faint traces of day-old aftershave. She knows he loves his sister, but he hates touching people like this. He never knows what to do with his hands.

She pushes away him away, guiding him out the door.

"I'll be fine," she says, shaking her head ruefully and sniffling against the back of her hand. "Thanks for coming. Really."

He looks uncertain, but also a little relieved. *Poor man*, she thinks. *He'll hate the funeral. All those grieving relatives to comfort.*

"You sure?"

"Yeah. Richard's great, really. We're great. I'm going to love living with him." The words are stones.

"I'll see you Friday then? For Dad's thing?"

She nods and wipes tears from the corner of her eyes. Jamie is already halfway to his car by the time she opens her eyes.

"Thanks," she says. "It really was sweet of you to check up on me. Tell Richard I'll see him soon."

She retreats into the house, and finds herself staring at the key. Her hand hovers over the phone. She remembers Richard's number, his smile, the way Amanda's heart hitched a little when he walked into a room.

She dials.

"Hi Paul. It's me."

VII.

"Where did you come from?" Paul whispers, teasing a tongue down the length of her thigh. "God, you're an angel."

"I'm not," she mumbles. Her arms are bent at a ninety-degree angle, propping her up on the leather cushion of the couch. She wants to be sad, but she is not. His fingers touch her again, and then his tongue.

Clarissa cannot remember how many times she has folded clothes, placed them in boxes, written steepled messages in magic marker across the tops. She has lived inside of so many different bodies. She has died inside them all, sheltering that small, shuddering spirit and then gently releasing it once the pain has ended.

People do not realize how early the body senses its own death. Time travels backwards, sending ripples from the shock that spin out in all directions. There is always a moment before when that sharp knife of fear seizes the mind. *I will die.*

Time is moving strangely for her now. Paul is very gentle but very persistent. She rocks from her perched arms onto her back, and he follows, never stopping. Her body hums like a plucked string.

"I'm gonna die," Clarissa whispers into Paul's hair, fine like cobwebs on her lips.

He doesn't hear. The unready body is taught to ignore those words.

Death tastes strange in her mouth.

VIII.

It is eight in the morning on Thursday, and Clarissa is staring into the mirror. Paul waits, shirt off, warmly naked, in the other room while she brushes her teeth. Except her fingers have forgotten how to move. The water is running, and she stares at the face in the mirror. Pretty enough, even marred by sleep. Grey eyes. Hair like lace. The curve of a petite nose and a slightly stronger chin. She moves in the light, watching shadows fall in different places, over lips, cheeks, hands when she holds them up.

"This is yours," she whispers. "Come take it from me. You should be doing this."

Nothing. Amanda is silent.

She remembers her first death. She was twelve years old, and there was something growing inside her brain. Her parents had nothing for her but brittle, plastic smiles and too many hugs. But she hugged them back, although they were strangers, and laughed and ate ice cream. Joked with the doctors. Befriended the other kids in the ward. Smiled as the tubes went in and the lights, slowly, went out.

Her name had been Clarissa.

She had thought that was what she was supposed to do. That tiny voice in the back of her brain had been so scared, urging her to make it all right. She didn't want the people around her to be sad.

"Hey beautiful!" Paul calls out from the other room. "I'm going to pick up some breakfast. The fridge here is empty."

"I'll be out in a moment. There's a great bagel shop down the block."

"Bagels it is!"

And he is gone. Part of her drifts out the door alongside him, ethereally hooked around ankles and wrists. She can feel it unwinding like a garden hose inside her belly.

She brushes her teeth, cleans the bowl, wipes down the mirror.

Ten minutes later, the apartment door opens, and Clarissa turns to greet Paul.

It is Richard.

His arms hang limply from sodden shoulders, and his face is hangdog.

"Richard," she says.

"You wouldn't answer my calls."

"I was busy." She twists her hands. *Amanda*, she says, *you must do this. He is yours. He is not mine.*

"You should've called back." He is not moving, so she does, walks towards him, and takes his hand.

"I know, sweetie. Richard." She stumbles. "I should have. I was packing . . ."

His fingers unconsciously link around hers, though she is intensely aware of their pressure, the feel of their smoothness. Her body remembers them.

"You . . . you still want to move in?"

She swallows and lies. "Of course, I do. I love you."

Relief. His frame slumps, reboots, becomes animated. "I was so scared. You wouldn't talk to me. Don't do that again!" And then: "I don't know what I'd do if I lost you."

She kisses him softly on the cheek, and then again on the lips. Her hand snakes up along his side, runs along his jaw to his ear.

Please Mandy, she whispers. *I don't want to do this.*

But his arms have already encircled her now, and his mouth is on hers, and she is falling, falling backwards into the couch, the nestled blankets where she and Paul had slept an hour or two before.

"I love you," he whispers. "I love you I love you I love you."

The sounds blur together, and she doesn't answer back.

IX.

A bag of bagels lays discarded on the bench by the door.
Clarissa is crying and she can't remember why.

X.

The crowd moves around her like the muscles of a giant lung breathing in and out. She needs to find him, needs to find Paul. She thought she had seen him moving this way, into the mouth of the subway, down the stairs, through the turnstile.

Grief is a crazed thing inside her.

There is a shock of blond hair in front of her. Now it is gone. Where is he? Where is he?

It wasn't me, Paul. It wasn't me. There is another woman living inside my chest and she loves him, and I didn't want him to hurt so much. I'm sorry.

Someone who looks like Paul is buying a newspaper from the vendor. No. Paul wouldn't buy a newspaper, not now. He'd be angry, hurt.

It didn't mean anything. He was just someone using this body. It wasn't me.

There, by the edge. She elbows her way through the people: the mothers with their strollers, the ones with yoga mats and shopping bags. She is pushing past, beyond the yellow safety line, searching for him.

I'm just using this body all up until it's gone and I don't want you to leave me.

People are impatient now. There is a light, displaced air, the incipient roaring of the train riding the tracks.

I am here. I don't want to die today. Paul, where are you? Hold me, Paul. I'm scared. I'm so scared.

Someone calls out behind her. "Amanda!"

She turns. Richard is wading his way through the crowd, but her eyes never make it to him. They are transfixed with the single eye of the train speeding toward her. She stands there, frozen, feeling the air rush past here, and the noise like a kind of applause in her chest. She cannot move. She cannot look at him.

Paul, she thinks. *I don't want to die.*

And something within her grabs hold—the sweet girl from the mirror, petite nose, strong chin. Hair like lace. That little-girl voice hidden behind the ribcage, the beating heart, now swells up inside her. Synapses fire. Her muscles are not her own.

I will do this, the other one says.

She teeters on the edge of the track.

A last sliver of light, the knife-edge of consciousness. *Paul*, she thinks desperately. *I am afraid.*

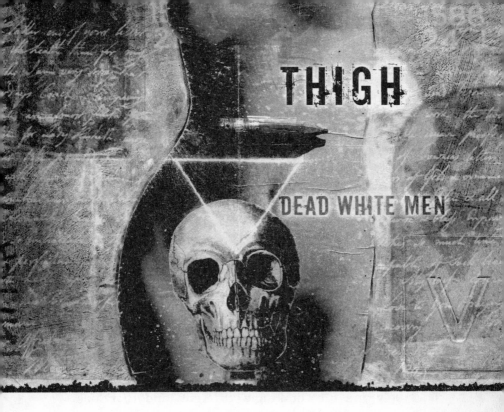

[thigh]
DEAD WHITE MEN

Celia was *that* girl, every bar has one, the strange girl, the beautiful girl, the untouchably *perfect* girl—she was short, yes, and thin enough, blonde, though not super-blonde; she had the mascara, the glitzy eye shadow, the black, shiny dress and the high heels—very high, at least four inches, so that she seemed to stab the ground as she walked on it. But there was something different about the way she watched the crowd, always on her own, never with friends, never seeming to talk to anyone for more than a moment or two. And so Ernie found himself watching too.

He watched her. And he watched her eyes scanning the crowd, bored, disinterested, as if she didn't really want to be there at all, as if she had better things to do. And he watched as, one by one, despite the boredom and disinterest, despite the *something differentness* about her, she never once seemed to turn down the men who came to her.

Some of the others—that vast confederacy of perpetually and happily single men who go to nightclubs to sleep with women—noticed Ernie looking. "It's not worth it, mate, it isn't worth it," one of them said, sliding a pint of Carling over to him as the night was beginning to wind down. On Mondays the pickings tended to be slim, and even the most ambitious of the lot tended to settle down for a pint, a loose camaraderie falling over them that would burn off like fog by Wednesday or Thursday when the competition became fierce. When Ernie asked why, every one of them went silent, still as the grave, and got a look in his eyes that said, don't ask anymore, just let it drop.

But Ernie didn't let it drop—couldn't let it drop. He didn't even know himself why except there was that thing in him, alert to that vital knowledge that Celia was, somehow, shockingly and breathtakingly different, and that look, the look the others had in their eyes, he wanted to know what it was, what it meant; he wanted to have it too. And so that Friday, the Friday after when all the others were still playing it safe, still keeping a little ring around Celia and her oddness, Ernie made his approach. He tried to play it cool. He tried to touch her arm with that special touch that said he was a *man*, that he wanted her, and that he could please her like no one had ever pleased her before—all men have, at some point in their lives, attempted this touch or some Platonic shadow of it. Ernie was surprisingly good at it, perhaps only two or three removes from the Male Touch that existed in the Universe of Ideals. But his hand was clammy from holding the lager, and so even though he wiped his hand, successively, on his pants before the approach, she still nearly jumped when his finger grazed her arm.

And then she looked at him. It was not a casual look, that; it was not a look that glided over the body, a copped feel of a glance. This was an invasive, probing stare that assessed every damp spot on his clothing, every misplaced hair, every personality defect from infant bedwetting to unpaid parking tickets, the tone, subject, setting and quality of every wet dream he had ever had; all of these counted up, processed, assessed behind eyelashes stiletto-sharp with mascara. This—this was the Platonic ideal of all Female Gazes.

Ernie felt himself begin to sweat. He tried to speak. "Hello," he wanted to say, but already he was forgetting how the words fit together, how the *h* might glide into the *e-l-l-o*. But then she leaned in close, her mouth next to his ear, voice soft and low and sexily British, the way he imagined, dreamed, it might be: "Meet *here* in two hours"—those long, stretched vowels and gently curving *r*'s.

Ernie was so surprised that the seduction had taken place, that *he* had been the seducer, he barely knew what to say in return. But that was a good thing, because by the time *he* recovered, *she* had already disappeared, and he was left holding a scrap of paper in his lager-sodden hand.

And that was how it began.

ST. GILES-IN-THE-FIELDS, LONDON
ANDREW MARVELL
1621-1678

Ernie forced himself to coolly suck down the last of his pint of Carling, to smile easily at the girl at the bar, tip generously, walk slowly outside into the cool London air where a heavy fog still hung close to the ground. He would play it cool. He would play it calm. He would not rush, he would not hurry—no, he knew better, he was wise in the ways of women and a savant in the accompanying mathematics of lateness arrival politics.

But.

The address was not easy to find.

His difficulty came not because it was out of the way. On the contrary, Ernie found himself in the West End in an area he knew well, just east of the Tottenham Court station. His difficulty came because it was a place entirely unexpected, and so he spent a solid twenty minutes tracing and retracing his steps, his eyes unwilling to find the required address. So when he finally did spot Celia, he was out of breath and sporting a brand new set of damp patches around the underarms. She on the other hand was perfectly cool, as if she had been leaning against the wall of an old church for all of eternity, cigarette clutched between two fingers, quiet puffs, and her uneager eyes glancing up and down. She had changed out of the shiny black thing she had been wearing earlier, and now she was dressed in a comfortable black turtleneck and loose pants.

"Hi," he said, and the word came out smoothly for which he was desperately glad.

"Hi," she said.

She blew out a stream of smoke through her nostrils. Should he kiss her? It was hard to tell. He took a step forward but before he could close the gap to kissing distance, she stubbed out the cigarette and motioned for him to follow. The puddles beneath his arms spread like creeping mildew.

"Bit of a maze, isn't it?" he asked.

A stupid thing to say. But she was busy now with a set of lockpicks at the side door. When she didn't answer, he puffed at his hands to keep them warm. They stood together like that in the stone arch of the doorway, Ernie unsure what to do with himself. She was shorter without the heels, her presence smaller, but somehow more intimidating. There was a quiet "click" and then, for the first time, she smiled, and she looked at Ernie, and Ernie looked at her, and she led him in.

Ernie hadn't been in a church—not a real one, not something more than the high school gymnasium—since his confirmation at St. Christopher's in grade eight. His parents hadn't been much for religion, were barely talking at that point and hardly seemed invested in the sacraments they had ostensibly subscribed to. This was a proper church, though, and it felt strange for Ernie to be there, surrounded by the bare, white outlines of saints and prophets and, somewhere up above, the watching eyes of a Jesus affixed, grimly, to the cross. The air was different; Ernie's sense of space distorted and he found himself not wanting to be in this place. But even then, even as he recognized the growing sense of unease, he could feel Celia keeping hold of him, her hand warm in his—despite how cold it at had been outside, it was very warm—and his penis twitched in a half-stutter of desire and began to press against the front of his trousers.

"You're very . . . beautiful," he said, his tongue almost-but-not-quite tripping. A moment of panic. *Breathe*, he told himself. He could hear the sound of their shoes, had forgotten what shoes sounded like against a proper stone floor: *tap, tap, tap*, they went. "I've seen you before, you know, at the club. I come in most nights. After work. And sometimes I see you there." She led him past the aisles and benches. She seemed to know her way. And then the tapping stopped, and she tugged at his hand very gently. "I never thought we'd, well, you would, you know—" God, he was an idiot. "I wanted to talk to you before. I think you're, oh, right—"

It took him by surprise, the sudden feel of her skin against his, the light press of her lips and the flick of her tongue against his teeth. He didn't know if he should say something else, but he'd tried, hadn't he? Maybe *that* kind of girl—Celia—wasn't chatty, maybe she just didn't want to talk, that was all right, wasn't it? And then her mouth was gone from his, and she whispered to him, "Can you be very quiet?"

Ernie knew what to do; he had done this dozens of times before and he managed to find his way around the precise combination of breasts and thighs and arms and legs that was Celia even in the dark; and then they were both of them on the cold flagstones of the church, her nipples as sharp and cold as bullets, and she was guiding him into her so that when he entered, his desire having quickly ratcheted up past his uncertainty, it was like slipping into a warm pool. The ground was hard underneath them, and he was sure it must be uncomfortable.

"Do you want me to . . . ?" he asked, but he didn't know what to say.

And Celia said, "No, it's fine. I'm fine *right* here," and then she moaned.

And she did something with her hips and so did he. He thrust away, and he felt his knees grazing against the cold flagstones, he got sight of a name and a date underneath her, but, really, it wasn't the time for sightseeing, it wasn't the time to be thinking about anything except . . .

That's when it happened.

That's when he felt something shuddering through him and it wasn't quite normal, not quite an orgasm, it felt like something was pushing against him, something cold and silent and it wasn't part of him, it was stealing into him and pushing him out and then—pop!—

Ernie thought he might be dead. He thought maybe, maybe, he had had a heart attack like his Old Man had, forty-seven, strong as an ox and healthy as a man could be, but cursed with a body that nevertheless had up and stopped one day. But he hadn't felt any pain, had he? Surely there would be pain? And darkness, he thought, or light, very bright light—but it was still the general dimness of the church, lacking either the black of eternal damnation or the brilliance of Heaven.

And Ernie looked around him but there was his body, still very much alive, there it was, thrusting away. And it looked curiously funny, all those flailing arms and legs, all the bits of him pretending very much they knew where they were supposed to be going and what they were supposed to be doing when really, he didn't know all that much about it at all. He tried to imagine a form of punctuation that might describe that body, but all he could figure out was a series of imaginative symbols pulled from the top row of the keyboard accompanied by something that might have been an umlaut.

Ernie felt very scared, and as the thrusting came to a crescendo, the grunts turned into a series of guttural engine grinding noises—"G-g-g-g-g-g!" He wondered if it was because he was in a church, if the sound echoed differently here, if God had struck him down for what he had done, if God was real and he had determined Ernie was a sinner, a real sinner. . . .

But then his body climbed off Celia, and she had a look on her face, a look he had never seen before, a look of . . . peace maybe, happiness, almost certainly. All the cold was gone from her, all the aloof reservation, and she looked almost childlike, as if her face had been scrubbed clean of the mascara and makeup until it glowed. His body collapsed on the tiles beside her, its eyes were closed, but it was definitely *his* face. Definitely *his* lips that now nuzzled her nipples and when it spoke, it was *his* voice that murmured into her ear. Celia laughed, and she smiled, and Ernie suddenly felt very awkward watching himself, awkward watching Celia with him.

Sometime later, there was a gentle tug, as if someone had a set a hook inside him and that someone now slowly, inexorably, was reeling him in. They were twined together—Celia and his body, and her head rested against his—its?—chest. He slipped back into his body like coming home after a long vacation to find all the appliances still worked the way he remembered they had. His fingers flexed involuntarily, and then Celia was awake, she was turning away from him. The place where her head had rested felt cold and empty.

She slipped on her turtleneck. She slipped on the loose-fitting black pants, and when she turned back, there was that look in her eyes again, that look that all the girls had when they looked at Ernie the morning after. And he tried to smile, he tried to give her that boyish charm, but the disappointment was so thickset in her eyes that Ernie suddenly felt ashamed that he wasn't whatever it was that she was looking for.

"We should leave now," she said. "It won't be long before someone comes." And this time it was Ernie who was nodding, though he didn't quite know why. "You'll be able to find your way home?" she asked.

He bobbed his head again, and he wanted to say something else to her, something that might unravel in some small way the secret of what had just happened, the secret of the church and the thing that had been inside him and what they had said and why, despite all that, despite the strangeness and the fear, despite whatever the answer to those question might be, that he still wanted to be near this woman. "Please," he said.

Celia looked at him with surprise. "You can't fall in love with me, you know. This was just sex." Ernie didn't say anything. After a moment, something in her expression cracked just a bit, just enough. "All right," she said. "Bunhill Fields Burial Ground, tomorrow."

BUNHILL FIELDS BURIAL GROUND
WILLIAM BLAKE
1757-1827

Ernie brought a flashlight. Celia hadn't told him what time, and so he waited, nervously, in the courtyard by the Artillery Fields. The place was strange in the moonlight, where a thing half-glimpsed could be any other thing in the world. When Celia arrived she too could have been anyone, the light making silver tracks in her hair and polishing her skin to a semi-luminous glow, and it made Ernie wonder, just for a moment, if he too could have been anyone in the world. Ernie tried to kiss her, but she turned her head at the last moment so he grazed her cheek instead.

"I didn't know if you'd come," Ernie confessed.

"I'm here, aren't I?" she said and the words could have been hurtful, but she smiled slightly, just a little bit. She took his hand like two sparrows cupped in her long, slim fingers and she led him through the gates. When he tried to turn on the flashlight, she shook her head. "We can't use that here," she said. "The guards will spot the light." And Celia led him to a stretch of lawn by a big tree. "Here," she said, "here." And Celia leaned in to him, and she kissed him until something like vertigo, like the world was falling away from him, stole away the nervousness. She brought him down, very gently to the grass, and when she slipped off the turtleneck her skin was pale and her ribs were a lattice above the contracting muscles of her stomach. "It's cold," she said, and the word puffed out of her mouth like a speech bubble.

"Sorry," Ernie said, "I should have brought a blanket." And he felt stupid saying it, but she smiled anyway and so did he.

Ernie tried to take his time; he tried to explore around her, to tease the ridge of her ear with his tongue, to suck gently on her lower lip. "No," she said, "could we just have sex, please?" And this time she didn't smile.

So Ernie entered her carefully and the feeling was rough and unforgiving, but it still felt good somehow, it felt really good, this just sex. He pushed against her and her body gave beneath him like the chassis of an overburdened car. He thrust again and again but as he did, as her body grew softer and pliant beneath him, Ernie felt something reaching into him, something eager and insistent, and the hands were cold, and he could feel himself inside Celia, moving there, but now his spirit—he supposed—was deposited beside his body on the lawn. And they were moving and they were moving, his body and hers, in the obscene gridlock of punctuation you only saw in comic books or Internet chat rooms. The noises she made were different somehow, as if they came from a different throat, a different set of lips, but his were the same, annoyingly familiar. When they stopped, when they were finished, they whispered to each other in the darkness. . . .

Ernie waited. He stayed away, he tried to stay away but the tether wouldn't let him go very far and so he sat on the grass, ten feet away, and he tried not to listen. But he couldn't help it. It was his voice, wasn't it? His voice. Ernie hated the sound of his own voice, hated listening to the message he had set up on his answering machine but this, this voice, it was still his, he knew that, but there was something to it, something deeper, resonant, a gentle purr to the way his body—he—spoke. Ernie had a moment of almost visceral jealousy to hear his voice doing that—a jealousy that went beyond seeing what his body had done with Celia, and how she had responded. This was something else. This went deeper. And Ernie listened. And then, slowly, he felt himself being drawn back into the body, into *his* body, and as he did there was a feeling of recognition, as if he were passing someone in a crowded hallway, someone from high school, someone he had met a long time ago. He opened his eyes, and they were *his* eyes again, and Celia was already looking away.

"Celia," he said, and he realized it was the first time he had said her name out loud. She looked startled.

"It's not—" she started, but then she stopped. Changed her mind. "The guards, they'll be coming. They don't like trespassers." She paused, looking at him uncertainly. "So, hurry, please, if you don't mind."

Ernie slipped into his jeans once again, and he tucked away the flopping penis. A thin layer of sweat slicked his chest and his neck so that the wind suckled heat from him in quiet little bursts. There was a crunch of gravel somewhere in the distance, and he tensed. Celia was moving slowly, and her eyes seemed wide and angry; she was trying to hook up the back of her bra behind her, but she couldn't quite manage to snag the clasps. Her fingers were shaking. There was more crunching—closer this time. Her fingers continued to shake. She arched her shoulders backwards in frustration, a parenthesis with no partner.

"Do you hear it?" she whispered. "Damn it, damn it all!" Ernie leaned in close, caught her fingers in his. Tentatively, she let go and Ernie hooked the bra. The noise was closer now. It couldn't be more than ten, twenty feet. "We have to go *now*. They won't be happy to find me here again. Or you either, I imagine."

The two of them bolted across the lawn, dodging headstones and weaving toward the gate drunkenly. Celia hadn't managed to put her shirt on; her shoulders were like marble, they looked like they belonged in this place, where every word was written in capitals. She charged through the gate, and it rattled and shook with a fierce grinding sound. A thing coming to life. A thing being slammed back into stillness. Then they were out, and they were running, and neither of them knew why anymore but sometime during the process, Ernie found that he had taken Celia's hand, and they were running together, down the deserted street.

"Tell me," he said when they were both leaning up against a brick wall, heaving the air in and out. Celia was giggling, but she was shivering as she giggled. Ernie put an arm around her, and the word came out in a puff of white, evaporating breath between whooping, heavy intakes.

Celia said nothing for a moment, but she seemed to burrow into his chest, pulling the edges of his jacket around her. After a moment: "I don't wuh-w-want to. You . . . you wuh-w-wouldn't believe me." She stuttered, and her teeth clicked together. "It's crazy. Just . . . don't ask."

With the elation beginning to dim in his mind, Ernie felt something curious and sad stealing into its place, and he half-wondered if that thing would push him out as well, leave him standing ten feet away, watching his body comfort and warm this beautiful, beautiful girl. "I'm asking," Ernie said, and he pulled his arms tighter around her as if by doing that he could keep hold of himself, keep his soul firmly anchored, hooked inside his body.

"It's the name, you see—Bunhill," she had told him after that, laughing and shivering as her fingers twitched, wanting to stub out a cigarette she hadn't lit yet, sitting across from him at an late-licensed pub. "They say it's from Bone Hill. They used to dump cartloads of the things here in the sixteenth century, just dropped them on the moor and sprinkled on a bit of soil to could free up the space at St. Paul's." Another giggle. "Everyone wanted to be buried in St. Paul's. They've got Donne over there for Chrissake, and, God, if you've ever read any Donne you'd understand . . . but," she said thoughtfully, "tonight isn't a good night for St. Paul's. For Donne."

She had been beautiful then, but in a completely different way than she had been in the bar. Ernie had wrapped his jacket around her, but he could still see hollow of white flesh beneath her throat, palpitating as she spoke, as she inhaled and exhaled. "I like to fuck the dead, Ernie. That's the truth of it, plain and simple." Her hair glinted a coppery gold where it was plastered in thin lines against her forehead. He said nothing. He tried to imagine his face at this pronouncement. Did he look surprised? He wasn't, not really—he had felt it after all, and there way maybe a bit of relief in knowing, in knowing what it was and in knowing that she was telling him what it was.

"It's out of fashion to like dead white men, did you know that? Dead white men. What a ridiculous thing to call *them*." Her nostrils flared beautifully, opening up like sails. They were marvellous, Ernie thought, that nose was the most beautiful nose he had ever seen.

"Have you ever been in love?" Celia asked suddenly, maybe because of the look on his face, maybe because he still had not spoken. She looked at him in such a way that Ernie almost said "yes" right then because, he knew it, he was in love. He was in love with that nose and that moving throat and the latticework of her ribs covered by his oversized jacket, with the way her fingers twitched, and her eyes stuttered, the way she never looked at him while they were talking, only after, as if she was addressing the speech to someone else and he was just the audience, lost in the shadows beyond the stage. He shook his head.

"No," she said, "I didn't think so. But I'm in love. I'm in love right now." Her voice went soft and intense: "I will tell you that it is the grandest, most glorious thing in the entire world and it never, *ever* goes out of fashion. Love is the one thing that never gets tired or old, not real love, not love like mine. You should be in love . . . Ernie, isn't it? Yes, that's right. Ernie. You should fall in love, Ernie. Go find some nice woman and fall in love. You'll be happier. Whoever it is you're looking for, she's not me. "

And he thought that maybe she was wrong.

That night, Ernie went home and wrote down the things that he had learned from the conversation. Ernie had never really written much, besides the odd scrawl of his phone number on lunchtime receipts and expensive, abstract-looking business cards. He found he liked the appearance of his handwriting, he liked the way it lined up in the neat, authoritative spaces between the lines of the notebook. He liked the way that the words did exactly what he wanted them to do, unlike the words in his mouth, which needed to be coaxed and wheedled. And these are the things Ernie learned:

a)   That "dead white men" was a derogatory term that referred to a purportedly disproportionate academic focus on contributions to historical and contemporary Western civilization made by European males.

b)   That Celia was, herself, an academic of the sort who might know what contribution had or had not been allegedly made to historical and contemporary Western civilization by said dead white men.

c)   That a large number of her colleagues who questioned the sexuality of certain writers were demonstrably wrong, although she did not say which ones—colleagues or writers—but Ernie found himself impressed nonetheless.

d)   That he, Ernie Wheeler, was in love with Celia.

e)   That Celia did not appear in any way to be in love with the aforementioned Ernie Wheeler.

f)   That neither of the two points mattered in the slightest when it came to the possibility of future relations, provided, of course, that they took place at a time and place of her choosing.

St. Nicholas Church, Deptford
CHRISTOPHER MARLOWE
1564-1593

And so Ernie began to read about those dead white men. He knew it was stupid. He knew he should go find a regular girl, a girl of crooked teeth and reasonable attractiveness who nevertheless wanted to sleep with *him*—or at least the reasonable facsimile of him that came with low lighting and alcohol—but all he could think about was *Celia*. And all Celia could think about, it seemed, were *them*. And so Ernie would think about them as well. He would learn what it was they had said, why they had said it, and what special power they had that they could still return, all these years later, and possess the hearts of women like Celia. Ernie had read admittedly little up until this point in his life beyond the odd John Grisham novel found abandoned on the Tube, and he had a sneaking suspicion that the kind of writing he would find in the books of the dead white men would bear very little resemblance to the kind of books you found, dog-eared, hidden underneath discarded newspapers and cardboard burger boxes.

And Ernie discovered that most of what it was the dead white men said had to do with sex. Take Marvell for instance: for all the fancy wordplay, all he really talked about was how to get a woman in the sack, and once in the sack, what she looked like in the sack. Ernie thought there was probably not much difference, really, between Marvell and himself. Not when it came down to it. Not when you stripped away the iambic pentameter.

But as he continued to read, as he scoured the libraries and jumble sales, as he very quietly began to amass his own personal library of books written by the dead white men, he began to see that maybe there was something to it after all. Because he found he wanted to say things to Celia. And the things he wanted to say were things he had never wanted to say to another woman before. He wanted to tell her that the most beautiful sound he had ever heard was the sound of her breathing, and that sometimes his desire was like air and filled his lungs, and he dreamed it might whisper out of his mouth and into her; and sometimes his desire was like water and he knew what it meant to be a fish with the sides of him aching and split open and dying to breathe. He wanted to tell her his desire was shapeless and formless but as potent as a lightning bolt, shot through with colour and a sound that came ten seconds too late. He wanted to tell her his desire, even when it was just the barest spark, had a weight and a substance to it so that he could wrap himself around it over and over again until it grew large and round and pearlescent and perfect.

But he never told her anything like this.

And he wondered what they told her—Marvell and Blake and all the great lovers, all the dead white men that paraded through him and paraded through her.

There had been one night when he had agreed to take her to Greenwich by riverboat. They had shared a glass of overpriced wine while they bobbed along the Thames and watched the city drift by, as self-absorbed and self-deluded as both New York and Palo Alto had been but with a kind of extraordinary, shabby European charm nonetheless. He had paid for the wine. He was used to paying for drinks for women and the habit still came to him naturally, so he over-tipped the bartender, who had the look of the type he normally left a business card with, but he refrained from doing so this time and instead wandered, drink-laden, back to the seat. Celia was still looking out the window, and the last of the evening light slanted down so that it touched the edge of her nose and her lips and her chin. Ernie was actually taken aback by how beautiful she was. He slid the glass up to her, and their fingers brushed. She still did not look at him, but she was humming something soft and sweet under her breath.

For a moment Ernie was terribly happy.

And then he was terribly sad.

He was terribly sad because he knew that Celia was not humming for him, that they would not go to Greenwich with its riverside pleasantness, the postcard architecture of the Old Royal Naval College and the Queen's House, as the bartender might have. They would not walk hand and hand along the curving street with a hundred other couples, buy ice cream or watch the water from the hill of the observatory. Instead they would disembark at the South Dock and then they would walk along the wharf; at some point, Celia would tug at his jacket and they would head south to a churchyard whose gates, he had learned, were adorned with two quite famous skulls-and-bones, whose pictures he had found on the Internet: ghastly things, with long, drawn-out jaws and sadly arched eye sockets. Beyond those gates, there would be a plaque and somewhere nearby, the unmarked grave of Christopher Marlowe. Marlowe, Ernie had learned, had died when he was twenty-nine, and George Peele had called him, "Marley, the Muses' darling," and he had written six plays, at least, that had survived, of which Ernie had liked *Doctor Faustus* best but had sympathised with *Lust's Dominion* most (which he had, after the reading, learned was probably not written by Marlowe after all); or perhaps he had not died at all then, under mysterious circumstances in a Deptford house, perhaps he had been *Shakespeare*, in which case, he had written approximately another thirty-seven plays and Celia was in for a disappointment.

Ernie himself was twenty-nine, and he thought maybe there were a few people who might remember him should he die. And he said, "How many times have you been this way?"

And Celia did not look at him, her eyes locked on the passing buildings.

"Oh, I couldn't tell."

And Ernie asked her, "Do you love him?"

Celia took the glass of wine to her lips, face still beautiful in tableau, now with the wine caught in the light. "I love them all, Ernie. I don't know why, all I know is I do. That's what makes them great men."

POETS' CORNER, WESTMINSTER ABBEY, LONDON
GEOFFREY CHAUCER (1343-1400), ET AL.

And that was when Ernie began to fight back. That was when Ernie decided he had had enough; that although he had now read his way through the majority of the *Norton Anthology of English Literature*, had, in fact, fucked his way through it and half the cemeteries of London and the surrounding counties, he had decided that he wasn't impressed; that all these men, no matter how great they might have been, they were all dead while he, Ernie Wheeler, was most definitely alive, and what was the point of being alive if you felt like a ghost haunting your own body?

For her birthday, they decided to spend seven consecutive nights in Westminster Abbey. It took weeks of planning— oh yes—and Celia's not inconsiderable skill with lockpicks along with, in at least one case, out-and-out bribery. But when all was said and done they had managed to eke out for themselves a period of no more than two hours a night of total privacy in one of the most famous landmarks in England, a place of kings and queens, where only a year ago William and Kate had tied the knot (as well as tying up the traffic of most of downtown London) in a lavish ceremony fit to bankrupt the royal coffers.

On the first night, they began at the cramped and awkward

tumulus of Geoffrey Chaucer—where Ernie had been sure he would brain himself on the low-hanging statuary—and worked their way toward the to the equally awkward if less dangerous marble monument to Edmund Spencer. Over the next several days it was Kipling and Dickens, Dryden and Hardy—Ernie had to be careful, the placement precise, lest the writhing or a sudden change of position evict one great man and usher in another. Ernie felt as if his body had become the King's Cross Station of the English canon, with departures and arrivals scheduled meticulously and choreographed by an invisible traffic director.

But when they came he was ready for them, and when they pushed, he pushed *back*. He had decided he would not go gently into that dark night, and so he raged, he raged against Chaucer and Spenser and Kipling and Dickens and Dryden and Eliot and Hopkins and Hardy and Browning and Tennyson and Drayton and Garrick and once, accidentally, John Roberts, Esq. (the very faithful servant of the right honourable Henry Pelham, Minister of State, died 1776) who hardly put up a fight at all. But the others did. They came with their cold, grasping fingers and their hot, hot passions and their words, most of all, their words—the words that Ernie now knew, had admired, had read for months upon months in preparation. Not just their words, either, but the essays and monographs that had followed upon them, the books of scholars that performed autopsies and dissections and cut them into tiny pieces, and, from those pieces, reassembled them and breathed new life into these oh-so-very dead white men. And the grunts and shrieks of Celia's orgasms sounded off the South Transept, and still Ernie fought, and sometimes he lost, but sometimes, sometimes, he won, and then it was *his* orgasmic joy that rang out alongside hers.

When it was finished, when they lay sweat-soaked and cold, Celia turned to Ernie.

"I'm sorry," she said. "I'm sorry this isn't working." She was beautiful even then, though Ernie could still read the faint etching of "1756-1826" on her arm. She was always beautiful. "It's not you," she said, stopped, and scrunched up her brow, her nostrils flaring as they did when she was deep in thought, a look that Ernie had come to know and to love. "It *is* you, isn't it? That's the problem. It's *you*."

POETS' CORNER, WESTMINSTER ABBEY, LONDON (REPRISE)

Ernie did not see Celia again. He did what any self-respecting man would do. He went back to his apartment and he burned the books, burned all of them, burned the *Norton Anthology*, the *Cambridge Guide*, the *Oxford Illustrated Guide*; he burned *English Literature: Its History and Its Significance for the Life of the English Speaking World*. He burned the very expensive editions of the complete works of William Shakespeare, purchased from a down-and-out graduate student who had decided to give up a life of solitude and learning in favour of dentistry. He burned every book he owned, every book except the notebook he had started after that night in the Bunhill Cemetery.

He returned to the bars and the night clubs, but he did not see Celia there. He took home an ever-widening variety of girls with super blonde hair and super white teeth for it seemed as if that had become the fashion over the last year and, indeed, Ernie found himself thinking that the poor, former graduate student had probably made a career change for the better. Sometimes Ernie would read these women what had been written in the book, and what he had later added to it, after Celia, and they would no longer look at him with that look of sad and subtle disappointment. Their eyes would go delicate and a little shiny, and it would be a look that spoke to him of love, or at least the first stirrings of it, a look that softened the superlative qualities of their super blondeness and made them rather lovely.

And one of these women turned out to be an editor for a very posh literary magazine. Her eyes went extra delicate and extra wide, and when she curled into him that night, after the sex, he decided he liked the sound of her breathing; he liked the sound of her accent which might have been from Sheffield, and, most of all, he liked the way that her body twisted alongside his like an ampersand. The next morning, he made her breakfast; the next month, he proposed; and a year later, his first book was met with general critical acclaim.

He lived happily with his editor—she turned out to be named Eira and her hair, when it grew out, was a mousy brown that Ernie loved for being mousy brown—for several years. His books sold well. They moved into a nicer house in the north end of the city, a sprawling Edwardian monstrosity with several floors which Eira filled with many bookshelves. They bought towels beautifully monogrammed with "E&E" and lived together in the general domestic bliss that sometimes occurs in novel interludes and rarely occurs in real life until Ernie began to realize that when Eira looked at him she did not see him—she did not see Ernie Wheeler—she saw a byline with his name, and she saw an author photo of him posed in a thoughtful position with a cat, and when she told their friends about him it was all in the style of an author biography—which is to say it went something like, "Ernie and I live together in the north end of London in a sprawling Edwardian house filled with bookshelves, monogrammed towels and two cats."

The divorce was messy, but not unprofitable as it gave Ernie enough emotional material for a memoir and three novels.

It was after the second of these novels that Ernie realized he had, by accident, turned into his father, after all. He had the same slightly padded gut, the same slightly receded hairline, and the same lack of investment in the sacraments he had ostensibly subscribed to. It was after the third of these novels that Ernie had a heart attack, like his father, at the age of forty-seven, despite the fact that he had been strong as an ox and healthy as a man could be. As Ernie lay there, gasping, as he felt the cold fingers of something coming from him, the familiar sense of displacement, he thought, *This is it. I know what this is*, and he felt something stealing into him and pushing him out and then—pop!—

There was darkness for a time, and then there was light.

His body pumped furiously away, and her hips ground furiously up into his, meeting him, giving way like the chassis of an overburdened car. She was older than the last time he had seen her. There were streaks of silver in the gold of her hair, and a nest of wrinkles accreting at the corners of her eyes. Her breasts were just a touch heavier than he remembered them having been, suffering more from the ill effects of gravity. Her skin had a spongy feel to it. But, he supposed, his own body was hardly in better condition if he was being honest.

The sound of their grunting and their moaning rounded off the walls of the South Transept, and, afterward, when they were finished and he lay beside Celia, the length and breadth of her body more familiar to him than that of the one he now inhabited, she said, "It's you." And he said nothing. And she said, "I love you, Ernie." And he said nothing. But he took her hand, and they lay there, in the quiet and the coolness, with a set of dates monogramming themselves into their flesh.

[breast]
ETERNAL THINGS

*This aforesaid Africanus took me from there and brought
me out with him to a gate of a park walled with mossy stone;
and over the gate on either side, carved in large letters, were
verses of very diverse senses, of which I shall tell you the full
meaning. . . .*

— Geoffrey Chaucer, *Parliament of Fowls*

I am the way into the doleful city. . . .
Before me nothing but eternal things
Were made, and I shall last eternally.

— Dante Alighieri, *The Divine Comedy*

I meet Stephen at the Turf on one of those rare, hot days in Oxford where the air seems to cling like a fevered hand to your wrist, and the sun is like a blanket smacking a wall, somehow hard and flat and palpable, but not really there at all. There aren't any tables available outside—too many tourists—and neither of us wants to spend an hour sitting inside, with the stale breath of the beer-soaked floors on our necks.

"I can't stand the tourists," Stephen says with the kind of smile worn by the kind of person who hates tourists.

I feel like a tourist. I am checking him out. I am freezing gorgeous little pictures of him in my mind.

He buys us both pints of summer ale. Mine tastes warm and soapy with a sharp, sweet bite of hops underneath it all.

"How is your research going?"

I shrug. Everyone is always asking about research.

"The library's cold. I had to buy a pair of finger gloves."

A year ago I would have given a forty-minute monologue on the importance of scribal dialect shifts on the reception of Geoffrey Chaucer. He waits a beat as if he's expecting more. There isn't anything more. I stare at my hands—chapped even though it's the middle of summer.

"There's a position at St. Andrew's in Middle English, you know." He has one of those polished, posh Oxford accents. "Not tenure track, not exactly. But it's a good position. I'm interviewing for it next week." His words are like beautiful stones, but there isn't any give to them. You couldn't find your way into them, crack them open.

I wonder if I want the position. I wonder if I am jealous. I wonder if I'm in love.

Three weeks ago, I had met a friend from back home in London. She was up for a position at Birbeck College, teaching women's history. Nervous, almost shy, she had whispered to me that after spending twelve hours a day on her dissertation for four years straight, she didn't really want to be an academic, after all. She was going to blow the interview. Move back home to California and find herself a husband. What was feminism if you couldn't choose for yourself?

I think about this as Stephen goes on about linguistic change in the early thirteenth century. He's rehearsing the arguments of scholars—one or two I'd met on conference—tearing into them, but doing it daintily, like he's ripping little chunks off with his teeth, chewing, swallowing. I wished he'd do it properly, just go for the throat and not mind much where the blood spilled, but that's not how it's done in Oxford. I can still tell he enjoys it though, that restrained viciousness: Stephen, with his posh, smooth accent and these beautifully clear eyes, the kind that could be light blue or light green, but always seem silver when you think about them, colourless, like glass. His face is smooth, boyish, with high cheekbones and a good-looking nose.

I wonder what it would be like to kiss him. I don't know what exactly we are doing here. Are we just sharing a pint? Is he scoping out the competition? Am I?

I don't think I will kiss him.

We are two pints in now. The sound moves in Doppler swirls around the courtyard. I drink my ale and imagine kissing Stephen. I imagine the taste of his mouth, perfumed and sharp from the hops. I imagine his lips. I imagine his tongue. I imagine the press of him against me.

"Could you share?" he asks.

"Share what?"

"The list," he says, "of manuscripts that mention the translation of northern English into southern. It might be useful for the interview."

I am thinking about kissing him. He is thinking about the levelling of inflectional endings.

"I thought you wrote on Chaucer," I say.

"Chaucer, well, he's annoyingly popular now, isn't he? I need something esoteric."

"Yes," I say. "I imagine you do."

Stephen smiles. He touches my arm lightly, and now he is guiding me out of the Turf, walking me through the streets of Oxford to a French restaurant on Little Clarendon.

"I'm not sure they'll have room for us," he whispers in my ear, but when we get there the place is half-empty. The menu is full of things I can't really afford, and there's a single wilted rose in the vase on the table.

Stephen samples the shiraz he has ordered for us both. "It's too warm," he says. "We'll keep it though. I hate to send wine back for being the wrong temperature. Unless . . . ?"

I shake my head. The wine is nice in that way bad wine sometimes is.

We both eat our expensive meals. Mine is very good. I assume his is as well. There's some awkwardness over the bill as I hand him a twenty pound note and some change for the tip. I can't tell if it's because I haven't paid enough or because I've paid at all.

We live in the same end of town, out on Cowley Road, which is probably the least posh area of Oxford to live in. There are sports bars and gambling dens. Sometimes people get mugged. A couple of months ago, a woman was dragged to a nearby churchyard and raped. She was about my age.

Stopping in front of Tesco's, there's a kind of magnetism looping its way around us, its bands drawing us closer, closer, tightening concentric circles like ripples on a pond moving in reverse.

His arms are around me, and we kiss after all. His mouth reminds me of the wine, a little too warm, maybe, but still sweet. Our teeth strike once or twice, click awkwardly like heels, and then our mouths are free to make wet circles around each other. *This is nice*, I think.

"We're making a scene," he whispers, smiling, maybe serious, maybe playful.

"I don't mind," I say, and kiss him again, running my hands along his arms.

We stand like that, locked together, for a few more seconds before he says, "Fancy coming back to my place?" I think it's funny, him saying that, like we're an old Victorian couple.

Chaucer was always writing about love. He claimed he was a bad lover. Too fat. Too old. He got into quarrels with the god of love after screwing over poor Criseyde, making her ditch Troilus and take up with Diomedes just as the whole Trojan War went tits up.

But who can blame her, really? Everything loses its edge over time. Sometimes it takes six hundred years. Sometimes it takes six months. Maybe Chaucer was doing her a favour. Maybe he was giving her a way out.

I've been over here for about nine weeks now, researching fourteenth-century manuscripts in libraries across England. I'm consistently amazed by the dullness of it, the way I had been so excited to see my first manuscript, oh, years ago now I suppose, and I still feel that tingle the first time I get one, but it fades quickly now. I can reduce the wonder of touching something six hundred years old to flat boredom in the space of minutes.

I use a plastic ruler I bought at the British Library to measure them, to track their layout, the width of margins, the size of titles, how much space is blank on a page, the shape of punctuation. It all means something, I believe this very firmly, have argued it in countless grant applications, successfully enough to pay for a four-month trip.

It is nine weeks today, and though I've hit the tipping point, crossed the threshold between time marked from departure and time marked until return, I've found a creeping anaesthesia, what Peter, my colleague, calls "numb productivity." I can put in twelve-hour days, easy, but I've lost track of what I'm doing, why I'm doing it. Sometimes when I talk with other graduate students, I can feel that rush again, the way you can fall in love, momentarily, with someone you've begun to get bored with just by hearing another woman talk about him.

I hoped that would happen with Stephen.

My fingers measure his skin—*this many inches from shoulder to shoulder, this many from ear to jaw*. He has a button-down dress shirt on, and I think about tearing it off him, scattering the buttons, but he turns away from me, on the bed, to unbutton them himself where I can't reach. I lie back, rest my hands under my head, like I'm watching clouds, until he's ready again.

Shirtless now, he kisses me and kisses me. Though he's got those beautiful clear-glass eyes, I find them comically lifeless. I want to see something in them, a spark of real desire. He hasn't told me I'm beautiful. I still don't know if he even likes me.

I decide that I don't like him. His voice is too posh, and his scholarship is dry, all those descriptions of marks in manuscripts, like it matters so much.

———————————

I wake up in the middle of the night, and have that instant sense of strangeness, of being in the wrong place. He's snoring next to me. I lean over and kiss him on the shoulder, the neck. He doesn't stir. I wonder if I should go home.

It's late now, or early, and outside Cowley has started to settle into that grim monologue that some cities have after three in the morning: conversations with themselves, the single voice of a dog barking, and then, minutes later, a door shutting. Never two sounds at once.

I feel used to waking up in strange places. I've been moving for nine weeks. It gets easier, each time, to run alongside strangers, find easy, quick friendships to get you through dinner, that stretch of hours between the library and midnight. They could be lonely hours, if I'd let them be lonely. But they seldom are now.

I listen to his breathing, count the measures between inhales, decide he really is asleep.

I realize there's a second set of breaths, and they are not mine.

I'm not terribly alarmed to find there is someone else in the room, I don't know why. I see him sitting in a chair by the corner, an old man, slightly pudgy, hair a salt-and-pepper crow's nest. He has a book open, and large, moist eyes. His breathing is shallow, slightly out of sync with Stephen's, and every now and then he wheezes.

I sit up in the bed, and I pull the covers up to hide my nakedness.

My clothes are strewn about the room, and I can't get at them, not with him in the corner.

Finally, he looks up, and there's something familiar about him, those sardonic eyebrows, the double-pointed beard. He's an old man, and his body creaks like a swing set.

"You're one of them, then?" he says, though that's not quite right. His words have some foreign element to them, the vowels long and stretched like taffy. I can understand them, but they make me think of my undergraduate English class, my first taste of medieval literature, reciting the first ten lines of the *Canterbury Tales* over and over again until Pilcher was satisfied that we had an ear for the rhythm of the language.

"Poetry," Pilcher used to say. "You have to remember that it is poetry. You have to hear the music in it."

I look at the old man: he has Pilcher's watery eyes, veins on his hand as thick and purple as rain-soaked worms. I nod.

"It's a shame," he continues in that taffy-stretched speech of his. "You seem like such a nice girl. You should be out doing better things with your life."

"I'm not a nice girl."

He chuckles, and this makes me absurdly happy. I'm not sure why yet, though I think I'm starting to realize by this point, to get past the strangeness of this. Because I recognize him, somehow. "Did you read his dissertation? *He* is not a nice boy, never was. He was dreadful as a student, cutting down his classmates. He never loved it."

He runs his hand along the book like he's smoothing a child's hair. "Little prick," he says.

It is Stephen's dissertation, the leather-bound kind rich students have made when they graduate.

"Are you much like him?" the old man asks.

I shrug. "I might be one day. In a few years." But when I think about it I know that won't be true.

"What's your argument then?" the old man asks.

I start to tell him about the form of medieval manuscripts, how in the early fourteenth century there's so much experimentation because the writers didn't have vernacular models to draw on, how it was important to find a context for English that placed it alongside French and Latin, somehow distinct but somehow linked to other literatures circulating in the period.

I tell him about the translation of scribal dialects.

I tell him about the levelling of inflections.

I falter.

"You started something," I say. "Something huge. How did you do it? How did you make something that would last so long? Something that would send people like him and I scrabbling after you with our rulers and our research and our righteousness?"

"Eternal things," he says with a little smile. "It matters then, does it? How big we drew our letters, how we ruled our margins?"

"A little," I say. "Maybe."

There's a long pause, and I listen to the sound of Stephen breathing. I find myself wanting to touch him.

And then finally, I ask, "Are you ever scared?"

He seems surprised at this, and he squints. I had forgotten how bad his vision must be, working in near darkness; glass for windows was still expensive, and candles too. Though he had written about reading late into the night, I remembered that.

"I was once." He pauses again, touches the book on his lap. "But now I feel like I'm just waiting. There's a door, a gateway I was shown once, with words written in black and gold. 'Through me men go into that blissful place.'"

"'Through me men go,'" I say half musingly, "'Unto the mortal strokes of the spear.'"

He nods, looks pleased.

"You wrote about it."

"Two sets of words, one doorway. I thought I dreamed it. But Africanus said the words weren't for me, that I could pass through the gate and never mind the black and gold, I wasn't the one they were for." He looks tired. I think he must be very old, if age means anything to him, but I think it does, it must. Even for the dead.

He stands up from the chair then, and I can see black robes like a judge's, or a shroud. They rustle as they touch the ground.

"I was never a very good lover," he continued, "too busy with books when I was young, never had quite the temperament for it. I wrote books on the subject, certainly, but when it came to that gate, he said it wasn't for me, the good or the bad, the well of grace or the prison of love. I don't think he meant to be cruel. Meant to help me, actually, to make it easier."

"Did it?"

"I'm here now, aren't I? Not lonely, exactly. It's a kind of curse, I think, though Lord knows what I did to deserve it."

"I don't think we ever really deserve the things that happen to us," I say. "They just happen." I'm surprised to find that there are tears on my face. Geoffrey notices, he stops pacing, comes to the side of the bed.

"You don't need to be afraid." He takes my hand, and I can feel the parchment toughness of his skin, brittle, like it had been soaked in lye and stretched over his knuckles.

"I do." I sniff, hate myself for it. "It's not enough, all these books, they don't mean anything. They don't tell me anything anymore."

"I know," he says. "That's the way of it. Always. For all the ones who came before you."

He stands, and I cling to his hand a little longer, because I can already see him starting to fade around the edges, like smudged ink, and I don't want him to go just yet. I'm not ready to see him go. I want him to tell me things, I have so many questions, but I clutch that hand and think, *He's just a tired old man, and he's not allowed to go home, after all these years, he is so far from home.* I feel sad, and I let go of his hand, let him drift away. But before he does, he kisses me on the forehead, and his breath is sweet and warm.

"Be well, my darling. Live well, die well, love well."

And then he is gone.

I lie in Stephen's bed, feel its strange give beneath me, the lumps I don't recognize, and I let myself cry gently. Then I pull away the sheets, meaning to get up, to find my bra and panties. Stephen murmurs something, and his arm snakes around me. I let him cling to me for a moment, remembering his hands on my breasts, earlier that night. I feel sad, sadness has soaked into every pore of me, like all that ale spilt onto the floor of the pub.

Stephen had been thorough, earlier, almost mechanical about the whole thing, but in a way that showed very much that he knew what he was doing, and I wasn't the first girl to end up in his bed.

The heat of him lying against me is both delicious and oppressive. I want to kiss him, feel a little less hollow inside.

His hands had been everywhere, and now, I run my own hands against my breasts. I feel the lumps there, just beginning, and am glad he hadn't found them. I am tired of the things people say to me when they find out.

I wait, breathe in the night air, warm and whispering with smells from the street. I want to be out there, not in here, and I move to collect my things, and I feel the arm slip away into the warm space I left in the mattress.

It is then I stop, something catching my eye, glinting, from around the doorframe. There are words written in letters of black and gold, old words.

"Through me men go into that blissful place." And then: "Through me men go unto the mortal strokes of the spear."

The breath catches in my lungs, and buzzes around like a fly, a trapped bird, until I let it out in one long stream.

"You knew, didn't you, you old bastard?" I whisper.

I am naked, but the air is warm around me, and I go to the door. I think about what he—the old ghost— had said about the well of grace, and the doorway not being for him. I think about Stephen. In the morning, he might wonder where I have gone. No, he had his interview, would be off on the train to St. Andrew's tomorrow, he had said that. He wouldn't wonder at all, would probably be happier.

I don't know which place I want to go to, the blissful one or that other, the words of gold or the words of black. And then I remember, they're both really the same place, there's only one door, even if there are two sets of writing.

I step through.

THIS FEELING OF FLYING

Meanwhile:

You awake afraid—terrified even—to the feeling of the plane bucking around you, your head pressed against the window and your immediate view a stomach-clenching shot of thin cloud cover and the thousands-foot drop to a patchwork of green and yellow farmland below. It takes a moment for your nerves to calm, for the adrenaline pumping into your system to fade. You are a thinker, Elspeth loved you for your brains first, but at this moment you are tired. Sleep drags at the edges of your vision: sleep, a palpable weight, a dark bag dropped over your eyes, tightened at the throat. You do not quite remember where you are, what the stretch of land underneath you might have been. Your body is trained to a different time zone, but that has been left behind ages ago.

"Sometimes it feels as if the world is catching closer around us," a voice murmurs from beside you, strangely accented. "The entire world pressing so close, so close. It is as, yes, two fingertips touching that have been long apart."

You do not recognize the voice, do not remember the grizzled man it belongs to: skin like olive wood, layers of colours, light and dark, pressed together in the folds of his wrinkles; hair black shot through with silver, joints a collection of unrolled dice, things you might play knucklebones with.

"Shush now, *pouli*, it will pass, do not trouble him." A younger one, cut from the same cloth as the first, but broad-shouldered, young in a way you don't feel. "I'm sorry, he does not like to fly."

You nod. You don't like to fly either. The Valium buzz is like a neural hypnotic and every part of you is singing, but you can feel the crash coming, maybe it's already there. You try to stretch your legs but your knees crowd against the tray table in front of you.

"It is hardest for the old men," the guy says, and you wonder if maybe he is talking about you. Your hair has just the beginnings of grey, but who is he, really, to judge? The young have a different way of counting age.

"Sure," you say, "of course, it is." But you don't quite know what you're talking about. He flashes you a smile, the young one—the old one is holding his head like he's nursing a hangover, and you think to yourself, *It must be hard for him, for all the old men.*

The young one winks, and there is something strange about it. He stretches generously, unbuckles himself from the seat. He places both hands—his delicate fingers with black wiry hair—over the old one's gnarled tree-root hands. He kisses the old man affectionately on the head.

You find yourself wanting to look away, but the close proximity makes this little piece of human drama uncomfortably close. You don't want to watch. You watch anyway. The old man looks up, for a moment, and there is something terribly sad in his eyes. The young man makes his way down the aisle, body pantherine in slim-cut jeans, a plain white t-shirt that showed off the solid muscles beneath. You leaf through a brochure on cheap watches, garden furniture, deluxe pet carriers. Who buys this stuff, you wonder—who needs it?

Your eyes flick up, and he is whispering into the ear of an airline stewardess—the generically well-turned-out type—and you see his hand touch lightly against the small of her back, see her shiver as if something warm and sweet runs down her spine, see her eyes follow him behind the first-class curtain, see her trail after a moment later, tentative, excited.

"My son is too young, I cannot watch him but feel myself age," the old man mumbles, lips looking as if they long for a cigarette, something to smoke. You put away the brochure. "He had two mothers, that is the problem, he likes the insides of women so much. *Fah*,"—you think he might spit but he doesn't—"two mothers is too many for any boy to grow up properly and now he is half-woman himself, no beard, hairless all the way down I swear, like a little girl."

You are used to the rants of old men on planes, young men, the ones who have so much bulk they spill over onto the seats beside them, full of noise and boisterous good cheer and general ungraciousness; the children screaming as their ears grow full and painful, fit to burst. One boy had told you—mischievous, bored, rebellious, and undeserving of the look of disdain he wore—that he didn't need the plane to fly, that he could step outside into the wide-open air and his spread wings would take him higher than any fucking plane, higher than God. You asked him why he paid for a ticket. The boy had shrugged, scratched at his shoulder, and turned away, bored already with the conversation.

"I fear for him, all those women. He moves too easily, he doesn't fear women the way he should. A woman can hurt you in so many ways."

You find yourself nodding at that, thinking about your wife, Elspeth, and how much she hates it when you leave. You tell her it is for business, you tell her that you have responsibilities, and sometimes she smiles and sometimes she turns away but you can always tell how hurt she is. Her hurt is its own knife, but you go anyway, whenever they offer, wherever they offer, because as much as the knife cuts, you hate to be in one place for too long. You are afraid of what will happen if you stay on the ground.

The airline stewardess is slipping out between the curtain to the first-class cabin, a dreamy look on her face, knees drunk. The young man appears behind her, a dark shadow, the two almost the same shape, one the silhouette of the other. He is smiling. You turn to the old man.

"Where are you going?" Your first words. The old man looks up, startled.

"I go to the new land, the land of promise." The old man pauses, lips forming around the phantom cigarette, breathing. "The land will not keep its promises. The land is sick. The people are sick. Nothing works properly anymore, the universe is broken, it broke with the towers, when they burned." Another pause, and then an intense look. You flick your gaze away, sorry you have engaged. "Do you know, do you see it?"

Eyes to the window. You stare at the wing of the plane, the perfect geometric shape; you imagine the boy in the air beside it, wonder if his arms would be so smooth, so perfect, or if he would plummet like a stone. Your face so close to the glass, the space is not so much—the distance between sitting, safe, here, listening to an old man ramble and the sudden drop. No more than a handspan of inches. There is a kind of magic to it, that the plane should remain in motion at all.

"I see it," you say, and you do, you really do. The universe has cracked like an egg and out has flown these magic birds, these things unbound by gravity. "Do not leave the plane, do not ever leave it."

"Ah," the old man says, "you do see it then, you are wise,

more so than my boy who loves chaos and broken things and magic that does not work the way you intend it."

You awake to a distant chime. The air is stale, breathed too many times by too many people. You can feel the time now not by your own circadian rhythms but by the murmur of restlessness in the people around you, legs that were once still now kick ferociously against seatbacks, feet twitch in the aisles.

There is a woman beside you when you wake and she is the most beautiful woman in the world. You do not wonder about the old man and his son. You may have left them several countries back. "Do not get off the plane," you told the old one, but you know now that no one gets off the plane. The plane is always in motion. It does not land.

But you do not think about this. You do not think about Elspeth at home, waiting for you, her fingers clutching a dress whose hem she has made threadbare with pulling and plucking and mending. You do not think about anything except for the beautiful woman next to you. Beautiful women have their own way about them, and you have not sat beside many on the flight; they tend to travel in pairs, in packs, protected, loved. Tickets for two, headed to exotic locations where the sun sleeps for half the time as the rest of the world. But she is alone.

You find yourself looking at her slantwise, slyly out of the corner of your eye—you *are* clever, after all. But then your gaze is drawn out the window, the flashing light on the tip of the wing and darkness all around. Slantwise, you look again, but find she is looking outside, straining a little in her seat.

A thrill of delight. You look at her looking out the window, meet her eyes as they slide back, half-guilty at being caught out.

And then she smiles, just once, and you think you might try speaking. There is an intimacy to planes, and you are allowed to speak, if you are seated together. "Do you see the world out there?" you say, playfully. "I do not remember it. Tell me what it is like."

The woman looks surprised, and she knits her perfect ivory brow and she looks at you with her perfect blue eyes, and then she smiles—a second time!—as if no one has spoken to her in a very long time. "There is no world out there," she says. "It has already come undone."

"I thought as much," you say. You like the way it feels to have her perfect blue eyes on you as you imagine all men do, and so it makes you foolish. "How will it be made again?"

"From the darkness," she answers. "From the pieces that do not fit together."

You are feeling giddy now, and your legs twitch—you have ridden in the plane for many hours and the blood has pooled beneath your knees and something tugs at your synapses. But she is there, and that brings a mad calmness to you. You love her almost immediately, find it impossible not to. She is not like Elspeth. You know that she must understand planes and flights and the fear of staying in one place. She is here, isn't she? You are faithful to Elspeth and you have never cheated, not on any of the trips. Travel is not made for that kind of escape. But she is beautiful and you are falling, and you can see that she can see this happening to you. She smiles sadly. A third time.

"Do not look at me like that, *anasa mou*," she whispers.

"You are the most beautiful woman in the world," you find yourself saying, because it is true and she is seated next to you so you are allowed to speak to her. Your hands and your voice and every part of you tremble.

"Have you not been told? A beautiful woman ruins many things."

"You make the world come alive," you breathe. "There was no world until you were in it, and we are all kept aloft by your will alone, you are magic, fire, the doing up of everything."

"I am a broken tower," she whispers, and her perfect blue eyes close. She touches your wrist, just once, but you feel every bone in your body jump, steel filaments when a magnet passes, reorienting.

"Tell me," you beg, because you can, because the magic of the airport, of the ticketing offices, of the blind fate of the universe has seated *her* next to *you*. And because the laws of airports and ticketing offices and blind fate have done this, she answers you.

"I grew up by the sea, I remember when the waters of the world were everything, and there was no dry land to be found. My mother told me that when my father came to her, he was a swan and he was beautiful. Her eyes would go shallow with the love of him, and her mouth would make an expression I do not know but some men might call it love, but it was not that, love is not that look. She would comb my hair, and she would sing, and sometimes her face went like that until she was no longer looking at me—*through* me— but, fingers running through my hair over and over again, I would wonder about him.

"One day when I was young, I came across a swan by a lake, and I called to it and it came awkwardly, for birds are not meant to walk on the land, but I was afraid of the water. And its neck danced like a snake and its body was a kettle balanced on tiny legs, and the circles around its eyes were dark. It laid its head in my lap, and I stroked the fine feathers of it, and I thought that perhaps what I was feeling might be love. And we lay there, the swan and I, until I tugged away the child-skirts my mother dressed me in, and I felt the feathers on my thighs, and I wondered if it was how my mother had felt.

"Does it matter so very much to be beautiful?" She pauses and her voice is the most beautiful voice in the world so you are sad to hear it end, although you have understood very little of what she says, not really, for you are not in love, you are transfixed.

"I would cradle you in my arms," you whisper, and you don't know why or what you are saying, and you have never felt like this before. It is not the way you love your wife. It is like madness. "I would crack the world for you."

"There is no true love in the world, and that is the thing I know, *anasa mou*, that we might lie together and I might stroke your hair, but then there shall be the fire, the devastation, and you shall hate me for my love."

"I would swallow the moon," you whisper. "I would make of my bones a house for you to live in."

"When I returned home, I watched myself in the mirror as I brushed my hair, and I waited to grow pregnant but I never did, and my eyes were never like my mother's. It was not love."

"I would make you ugly to be mine so that others would not look on you," you whisper. "I would cut off the ears of your enemies."

"And so I am here because the world is drifting faster apart and I am filled with so many holes now, so many absences, pieces that fit together badly like the swan with his kettle-body and his slender neck. I will fly and fly until the world rebounds and we are all drawn more and more tightly together, like a flock of starlings, and the pieces of me are one, a thing beyond love, beyond attraction, a thing whole and at rest."

She touches your wrist once again, and you grow silent, as if there is a radio inside your head that someone has just switched off. You feel as if you have been trapped in amber, that time has frozen you in a single moment, but then it releases, you are through it, and the people around you are twitching, yawning, stretching. A tray filled with peanuts and crackers trundles past you. The woman next to you is beautiful, but you have seen beautiful women before, and you somehow wish you were sitting somewhere else. Beautiful women make you uncomfortable, they make you feel older than you are, unlovely, vaguely ashamed.

"You are a sweet man," she says, "but the end has come and gone again, and there is no room for love."

You do not know how long you have been flying for. It is one of those slow patches when all the windows are shut, and it seems as if it could be minutes or hours before dawn. But when you lift the edge of the window neither light nor darkness spills onto your knees—instead, it is as if you have not lifted the window at all.

"Don't bother looking out there, son," a voice behind you remarks, a sluggish, molasses-thick voice, but pleasant to listen to, comforting. "Nothing to see anymore."

You try to turn in your seat, but there is not quite enough space to do so and the seatbelt light is still illuminated as if you are between bouts of turbulence. Perhaps that is what woke you. You knuckle the arms of your seat but nothing happens, and the plane is still, a solidly moving body.

"How long have we got left?" you ask companionably. The seats beside you are empty and you find yourself missing the company.

"Depends on your perspective, I suppose," he chuckles. "Some people would tell you that our time has already run out. We've hit the—what's it?—tipping point. Disaster's imminent. Disaster's already come and gone. How long have any of us got left? Don't make a lick of difference."

You like his bluff cheerfulness, and though you cannot see him, you see an image building itself up in your mind: a wide, red face, one of the few kinds that might wear a moustache and make it look practical. He sounds like he might from the south, some country's south, where gentility and politeness are bred into the bone. He is the kind of man you wouldn't share a beer with, not knowing any men like him well enough to do so, but the kind of man, should you see him in a bar, that you might wish you could share a beer with.

You check your watch, but find it isn't working. The hands have stopped.

"Where is the plane going?" you find yourself asking because you discover you do not know and, with his bluff cheerfulness, he must know and he must tell you.

"Plane's not going so much as it's coming, son. It's coming home. Where else ought a man be flying to?"

"Please," you say. "I don't want to go home."

"Everyone wants to go home. That's what home is. Home is the place you want to be coming to, even when you wish you were leaving it. The world is only so big and a man can only travel so far before he finds himself curving back to where he started from."

"No," you say to him, and you are glad you cannot see him because you are afraid, suddenly, that if you were to turn, you would not see the man you want to see in your mind; you would see something else: a tornado, a bloodslick, a breath of ash, something that was polite only as a mask to violence. "Home is where things stand still. Home is where life is rooted, and restricted, where you cannot move at all."

"Oh boy," he says, "have you got it wrong, son!" He laughs, slaps his knee like the sound of a thunderclap. "Where we are now—with seats pressed close together, and belts locking us in—this is where you can't move, this is where the moving happens for you." His voice goes low and soft, like a knife sliding in below the rib. "You can't stay here. You can't keep us here. They say I should not touch you, but I will, boy, I will rip you to pieces. There is nothing out there, nothing for a century's worth of miles, but there is *nothing in here*."

You are not surprised at what he says, not surprised but it scares you nonetheless because you know that he is not lying: you know that you are keeping them here, all of them, but you do not know why and you do not know how. He is so close to your ear: you know the words are only for you to hear, and you can smell the scent of him like cordite, like firecrackers, but still you do not want to move, you do not want to let him free. When the turbulence comes, your knees kick into the side of the plane, and your head knocks back against the seat. He is gone, whoever he was, and you grip the chair until your fingers hurt and the plane stops shuddering, but the light does not click off, and so you do not move. The belt presses against your stomach, jamming against your hip bones. You are happy for the safety it offers

It is the boy now. You remember him from the beginning of the flight, when he would not move his legs to let you slip into your seat, when the music from his headphones was so loud that it slid past his ears and into yours. This is the principal rule of air travel: you must never cross the boundaries from Seat A to Seat B, from Seat B to Seat C. These are sacrosanct territories, little floating islands. But the boy next to you does not know this, and does not care. He reminds you of your own son, Thomas—Tommy, he wants you to call him but you don't like making names easier to swallow so you never do—he's about the same age, with the same almost-rebellion in his face.

"You're still here," the boy says, flicking a meteor shower of glances up and down your body. "You don't think, maybe, it's time now?"

"Time for what?" you ask, but you know he won't answer you properly. Thomas never answers properly. He mumbles, he speaks out of the corner of his mouth, and, as a result, everything he says comes at you from an oblique angle, catches you off-guard. But lately, Thomas hasn't been speaking to you at all. You think, sometimes, that maybe he doesn't recognize you, you've been gone so long, and when you look at him you don't recognize yourself in his face. It is like he has been cut fully from the cloth of Elspeth.

"Time to blow this popsicle stand," he says, "time to shake things up. Time to, you know, get the party started— let 'er roll, let 'er roll."

You turn away. He is not Thomas. You don't have to listen to him.

"Don't be like that, pops," he says. "This is how it always goes: the world comes crashing down and then, zip, it's all back to the beginning again. Some of 'em, they just dragged on and on until the aches in their joints had aches in their joints, if you catch my drift. But not me, no sir, hot and fast—that's how I flew, and when I went down—" He makes machine gun noises and jogs his hands as if he is firing at German bombers. "—well, it was just, you know, blammo, down in smoke and flames!" He nudges you in the arm, another invasion of space. "This is how it's gotta be, it's why you're here, pops, it's why we're all here. When you've got to the end, all you can do flip her 'round and head straight back to the beginning again."

More silence from you. He hums a few bars from "Got the World on a String" and you try to imagine this wiry kid listening to Frank Sinatra, but the image doesn't work.

"Well," he says after some time, after the silence has become a living thing between you. "My old man was the same. He thought he wanted to go, thought he wanted to get out of the rat race, his own private prison block, and so he sent me out. Maybe I blew it, maybe I didn't. Maybe I just found the only way to go was up"—he paused—"until, of course, the only way to go was back down again.

"You treat your son well? You listen to him? You know, back then—back when you were on the ground?"

You try to think about Thomas, but now that you focus on him, you can't really remember the sound of his voice. Did you listen? Did he ever speak? It seems like back then, you, Elspeth and Thomas lived in silence.

"Nah, you don't know, do you? Of course, you wouldn't. It's all slipping away from you now. Memory, place, space, it's all just a cloud and we are driving on through—driving past, leaving it in the dust."

Yes, you think, that is exactly how it feels. You are flying into oblivion. And you don't want it to stop just yet. You want to leave them behind. You want the last time you saw them, when Elspeth walked you to the door, and Thomas handed you your suitcase, neither speaking, both tight-lipped, same-faced, to feel like an ending.

"I'll tell you a secret," he whispers to you, arms jostling alongside yours. "This is an old story, so old that my father told it to me back when it meant something different. Once upon a time, there was no earth, nothing, zip, zilch, *nada*, and the universe was empty except for, you know, all these birds, thousands of the things just zooming through the ether, through this infinite sky. Anyway, the lark, his old man bites the dust—metaphorically, 'cause there ain't no dust, that's the point—but because there isn't any earth they don't know what to do with the body. So, finally the lark, he buries his father in the back of his head, that's the only real estate around.

"My pops used to tell me that was the beginning of memory, that was how you honoured your elders, back then. You respected them. You kept 'em with you. But you know what I think?" He pauses, took a breath and let it whistle out through his teeth. "I think that was the beginning of forgetting. Because there ain't no voice you can ignore better than the one in your own damn skull, isn't that right?

"The others," he says, looking away now, that teenage boredom started to creep back into his voice, "they want you to land this thing, to let it all start again—you've carried them this far, sitting in the back of your skull, all these stories from the old country, all the dreams and visions and old gods and new gods you've picked up along the way—but I say, why let it start again? Who needs all these stories? Fly on, my friend, fly on. Nowhere to go but up, nowhere to go but nowhere at all, never touch the ground, isn't that right?"

The plane is not empty, but it feels empty now: darkness shrouds row upon row of seats that could be filled with ghosts for all you know. But this thought does not frighten you—thoughts seldom do, you've been a thinker all your life, known for your brains. The thought of ghosts sinks comfortably into your mind, where you let it roll around like a dried seed in a pod, rattling away, but comfortable. You try to think back on Elspeth and the boy, Thomas, but surely they have gone now, surely they are dead and buried somewhere, or else they are alive and the house is filled with the noise of a new man—husband, father—they would not wait so long as you have been flying; you know they would not wait because they told you, then, that there would be no more waiting. Ten years was enough, more than enough time to come home. But you do not want to go home, and you are happier this way, with them happy. Or dead. But silent, at least, in your thoughts.

You think on beginnings, and endings, and the many stories you have told yourself, stories as a way of remembering, stories as a way of forgetting.

You think the boy, the one beside you, is probably right. There is a way to end this, and it involves letting yourself touch the ground, letting the universe begin again, and time move forward as it has surely been moving backwards since the flight began. Away from disintegration.

All around you are the hungry eyes of the maybe-ghosts. The old man and his son, the one who was not afraid enough. The beautiful woman. The dangerous one with violence at his centre. You know what it is they want of you.

But it is so beautiful, this feeling of flying, of moving and standing still, the need not to decide, the need not to begin again. So you close your eyes and you dream the old gods powerless, fastened into their seats, waiting upon you and your clever brain to let them free. Maybe, you think, maybe soon you will touch down and feel the tarmac grinding underneath the wheels of the plane. Maybe soon you will face the homecoming, and that moment when you search the faces of the crowd gathering at the exit, and know, for sure, what you have lost. If you have lost anything at all. If there was anything to lose.

You take a breath, let the air fill your lungs until you feel weightless, adrift, flying.

Maybe soon.

Not yet.

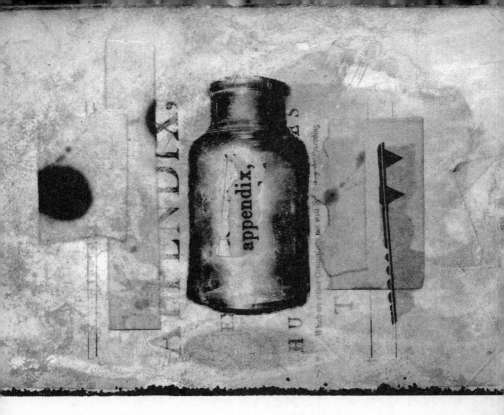

[Ejorum gratia est hoc opusculum]

ACKNOWLEDGEMENTS

The encouragement, companionship, praise, support, cursing, feeding, browbeating and handholding of many people have made this book possible. First among these must be Sandra Kasturi who has been a constant source of inspiration, dinner and good advice (all of which have directly contributed to the making of this book) and Robert Shearman—you showed me what it can be like to be a writer. I owe you so much for giving me the confidence to write this. And, of course, thanks go to the good folk of ChiZine Publications—Brett Savory, Matt Moore, Erik Mohr, Sam Beiko, Danny Evarts, and Beverly Bambury—for being the best kind of family and makers of fine, fine books. Also, to

Chris Roberts who has worked tirelessly to make this a truly gorgeous book. Lastly, Laura Marshall, who always deserves special mention and often gets the final word. If one person has helped me survive the mayhem of my life then it is you.

Further thanks go to the following people for kindnesses shown and friendships given: Nancy Baker; Bob Boyczuk; Peter Buchanan; Tony Burgess; Mike Carey; Julie Czerneda; Gemma Files; Ben Fortescue; Amanda Foubister; Alexandra Gillespie; Sèphera Girón; Emma Gorst; Simon Horobin; Andrew House; Michael Johnstone; John Langan; Claude Lalumière; Tim Lebbon; Kari Maaren; my parents Rosemary and Roy; my brother Justin, his wife Valerie, and their children Caitlyn and Miles; Clare Marshall; Jennifer McDermott; Yves Menard; Stephen Michell; David Nickle; Kathleen Ogden; Stephen Powell; Chris Pugh; Sophie Roberts; Michael Rowe; Tom St. Amand; Paul Tremblay; Halli Villegas; Daniel Wakelin.

Finally, I would like to thank the staff and instructors of Clarion West 2012: Mary Rosenblum; Stephen Graham Jones; George R. R. Martin; Connie Willis; Kelly Link; Gavin Grant; Chuck Palahniuk; Les Howle; and Neile Graham. And, of course, my fellow classmates: Brenta Blevins (earthy rum); Bryan Camp (sweet gin); Indrapramit Das (dark vodka); Sarah Dodd (sweet port); M. Huw Evans (scotch); Laura Friis (brandy); James G. Harper (isinglass); Alyc Helms (slivovicz); James Herndon (cognac); Nik Houser (Turkish vodka); Henry Lien (huangjiu); Georgina Kamsika (red wine); Kim Neville (tequila); Cory Skerry (also tequila!); Carlie St. George (bitter whiskey); Greg West (astringent liqueur); Blythe Woolston (strong whiskey). You all taught me so much, with such kindness, grace and good humour.

I gratefully acknowledge the Canada Council for supporting a draft of *Hair Side, Flesh Side* through the Grants for Creative Writing Program, the Ontario Arts Council for a Writers Works in Progress Grant and the Toronto Arts Council for a Level Two Writers Grant. I would furthermore like to thank the Social Sciences and Humanities Research Council for their support of my academic research into

English manuscripts of the fourteenth century through a Canada Graduate Scholarship and a Michael Smith Foreign Supplement for travel to Oxford, the undertaking of which provided much inspiration for this book.

A version of "A Texture Like Velvet" was published as "Skin" in *Future Lovecraft* (December 2011, Innsmouth Free Press). This story was inspired by a brilliant talk given by Bruce Holsinger at the New Chaucer Society Congress in Siena in 2010, which was published as "Parchment Ethics: A Statement of More Than Modest Concern," *New Medieval Literatures* 12, 2010.

AUTHOR

Aurora-winning poet Helen Marshall (*manuscriptgal.com*) is an author, editor, and self-proclaimed bibliophile. As a PhD candidate at the University of Toronto's prestigious Centre for Medieval Studies, she has presented widely in England, Canada and the United States on topics ranging from the width of medieval punctuation to fourteenth-century romances.

In 2011, she published a collection of poetry with Kelp Queen Press called *Skeleton Leaves* (*skeleton-leaves.net*) that "[took] the children's classic, [stripped] away the flesh, and [revealed] the dark heart of Peter Pan beating beneath." The collection was jury-selected for the Preliminary Ballot of the Bram Stoker Award for excellence in Horror, nominated for a Rhysling Award for Science Fiction Poetry, and won the Aurora Award for best Canadian speculative poem.

Her poetry and fiction have been published in a range of magazines including *The Chiaroscuro*, *Paper Crow*, *Abyss & Apex*, the long-running *Tesseracts* series and an anthology of Lovecraftian horror. She is a graduate of Clarion West 2012.

[about the]

Artist

Chris Roberts is Dead Clown Art. Among other things, he is a freelance artist, using mixed media and found objects to mask his utter lack of creative ability. Guess that also makes him a con artist. Chris has made mischief for Another Sky Press, Orange Alert Press, Dog Horn Publishing, Black Coffee Press, Kelp Queen Press, PS Publishing and ChiZine Publications; for authors Will Elliott, Andy Duncan, Tobias Seamon, Seb Doubinsky, Ray Bradbury and the wildly talented Helen Marshall. He also made the list of recommendations ("long list") for the 2012 British Fantasy Awards.

Chris would like to thank Helen for (foolishly) trusting him with the gobs of inside artwork he made for her stunning collection which you hold in your hands. This collection is something special because Helen is something special. Thanks also to his pretty and "planetary" wife, Kelly, and their cute and clever daughter, Amelia; for putting up with his moody hijinks, and for giving him the time needed to make all the silly things that he makes that were most certainly not here before.

You can watch Chris misbehave online at *deadclownart.com*, or on Twitter *@deadclownart*.

EMB
RACE
THE
ODD

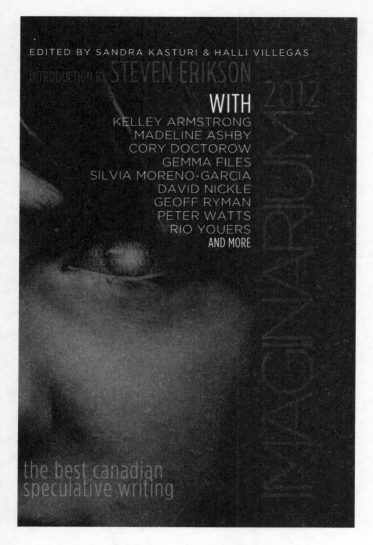

EDITED BY SANDRA KASTURI & HALLI VILLEGAS

INTRODUCTION BY STEVEN ERIKSON

WITH
KELLEY ARMSTRONG
MADELINE ASHBY
CORY DOCTOROW
GEMMA FILES
SILVIA MORENO-GARCIA
DAVID NICKLE
GEOFF RYMAN
PETER WATTS
RIO YOUERS
AND MORE

the best canadian
speculative writing

IMAGINARIUM 2012:
THE BEST CANADIAN SPECULATIVE WRITING
EDITED BY SANDRA KASTURI & HALLI VILLEGAS

AVAILABLE JULY 2012
FROM CHIZINE PUBLICATIONS AND TIGHTROPE BOOKS

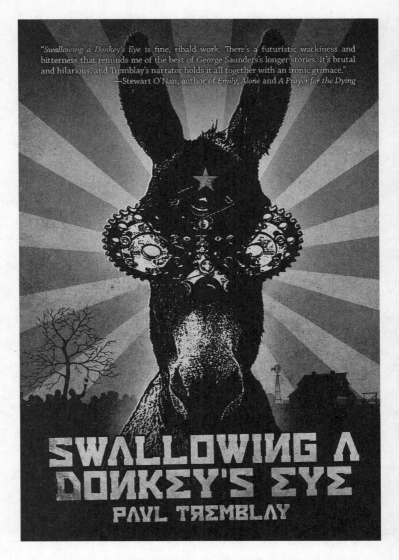

SWALLOWING A DONKEY'S EYE

PAUL TREMBLAY

AVAILABLE AUGUST 2012
FROM CHIZINE PUBLICATIONS

978-1-926851-69-3

CHIZINEPUB.COM

BULLETTIME
NICK MAMATAS

AVAILABLE AUGUST 2012
FROM CHIZINE PUBLICATIONS

978-1-926851-71-6

THE INDIGO PHEASANT
VOLUME TWO OF LONGING FOR YOUNT
DANIEL A. RABUZZI

AVAILABLE SEPTEMBER 2012
FROM CHIZINE PUBLICATIONS

978-1-927469-09-5

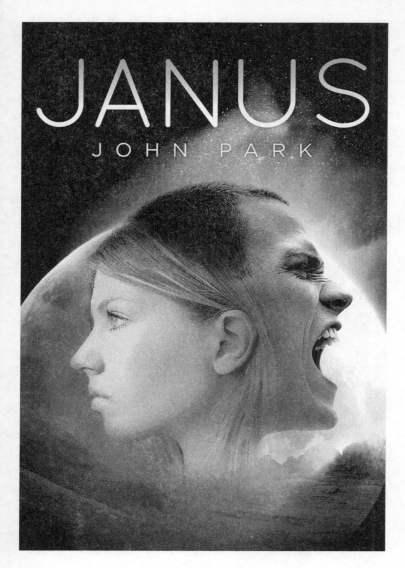

JANUS

JOHN PARK

AVAILABLE SEPTEMBER 2012
FROM CHIZINE PUBLICATIONS

978-1-927469-10-1

REMEMBER WHY YOU FEAR ME
THE BEST DARK FICTION OF ROBERT SHEARMAN

AVAILABLE OCTOBER 2012
FROM CHIZINE PUBLICATIONS

978-0-927469-21-7

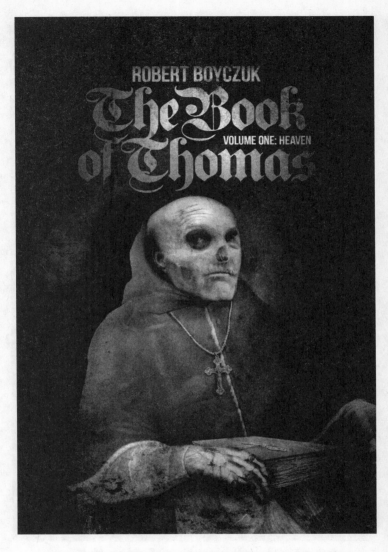

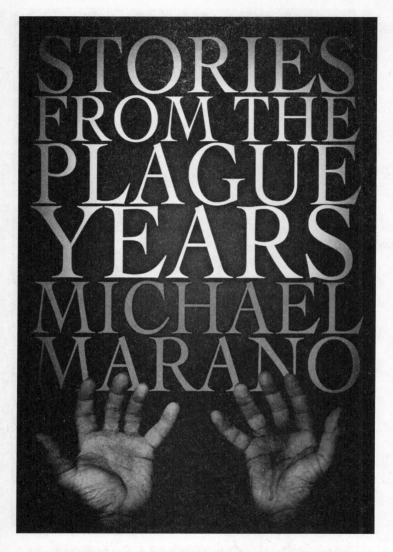

STORIES FROM THE PLAGUE YEARS
MICHAEL MARANO

E-BOOK AVAILABLE DECEMBER 2012
FROM CHIZINE PUBLICATIONS

E-BOOK ISBN 978-1-927469-31-6

978-1-926851-54-9
JOHN MANTOOTH

**SHOEBOX
TRAIN WRECK**

978-1-926851-53-2
MIKE CAREY, LINDA CAREY
& LOUISE CAREY

THE STEEL SERAGLIO

978-1-926851-55-6
RIO YOUERS

WESTLAKE SOUL

978-1-926851-56-3
CAROLYN IVES GILMAN

ISON OF THE ISLES

978-1-926851-58-7
JAMES MARSHALL

**NINJAS VERSUS
PIRATE FEATURING
ZOMBIES**

978-1-926851-57-0
GEMMA FILES

**A TREE OF BONES
VOLUME THREE OF THE
HEXSLINGER SERIES**

978-1-926851-59-4
DAVID NICKLE

**RASPUTIN'S
BASTARDS**

"IF YOUR TASTE IN FICTION RUNS TO THE DISTURBING, DARK, AND AT LEAST
PARTIALLY WEIRD, CHANCES ARE YOU'VE HEARD OF CHIZINE PUBLICATIONS—
CZP—A YOUNG IMPRINT THAT IS NONETHELESS PRODUCING STARTLINGLY
BEAUTIFUL BOOKS OF STARKLY, DARKLY LITERARY QUALITY."
—DAVID MIDDLETON, *JANUARY MAGAZINE*

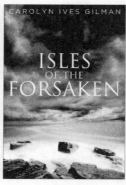

978-1-926851-35-8

TONE MILAZZO

**PICKING UP
THE GHOST**

978-1-926851-43-3

CAROLYN IVES GILMAN

**ISLES OF
THE FORSAKEN**

978-1-926851-44-0

TIM PRATT

BRIARPATCH

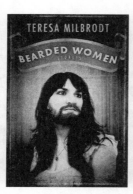
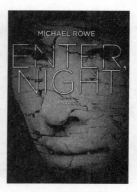

978-1-926851-43-3

CAITLIN SWEET

THE PATTERN SCARS

978-1-926851-46-4

TERESA MILBRODT

BEARDED WOMEN

978-1-926851-45-7

MICHAEL ROWE

ENTER, NIGHT

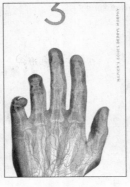

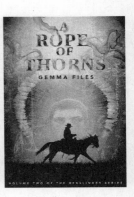